A Blood Stained Ivory Tower

by

Richard Kelly

First published by AuthorHouse 04/08/04

ISBN: 1-4140-7283-X (e-book)
ISBN: 1-4184-0804-2 (Paperback)
ISBN: 1-4184-0803-4 (Dust Jacket)

Library of Congress Control Number: 2004090785

This book is printed on acid free paper.

Printed in the United States of America
Bloomington, IN

Prologue

My name is Tom Evers. From the window of my second floor office on this beautiful spring day, I see clusters of college students moving along the sidewalks headed to their next class. Others are sitting on the grass talking with friends or reading while enjoying the warm sunshine.

This is a familiar scene to me. I've spent almost exactly half my thirty-five years on university campuses, first as an undergraduate, later as a graduate student, and most recently as a member of the faculty of a Midwestern university where I teach psychology. I'm so absorbed in the academic environment that I've developed an almost pathological dependency on it.

I find my job challenging and stimulating, and my work with students is highly rewarding. My colleagues are decent, dedicated scholars whom I respect and admire. I consider myself fortunate for the many friends I have among them.

The university provides the opportunity for such a wide variety of cultural and recreational experiences that I'm able to lead a rich and fulfilling life without ever venturing beyond the boundaries of the campus. I can attend theatrical and musical performances by highly talented amateurs and professionals, listen to lectures by individuals of national and international reputation, and watch gifted athletes competing in intercollegiate sporting events. The athletic facilities available to me are on a par with those found in exclusive health clubs.

It's a common perception that academics spend their lives in an ivory tower, which allows them little contact with the broader society. As a result, they lose sight of the issues and problems faced by those who live in the so-called real world. I see myself as an example of this not-so-complimentary stereotype. When I leave the campus to attend a professional conference or represent the university at a function out of state, on the edge of my consciousness is the thought that I've entered into alien territory, and I become uncomfortable. It's as though I experience symptoms of withdrawal, generated by an addiction which can be alleviated only by returning to the sheltered academic world I've become dependent upon.

It's ironic that while I work with intelligent, rational people in a tranquil environment, my wife Beth's profession brings her in contact with some of the most disturbing aspects of our society. She's a prosecuting attorney who deals with thieves, rapists, drug dealers, child molesters, and murderers on a regular basis.

I tell you this because I want you to understand how improbable it was for me to be involved in the strange events I'm about to describe and how totally unsuited I was for the role I would eventually play.

- 1 -

It was a few minutes before eleven o'clock when I stuffed a stack of file folders into my briefcase bag and headed toward the door of the university library. I was feeling quite pleased with myself. It was Friday. The fall semester wouldn't begin until a week from the following Monday, and I'd just finished preparing a syllabus and reading list for each of the courses I was scheduled to teach. Usually I'd end up scrambling around the day before the first class meeting trying to get these materials together. I routinely warn students of the dangers of waiting until the last minute to begin studying for an exam or starting a term paper, but I seldom heed my own advice.

In the three hours I'd spent in the library, the blue sky had changed to dull gray. There was lightning off to the west. I wondered if a storm was coming that might finally provide some relief from the heat. This had been one of the hottest and driest summers since the record-setting years of the mid-1930s. Already in August there had been fourteen days when the thermometer had risen into the nineties, and there were still eight days left in the month. The normally lush green areas on the campus were light brown, and the watering of lawns in the city had been prohibited for several weeks.

I was halfway across the main quadrangle on the way to my office in the psychology department when it started to rain. It came down with such force that it was useless to hurry to avoid getting wet.

The department is located on the second floor in Coomer Hall, a three-story, red brick structure dating back to the late nineteenth century. The appearance from the outside is deceptive. Several years ago, it was completely renovated. Those entering the building for the first time are surprised to find themselves in an ultra-modern space, which doesn't seem to match up well with the simple, traditional lines of the exterior. Though the contrasting architectural styles aren't aesthetically

1

pleasing, the classrooms, laboratories, and office complexes are well designed and the internal space provides an excellent educational environment.

The department offices are on two hallways extending in opposite directions from a reception area where there's a desk for the secretary and seating space for students while they wait to see faculty. Even though it was a weekday, the place was dark and deserted. Jean Mason, our secretary, wasn't due back from her vacation until the next week, and most faculty members aren't in their offices between the end of summer school and the time the students arrive on campus.

I turned on the lights, unlocked my office door, and checked to see if there were any phone messages. I hadn't heard from Beth since early the day before, when she left to attend a seminar for prosecuting attorneys at the state capital. There had been a call at 8:43. It wasn't from Beth. The caller identified himself as David Richardson. He asked me to call and left a number where he could be reached until eleven o'clock.

The message brought to mind painful events I preferred not to think about. In late March, on the first weekend after the students returned from spring break, David's daughter, Whitney, had been the victim of a brutal murder. The nature of the crime, and the fact that Whitney was one of the most talented and respected senior women on campus, sent the entire community into a state of shock. In spite of a five-month intensive investigation, the police hadn't been able to solve the case.

I glanced at the wall clock. Ten minutes after eleven. It was probably too late to call, but I dialed the number anyway. I was curious as to why David Richardson would want to talk to me. I was about to hang up after five rings when a woman answered.

"This is Tom Evers returning Mr. Richardson's call."

"Oh, Dr. Evers. My husband is on the other phone, the one he uses for business calls. Would you please hold?"

It was several minutes before David Richardson came on the line. "Hello, Dr. Evers. I'm glad you caught me. My wife and I were about to leave the house when my office called. I assume you know I was Whitney's father."

For some reason, his use of the past tense disturbed me. "Of course, I recognized your name. We talked briefly at the campus memorial service."

"I thought we'd met, but I wasn't sure. My wife and I were in a state of shock, and so many people came up to express their condolences." There was a pause. "The service touched us both very deeply. I apologize for not being entirely clear about our meeting."

"That's perfectly understandable. It was a very emotional time for all of us."

"Here's why I called. I'm a graduate of the university. For a number of years I've served on the alumni advisory board of my fraternity. Each year, at the beginning of the fall semester, our group meets with the house officers to go over plans for the year. It mostly has to do with finances. My wife and I will be arriving on campus early this afternoon and will be staying until after lunch on Sunday.

"We were hoping we might be able to meet with you sometime during the weekend. I realize our request hasn't given you much warning, and I know this must be a busy time for you with the semester about to start. If you could spare us just a few minutes, we'd appreciate it very much."

"I intend to be in my office the rest of the day, or I could come to campus tomorrow."

"We would like to get together with you as soon as possible," Mr. Richardson said. "Could we plan to meet after we have settled into our room in the Union Building—say about three o'clock?"

I said that this would be convenient for me and gave him directions to my office.

Since David Richardson hadn't given any indication as to why he and his wife wanted to see me, I began to consider possibilities. Because of my training in psychology, it wasn't unusual for students and faculty members to come to me for advice in times of stress. The Richardsons had certainly gone through a very difficult period and might seek counsel. However, it was doubtful they'd look to me for help. They lived in a metropolitan area where there were any number of highly qualified professionals in the mental health field.

It seemed more likely that the Richardsons were planning to make a donation to the university in memory of their daughter. Ordinarily, that would be handled through the University Development Office, which was responsible for fund-raising activities. But because Whitney was a psychology major, they could be intending to specify that the gift was to go to the psychology department instead of into a general fund. If that were the case, they might want suggestions as to how the money should be allocated.

Several ideas came to mind immediately: a scholarship for an outstanding senior psychology major, a prize for the best undergraduate research project, or a fund for the purchase of laboratory equipment.

I spent the next fifteen minutes preparing a list of possibilities and then walked across campus to the university cafeteria, intending to pick up a sandwich and bring it back to my office. I got in line behind two colleagues I hadn't seen all summer. We sat at a table together and ended up in a heated conversation. I don't remember what it was about, but it must have been interesting because it was almost two o'clock before I got back to the department.

When I went into my office, I saw that it was a complete mess. I'm not a neat person when school is in session. During the summer, I'm even more of a slob. Books, professional journals, folders, computer printouts, and unopened junk mail covered every inch of space, including the two armchairs that accommodate visitors—not the appropriate atmosphere to talk with potential donors to the

3

university. After a half-hour of clearing debris, things looked better. There was still room for improvement, but at least I'd be able to offer the Richardsons chairs to sit on.

At ten minutes past three, I heard footsteps in the hall. Mr. Richardson appeared in the doorway. Mrs. Richardson stood behind him and to the side. They seemed hesitant about entering the office without an invitation, something that students and colleagues never needed.

"Come in," I said, as I got up from my chair and walked around the desk to shake their hands. "Please, sit down."

The Richardsons were as I remembered them from the memorial service. They appeared to be in their late forties. Mr. Richardson was an inch or two over six feet and looked to be in good physical condition. His neatly trimmed, dark brown hair was beginning to gray at the temples. He was wearing a pale blue shirt with a button-down collar, tropical weight gray slacks, and highly polished loafers. An outfit that probably cost as much as my entire wardrobe.

Mrs. Richardson was taller than average, maybe five-nine. She had light brown hair, fine features, and a well-proportioned, trim figure that would be the envy of most women twenty years younger. She wore a simple, short-sleeved tan dress and plain, brown, low-heeled shoes. The Richardsons were a handsome couple.

"I apologize for being late," Mr. Richardson said. "The heavy rain we drove through most of the way slowed us down."

I nodded. "We've had quite a storm."

"We appreciate your meeting with us on such short notice. We don't want to take up too much of your time, so I'll get right to the point. It wouldn't be an exaggeration when I tell you that our family has been completely devastated by the loss of Whitney. We can't seem to get over the terrible effect it's had on us. Recently, Joan and I have come to the conclusion that we might be better able to get our lives back on track if Whitney's killer were found."

At this point, I was fairly sure the Richardsons weren't in my office to talk about a memorial donation to the university.

"The methods the police have employed in their investigation obviously haven't produced results. We've been wondering if approaching the case from another direction might be more effective. Though we don't pretend to be experts, it seems to us that a person capable of committing a crime of this nature must be suffering from a serious mental disorder. With this in mind, Joan and I thought that someone with professional training in psychology might be able to shed some light on the case. Because Whitney always spoke so highly of you, your name came to mind immediately."

David Richardson glanced at his wife. She nodded her approval.

"We're hoping you might consider conducting an independent investigation. We'd pay you at the rate you ordinarily charge for professional consultation. The form of the investigation would be entirely up to you. We're well aware that this would be a difficult task, so we wouldn't be expecting a miracle. If nothing came from your efforts, we'd certainly understand.

"I want to emphasize we don't want to appear to be presumptuous by raising this issue with you. We're making this request because it's extremely important to us that everything possible is done to find the killer. We think you'd be the person best qualified to accomplish that."

Joan Richardson nodded again.

In the course of my professional career, people had come to me asking for help with a wide range of problems, and I'd received some unusual requests, but never anything like this. While I was trying to decide how to respond, Joan Richardson frowned slightly and leaned forward in her chair. She seemed to sense that I was having trouble deciding if I would agree to undertaking an investigation.

"Dr. Evers, I think we should allow you some time to decide," she said. "We could arrange to get in touch with you before we leave on Sunday."

I started to accept the offer and then changed my mind. "It's thoughtful of you to suggest that possibility, but there's no reason to postpone my decision. I appreciate the trust you have in me, but I lack the expertise that would be necessary in an undertaking like the one you've described. It's always been my policy when someone comes to me with a problem that's outside my specialty to make a referral to a colleague who is better qualified. In this situation, I'd be little more than an amateur. I'd like very much to help, but, unfortunately, I seriously doubt that I can."

David Richardson responded immediately. "Your having said that makes me even more convinced that you're the person we want. When I give an assignment to a member of my staff and he, or she, is overly confident and optimistic, it's cause for me to be concerned. I've found I'm far more likely to get positive results from someone who recognizes the difficulty of the task and warns me of the possibility of negative outcomes. Could you at least give our request more consideration?"

"Please, Dr. Evers. It's so very important for us to do everything possible to find the person who took Whitney from us," Joan Richardson said, with a look of concern on her face.

In our brief meeting, I'd come to like Joan Richardson. Maybe it was because she reminded me of Whitney. There was no way I could refuse her request.

I nodded. "It is very unlikely that I'll agree, but I'd be willing to give it some further thought."

"That's all that we ask," Mr. Richardson said.

"I should make it clear that if I do choose to become involved, I wouldn't accept any payment."

Mr. Richardson nodded. "Of course, that would be entirely up to you."

5

We left it that the Richardsons would call me at home on Sunday morning for my decision.

- 2 -

I tilted my chair back, put my feet up on the desk, and thought about David and Joan Richardson. The agony they were experiencing brought back memories of the first time I'd met Whitney. It was in the spring three years before, during the week when students were registering for the courses they'd be taking in the fall semester, that she appeared at my office door and, in a very polite voice, asked if I had the time to answer a question about registration. I assured her that I did and invited her to come in.

She was wearing an oversized sweatshirt, jeans, and running shoes with a lot of miles on them. It was the standard outfit that year. On close inspection, she didn't conform entirely to the campus fashion code. She wore little or no makeup, which was certainly not typical. This might've been because she hadn't kept up with the current trends, but I doubted it. Whatever the reason, the absence of makeup served to highlight her perfect complexion, light brown hair with a natural curl, and eyes of such a pale shade of blue that her gaze could be distracting.

It turned out that Whitney, who was a freshman, wanted to sign up for my course in abnormal psychology, which was open only to juniors and seniors. To register for it, she needed special written permission from me. Several students come to me with this request every semester. Invariably I refuse because I've found that freshman and sophomores have difficulty competing with the more academically experienced upperclassmen. When I explained that to Whitney and suggested she plan to take the course later on, she was obviously disappointed, but she didn't argue the point as many students are inclined to do when they don't get their way.

The next semester, during the registration period, Whitney showed up at my door again, appearing more confident than when I'd seen her the first time. "You probably don't remember me," she said.

"Yes, I do. Last spring you asked me if I'd give you special permission to enroll in my abnormal psychology course. I suspect you're here to try again."

She smiled and nodded. Her persistence impressed me.

"While I don't feel I can make an exception for next semester, there is another possibility. The class enrollment limit is usually reached before registration is over. The juniors will be registering ahead of you in the spring, so it may turn out that you'd be frustrated again."

"I'm aware of that."

"If you can give me a convincing reason as to why you want to take the course, I'd be willing to guarantee a place for you next fall."

Whitney smiled. "When I came in, I knew you'd say no. This may turn out better than I expected. I'm in pre-med and have such a limited number of electives, I need to plan my schedule carefully. Last year, at the end of the first semester, I made a list of the classes I thought would be important for me to take before I graduated. Your abnormal psych course was at the top."

I'm not entirely sure why I signed the special entry permission form Whitney brought with her. I'd like to think it wasn't because she complimented my course. In the past, students had used that approach, and it hadn't worked.

There were eighty students enrolled in abnormal psych the next semester. Seventy-nine juniors and seniors and Whitney. At the first meeting of my classes, I emphasize that the examinations will be difficult and challenging. In spite of the warning, most of the students fail to meet my expectations on the first exam. Many simply don't put forth enough effort. Others, who work hard, devote too much time to rote memorization when they should be attempting to understand the material. Fortunately, I typically see a steady improvement in the performance of the class during the semester, and I'm pleased at the progress that has been made by final exam time.

The semester Whitney took the abnormal psychology course, the pattern was basically the same. In the first set of exams, I read one answer after another that indicated the student was capable of doing better work. There were only a few more papers to grade when I came across one that was of truly exceptional quality. In a clear and concise way, the writer demonstrated an excellent understanding of the material and even included relevant information that wasn't in the textbook or covered in my lectures. I reread the essays several times and concluded it was an Olympic Gold type performance. I turned back to the first page of the exam paper to see the student's name—Whitney Richardson.

I use a point system in grading. The students are given the total number of points they receive along with the letter grade equivalent. On her first exam, Whitney had achieved something that rarely occurs in my classes. She'd fallen short of the maximum possible score by just five points. On the next two examinations, she missed by a point or two, and then finished with a perfect score on the last exam before the final.

I write a note on each exam paper in which I comment on the student's performance. In Whitney's case, I found myself running out of superlatives. After the third exam, I wanted to tell her in person how impressed I was with her work. She sat in the back of the large lecture room and always left by the rear door, so I wasn't able to catch up with her at the end of a class. When I finished grading her fourth exam, I thought of a way to get her attention. Instead of putting an A on the paper, I wrote an F.

When I hand back exams, there are always a few students who come up after the class is over to ask questions about their grades. Of course, Whitney was in the group. She waited until the others had left the room before saying anything.

"I think you may have made a mistake on my paper," she said, as she showed me the grade.

I shook my head. "No mistake. I did it on purpose."

"That's what I figured," she said with a smile.

"I expected if I did that, you'd come to me after class to point out my error. Before the end of the semester, I wanted the opportunity to tell you how impressed I've been with your performance. You've done outstanding work. In fact, because of you, I may have to consider allowing more sophomores to enroll in the course."

"Actually, I intended to talk to you after class anyway. I've decided to change my major to psychology, and I was hoping you'd consider being my advisor."

"I'd be happy to discuss it with you. I'm tied up the rest of today. Are you free tomorrow at four?"

"Yes."

"I'll see you then."

The next afternoon at a quarter to four, Whitney appeared at my office door. "I know I'm early. I hope I'm not interfering with your work."

"You're not. Sit down and explain to me why you're thinking about changing your major to psychology."

Whitney sat on the edge of the chair with her hands folded in her lap. "Spring semester last year, I took Intro Psych with Dr. Gilbert. I really enjoyed it, and I learned a lot. I decided to take as much psychology as I could fit into my schedule. Your course has been even more interesting than I'd expected. Now I'm positive I want to major in psych."

"You mentioned earlier you were in pre-med. A switch to psych would not only be a change in major, but you'd also be making a decision about your future career."

Whitney nodded and frowned. "That's made it a difficult choice. Ever since I can remember, I planned to be a doctor. Then last year I began to have doubts.

9

Before that I never gave much thought to what it would be like to study medicine, which was kind of dumb of me. Now I know it wasn't the right decision."

"I suspect you're thinking of going to graduate school in psychology."

"That's what I'd like to do."

"Your post graduate education would take as long as training in medicine. When you got the Ph.D., you could expect to be able to choose from a wide range of interesting career options, but certainly none offering the level of income and prestige associated with being a physician."

"I realize that."

"I'm sure you've done very well in the pre-med courses you've taken. Well enough that you can be reasonably confident of being accepted to medical school."

"I've worked hard. My grades are fairly good," Whitney said, as she leaned back in the chair and rested her elbows on the arms.

"I want you to understand why I'm going over this with you. In every freshman class, about twenty percent of the students choose the pre-med curriculum. Less than five percent end up in medical school. Most can't get good enough grades in the tough science courses. Many of your classmates would think you're giving up a great deal. You've the option of waiting another semester before making the final decision. If you did that, you could still fulfill the requirements for a psych major without any problem."

"I've thought about this a lot. I'm sure that changing my major is the right thing for me to do."

"If you're that certain, I'd be pleased to be your advisor."

Whitney smiled and breathed a sigh of relief.

"Before you leave, I have a question. Have you discussed this decision with your parents?" That's something I almost always ask of students who want to change their major. I do it because in my years as an academic advisor, I've come to recognize that some parents are convinced they know what's best for their children. All too frequently when the child, or more accurately the young adult, expresses the desire to take control of his or her own life by making an independent decision, a conflict develops. However these disagreements are resolved, it seems there's often unhappiness on both sides.

My question had far more of an impact on Whitney than I'd expected. There was an immediate change in her mood. Her head dropped, and she looked down at her knees. After hesitating a moment, she said in a quiet voice, "I haven't told them yet. I wanted to get everything settled before I brought it up because I've been worried about their reaction. Don't get the wrong idea. My parents are great. It's just that my father feels so strongly about me becoming a doctor. He came from a very poor family and had to work his way through college. He always dreamed of going to medical school but couldn't afford it, so when he graduated he got a job in business. Even though he's been very successful, I've a feeling he's still living with the disappointment and frustration. I think that's why he's always wanted my brother and me to become doctors.

"My brother is two years younger than I am, and it's already clear he won't make it to med school. He's a really good athlete, and all he thinks about is sports. He's very intelligent, but he doesn't get good grades. As far as my father is concerned, it's up to me."

Not that unusual a story, I thought. "That makes me a little uneasy. Just keep in mind, you can't design your life to please your parents. Even though initially your dad might have a problem with your decision, it's likely he'll come to accept it."

"I hope so," she said with a sigh.

- 3 -

After that first meeting, Whitney and I spent considerable time together. She took two more courses with me and was enrolled in my senior research seminar at the time of her death. For three semesters, she served as my undergraduate teaching assistant. During that period, my respect for her continued to grow. She was extremely conscientious and always excited about learning. Though she seldom talked about her extracurricular activities, I knew she was active in student government, and she'd served as a volunteer in a community center for children with developmental disabilities. And there was Whitney's dry sense of humor that made working with her so enjoyable.

Looking back, it seems strange to me that I didn't get to know her better. I never saw her when she wasn't upbeat and enthusiastic about whatever she might be involved in at the time. It took a while for me to realize that behind the cheerful facade there might've been some inner turmoil and distress. Because it wasn't Whitney's nature to reveal her feelings, I'd never had access to any of this. In fact, the closest she ever came to mentioning a personal problem was during that first meeting in my office when she expressed concern over her father's reaction to her plan to change majors. She never spoke of that again.

We were only a few days into the fall semester of Whitney's senior year when she came to talk with me about getting her applications off to graduate programs in clinical psychology. I explained to her that there wasn't any advantage in applying early because universities didn't begin sending out acceptance notices until the first week in April. In spite of what I told her, she insisted on getting started immediately. Her completed applications were in the mail before she left campus for the Christmas vacation.

On the fourth Monday in March, I was in my office at seven thirty. I wanted to have time to prepare my lectures for the day. The students had just arrived back on campus from spring break, and it usually took a while for them to recover

12

physically, and mentally, from the exhausting adventures they'd had during the previous week and to reenter the academic world. Until that happened, it would be a challenge to get their attention.

A few minutes before eight, I heard someone coming down the hall. It was Whitney. "I hoped you'd be in early. I wanted to catch you before your first class," she said, as she dropped into a chair. If I hadn't known her better, I might've thought she'd spent a strenuous week partying on a Florida beach.

"Tell me why it's so important to talk at this hour of the morning."

"I still haven't heard from the graduate schools."

"Whitney . . . Whitney," I said, with an intentional sigh. "You can't expect to receive anything for at least a week. You've got to be patient."

"I understand. It's just that I have to get things settled. I need to know what I'm going to be doing next year."

"I can tell you that right now. You'll be a graduate student in psychology at a first rate university."

"You've told me that before, and I believe you, but I'm still worried."

"I promise you that within two weeks, everything will be settled, so stop worrying. That's an order."

Ordinarily, Whitney would've smiled at what I'd said. Instead, she got up to leave with a frown on her face. In a quiet voice, she said, "I'll try."

Before she reached the door I asked, "Did you have a chance to relax and have some fun during the break?"

She shrugged. "I stayed on campus to work on a big term paper that's due this week, and I got caught up on sleep."

The following Friday, on the way to my office after my ten o'clock lecture, I ran into a colleague in the hallway I hadn't seen all semester. We had a lot to talk about, so it was ten minutes past eleven before I got back to the department. Jean stopped me as I passed by her desk. "Whitney came in a few minutes ago. She has something to show you. I sent her back to wait in your office."

I found Whitney sitting on the edge of her chair. Without saying anything, she handed me two letters.

I smiled. "I take it I'm supposed to read these?"

She nodded.

When I finished reading, I handed them back. "Not bad. A letter of acceptance with an offer of a full tuition scholarship and graduate research assistantship from first rate universities. You must be feeling better now."

"I'm pretty excited."

"The only thing that surprises me is that you heard so early. They must want you badly. Keep in mind, you have ten days before you're obligated to respond to these offers, and by that time, you can expect to have heard from other schools."

"These two universities were at the top of my preference list. I want to get this settled, so after lunch I'm going to write an acceptance letter."

"Which one are you going to choose?"

"The one you say is best."

"They're both the best."

"Then I've decided. I'm going where it never snows."

I remember the next Monday because I was particularly pleased with my morning classes. The students asked questions, and they were eager to discuss the material. I walked up the stairs to the department after the second class, thinking about how rewarding teaching could be when things went well.

I ate lunch in my office and worked on revising some lecture notes. I had a one o'clock seminar. When it was over at three, I went directly to a committee meeting.

It always amazes me that six or eight intelligent, well-meaning people can have so much difficulty in making decisions. After more than two hours, the only thing the group was able to agree upon was the time to schedule the next meeting, and even that required a great deal of discussion.

When I got back to the department at five thirty, I was surprised to find Jean still at her desk. It was unusual for her to be in the office after five. If there was unfinished work at the end of the day, she preferred to come in early the next morning to take care of it. As I started to ask her why she hadn't gone home, I saw that her eyes were red and her cheeks, moist. She'd been crying.

"Tom, I waited around to let you know what's happened in case you hadn't heard. I can tell no one's told you." After a brief pause, she whispered, "Whitney is dead. They found her body sometime around noon."

I had a fleeting thought that what Jean had told me couldn't possibly be true, but, of course, it had to be.

"I can't tell you very much. Ed Rawlins came in an hour ago. He was pretty upset. He said on the way back from his seminar he ran into a group of campus police who looked like they were talking about something serious. He knew one of the guys, Pete Everett, so he went over and asked him what was going on. Pete told him that the body of a young woman had been found beside the road out west of the campus. It was Whitney. Ed said she was in his afternoon class, and he'd wondered why she hadn't shown up."

Jean picked up her purse and walked out without saying any more. She'd started to cry again, and the tears were running down beside her nose.

For reasons I didn't entirely understand, Jean and Whitney had become friends. Their lives were so different. Whitney, the brilliant college student, and Jean, wife, mother, and secretary. Whitney would ordinarily arrive early for an appointment with me, and while she waited, the two would always get involved in a conversation. Jean's thirty-fifth birthday had been a few days earlier. Whitney had brought her a single rose in a tiny vase.

The local TV stations and the newspaper filled in the details of the crime over the next two days. A woman on her way to pick up her daughter at nursery school noticed what appeared to be a partially clothed human form lying in a drainage ditch that ran beside the road. She returned to her home, which was a short distance away, and told her husband what she'd seen. He went back to investigate and confirmed his wife's suspicion.

- 4 -

It would've never occurred to me to get involved in an investigation of Whitney's murder if the Richardsons hadn't brought it up, but the more I thought about it, the more intrigued I became with the idea. By the time I left my office at six o'clock, I knew I wanted to do something, but before making a decision, I had to talk it over with Beth. She had a way of seeing things more clearly than I do and is far more sensible. If she had any reservations about what I was going to propose, I'd have to abandon the idea.

The rain had stopped sometime during the afternoon. The sun was beginning to break through as I headed across the parking lot behind Coomer Hall toward my twelve-year-old pickup truck. Beth and I have different work schedules. When we bought a house and moved out of an apartment, which was within walking distance of my office on campus, it was necessary for us to have a second car. I finally had an excuse to own a pickup, a dream I'd had since high school. It is, without a doubt, my most valued possession.

We live five miles from the campus. The road I drive on to get home takes me along a river, its banks lined with imposing, hardwood trees. Our house is on a four-acre lot, which backs up to several hundred acres of state owned forest. Our closest neighbor, a dairy farmer, lives a quarter of a mile away.

The first time Beth and I saw the property, we agreed that it was exactly the kind of place we'd dreamed about owning someday. We couldn't imagine a better environment for bringing up children. Even though our attempts to start a family ended in failure and disappointment, it turned out that the house was a perfect home for us. The two extra bedrooms made it possible for Beth and me to have our own separate studies.

The sky had turned dark again, and it'd started to rain by the time I pulled into the driveway. It was probably my imagination, but the vegetation in the yard seemed to be greener than when I'd left in the morning. The house was very warm from having been closed up all day. Neither Beth nor I like to be in a place that's sealed off from the outside, so the only air conditioning we have is a window unit in our bedroom, which we use on hot summer nights.

I opened the windows in the kitchen and living room to let in fresh air and checked the answering machine. Beth had called at five fifteen. Last night, she'd eaten some excellent Italian food. Was leaving in a few minutes to go to a Japanese restaurant. Might not get a chance to call later. Would be home around five tomorrow. Attended some good meetings. She missed me.

Beth enjoys eating as much as anyone I know, and she has a remarkable appetite. Fortunately, she's blessed with the metabolism of a hummingbird, so she can eat all she wants and never gain a pound. If she gets so busy she can't take time to eat regularly for a day or two, she'll lose weight. Within minutes after she'd arrived home, I could expect a detailed report on the meals she'd had while she was away.

I changed to shorts and a T-shirt and went into the kitchen to fix something to eat. After some deliberation, I decided on a sandwich. I checked the refrigerator and found some fresh tomatoes and an onion from our garden. We managed to salvage most of the vegetable crop by watering during the dry spell. We did that without feeling guilty because we irrigate by pumping water from a small pond on our property, which isn't affected by drought conditions.

I layered slices of tomato, onion, and Swiss cheese on French bread and spread on some mayonnaise. I opened a jar of herring in cream sauce, a package of fancy crackers, and a cold bottle of Molson Ale. I loaded it all on a tray and went into the living room. I drank the ale and ate herring while watching the rain through the sliding door. I had a second bottle of ale with my sandwich. Nothing like excellent Japanese cuisine but a pretty good meal for a warm summer evening.

After washing the dishes and cleaning up the kitchen, I stretched out on the sofa with a novel I'd started a few days before, which had been written by a graduate of the university. I really liked her work. I hadn't met her when she was a student, but the things she wrote about made me think she must be a very nice person.

It was close to midnight when I went to bed. I lay awake for a while thinking I might be missing Beth a little even though she'd been gone less than forty-eight hours. My sleep was interrupted by a series of bad dreams. Whitney had been in all of them. She'd needed help, and I couldn't do anything. There was a lot of blood.

When I got up at seven the sun was shining, and there was a cool breeze coming through the bedroom window. It was a perfect day for my morning run, so I decided to do an extra two miles. During the heat wave, I'd missed a few days.

A half mile from our house, there's one of the few remaining sections in our state of a two-lane highway that had once extended from coast to coast. To accommodate the increase in traffic, the road had been straightened and widened.

17

Richard Kelly

The stretches of the old road that had been preserved were those with houses on them. That was my favorite place to run. There was very little traffic and no dogs. Occasionally, I came upon a parked car with a weary traveler sleeping behind the wheel, or one with a couple demonstrating their affection for each other. My passing seldom interfered with either activity.

After a shower and a breakfast of shredded wheat and strong coffee, I went into my study and sat down at the computer. If I was going to get involved in an investigation, I needed a plan.

A half an hour later, the screen was still blank, and I was beginning to have some second thoughts. Maybe it was unrealistic to think I could accomplish more than the police. After all, they were experts. What kept me going was the thought that I might have some advantages over the police investigators. For one thing, I was much more familiar with the campus environment than they were.

Most people picture universities as peaceful places, free from the problems that are so prevalent in our society. To a large extent, that perception is an accurate one. However, as much as I hate to admit it, my ivory tower isn't as idyllic as it might appear to an outsider. Members of the academic community don't always behave in a civilized manner.

Because of my professional training, university people sometimes come to me for advice when they have a problem. In the previous two years, I'd talked to three faculty wives whose husbands were having affairs with students. I spent several hours with a colleague who was desperate because his alcoholic wife was physically abusing their preschool age children, and I'd referred the wife of a high level administrator to a professional colleague who specializes in the treatment of battered women.

The lives of students are affected by discomforting trends. Alcohol abuse is widespread among both males and females, most of whom haven't reached the legal drinking age. One of my cynical colleagues maintains that the one thing you can be sure a young person will learn in college is how to drink.

As I thought more about getting involved in an investigation, I wondered if there could be some advantage in my being a member of the academic community; perhaps people on the campus might feel more comfortable revealing things to me than to the police.

After staring at the computer screen for another half-hour, thinking about how I might approach the investigation, it occurred to me that I was making a mistake in trying to develop a master plan. The only way to start was to interview people who could possibly provide me with significant information.

When I completed the first entry in my new investigation file, it was limited to a list of names of a few students I knew who might know something about what had been going on in Whitney's life in the period before her death.

After lunch, I read awhile and took a long nap. By the time I woke up, it was time to start thinking about dinner. I expected Beth to be home in a couple of hours. The evening meal is an important part of the day for Beth and me. We enjoy preparing food, and it is a time when we catch up on each other's day. I decided on pesto, a salad, and garlic bread.

- 5 -

I'd just finished cleaning up the kitchen after making the salad when I heard Beth pull in the driveway. I went out the back door to greet her.

"I missed you," she said.

"Same here," I told her, as I got her suitcase out of the back seat.

She grabbed her briefcase, and we walked toward the door together. We're not much for kissing out in the open, so I settled for putting my arm around her shoulders. I had to reach down quite a bit. At five feet four inches, Beth's shoulders are fairly close to the ground.

"I want you to tell me what you've been doing while I was gone, but I have to get out of these clothes first."

Beth's demeanor changes with the clothes she has on. For work, she prefers dark-colored, tailored suits. In her role as prosecutor, she's highly businesslike in her manner and, I've been told, some of her adversaries in the courtroom see her as intimidating. There's a calculated casualness about the clothes she wears when we go out socially. At parties, she lets down and relaxes.

Around the house, Beth wears things that wouldn't be acceptable as a donation to the Salvation Army. Most of the time, they're two sizes too large and so worn and faded that the original color is a mystery.

She came out of the bedroom wearing a familiar outfit, sweats that had been altered so they'd be suitable for summer wear. The sleeves of the shirt were cut off at the shoulders, and the pants came down to a point just above the knee. She had on canvas sneakers with no laces.

"I feel better now," she said, as she sat on the sofa and stretched her legs out on the coffee table.

"I have to confess, I was angry with you last night," I said.

"Why? I wasn't even here."

"That's the reason. It was a cool, peaceful, rainy evening. The kind we haven't had in a long time, and here I sat all by myself with no one to enjoy it with me."

"That's a shame. Maybe I can make it up to you in some way."

"It might be difficult."

"I'm still young and healthy. I think I can manage."

"When do we start?"

"I'll let you know later. Right now I want to hear about what you did while I was gone."

"No, you go first. How was the food?"

"Thursday night we went to an Italian restaurant Judge Forbes recommended. It was in a really rough neighborhood on a street that was lined with abandoned warehouses and boarded-up apartment buildings. The restaurant itself was a two-story brick of pre-WW II vintage. There was a uniformed attendant stationed in the parking lot who was carrying a gun. It made you feel right at home.

"It took me a while, but I finally decided on the fettucine alfredo with a minestrone soup appetizer. They brought one of those huge, all you can eat salad bowls for the center of the table. The meal was superb.

"Then last night, Jerry Okubo took us to a Japanese restaurant. It was just a store front in a strip mall on the east side of town, but what a meal. Jerry did the ordering for everyone. He had the waiter bring eight different dishes. It was arranged family style, so we could try some of everything. I had to restrain myself because I thought I might eat more than my share."

"How were the meetings?" I asked cautiously. I was afraid Beth was about to describe each dish in detail.

"They were good. But, as usual, the best part was getting together with colleagues, because it's comforting to find out that other people have similar stresses at work. Enough about my big city adventure. What's been happening here?"

"There is some news," I said. I told Beth about my phone conversation with David Richardson. "The only reason I could imagine the Richardsons might want to meet with me was to discuss setting up a memorial fund at the university in Whitney's name. I should have guessed it was something more important than that because David Richardson wanted to arrange a meeting as soon as he and his wife arrived on the campus."

"You've aroused my curiosity," Beth said. "What did the Richardsons want?"

"They asked me to conduct an investigation into Whitney's murder," I said.

Beth looked puzzled. "I don't understand. Why are they asking you?"

"The Richardsons feel they'd be better able to overcome the terrible effect the loss of Whitney has had on their life if the killer were identified and brought to justice. They seem to doubt that the police will ever be successful in solving the case. Because they're convinced the murderer must be a very disturbed individual, they think someone trained in psychology might be capable of coming up with information that would eventually lead to his arrest."

"What did you tell them?"

"At first, I said no. I pointed out that I have no experience or expertise in that type of thing, but Mr. Richardson was so insistent, I agreed to think about it and let him know."

"You'd like to do it, wouldn't you?"

"Why do you say that?"

"In the time we've been together, I've gotten to know you pretty well."

"I admit I'm tempted, and I've even given some thought about how I might approach it. See what happens when you leave? I lose all sense of perspective."

There was a long pause.

"You think I'm insane to consider it, don't you?"

Beth shook her head. "Actually, I don't. It's possible you might be able to accomplish something. The problem I have is a selfish one. It seems we never have enough time together. One weekend you'll be grading exams, and the next one I'll be preparing for a trial. I can imagine if you take on anything more, we won't see each other until next summer."

I nodded. "I've thought about that. If I go ahead, I'd have to be very careful not to become too involved."

"I say it's the thing to do, but only under one condition. You have to listen to me along the way, and if I tell you to slow down, or even to stop, you do it."

"You know I always listen to your every word. Your wise counsel has helped me avoid many a disaster."

Beth rolled her eyes. "I'll do my best to ignore what you just said. We can talk about it more later. Now, I want to think about dinner."

"We're having pesto, a tossed salad, and garlic bread."

"Great. That's one of my favorite meals."

To put that comment in perspective, you have to understand that almost every meal is one of Beth's favorites.

"I'll get you a glass of the expensive Chardonnay I bought to celebrate your return."

When I came back with the wine and a Molson Ale for me, we went out on the deck and watched the sunset. It was almost ten o'clock by the time we'd finished eating. After clearing the table and filling the dishwasher, Beth collapsed on the sofa. She'd stopped talking a few minutes earlier, a sure sign that fatigue was setting in rapidly.

"I know you were looking forward all day to a romantic evening, but I'm pretty tired," I said. "Would you be too disappointed if we just went to bed early and settled for a good night's sleep?"

Beth yawned. "I think I can live with that."

"Why don't you go to bed? I'll be in later."

There was no protest as she pulled herself off the sofa and headed for the bedroom. I knew as soon as her head hit the pillow, she'd fall into a coma-like state.

I sat for a while trying to understand why Beth hadn't expressed more reservations when I'd told her I was considering looking into Whitney's death. Then it came to me that I should've guessed she'd support it. The students who work with me on research projects have dinner at our house at least once a semester. Whitney came on several occasions. Each time, she and Beth had had a lengthy conversation. Beth thought highly of Whitney and had been deeply disturbed by her death.

The fact that Beth seemed to feel more strongly about unfairness and injustice than most of us probably contributed to her decision to study law. I'd seen her get upset in one of those rare cases when a defendant she'd prosecuted was unjustly acquitted. She'd become equally distressed when she'd gotten a conviction but considered the sentence the judge decided on too severe. The thought that Whitney's murderer was still free, and might kill again, was the sort of thing Beth would have difficulty accepting.

That night, I got eight hours of peaceful sleep. Having Beth beside me proved to be a good antidote to bad dreams.

- 6 -

The next morning, I left for my run while Beth was still asleep. When I got back to the house, she was sitting at the kitchen table drinking coffee and reading the Sunday paper. She had on one of my old, blue chambray work shirts that came down almost far enough to qualify as a robe.

"I planned our day while you were running," she said.

"I can hardly wait to hear about it," I said, as I got myself some coffee and filled Beth's cup.

"First, I want to talk about the investigation of Whitney's murder," Beth said. "Don't you think you should talk with Russ before you do anything?"

"Of course. What's the matter with me for not thinking of that?"

"There's always the possibility he might discourage you. If he thought it was all right for you to go ahead, I'm sure he'd share any information he has. He'd trust you.

"How does this sound? I have some work to do. You could probably catch Russ after lunch and be back here by mid-afternoon. I can be finished with my work by then, and we can relax the rest of the day."

"That sounds like a great idea. It's a little early to call Russ on Sunday morning, so I'll wait until after breakfast."

Russell Merrick is chief of detectives for the city police. Beth met him while she was preparing to try her first case as an inexperienced assistant prosecutor and was feeling a little apprehensive. She attributed her success in the trial largely to the advice and support Russ provided.

A couple of months later, Beth surprised me by suggesting we go out to dinner with Russ and his wife. I wasn't particularly excited about the prospect of spending an evening with a guy Beth described as a tough cop who was married to a woman named Rose. I couldn't imagine what we'd have in common to talk about, but I agreed because it was important to Beth. As it turned out, there wasn't any reason to worry. We had an excellent time at dinner and ended up back at our house talking until almost midnight. Ever since, we've eaten a meal together half a dozen times a year, with Beth and Rose taking turns preparing their specialities or trying new recipes, and I consider Russ one of my closest friends.

At ten thirty, I dialed the Merrick's number. "I need to talk to Russ," I said, when Rose answered.

"I'll see if I can get him to the phone, Tom. He's out on the patio watching the grass grow."

"Did I hear you say watching the grass grow?"

"That's right. You remember back in July he bought a new riding lawn mower. I told him our lawn wasn't big enough for one of those things, but he'd always wanted one. It hasn't rained since he got it, so there's been nothing to mow. After the rain on Friday, he thinks the grass will be high enough to mow by this afternoon. I haven't had the heart to tell him it probably won't work out that way."

"Don't interrupt him. Just tell him I'll be stopping by after lunch. I want to talk to him about something. Maybe I can take his mind off the grass."

"A few minutes after I hung up the phone, David Richardson called. I told him I hadn't decided if I was going to get involved in an investigation and said I'd let him know my decision in a few days.

It was half past one when I pulled into the Merrick's driveway. I drove on to the back of the house expecting to find Russ on the patio or riding his mower. He wasn't there, so I went to the kitchen door and looked through the screen. Rose was putting away the lunch dishes. She's of medium height, with what might be described as a round figure, and had curly brown hair without a touch of gray. What makes her stand out is that she's always in a cheerful mood. When she saw me, she motioned toward the living room.

"He's watching a ball game. The grass didn't cooperate."

Russ was sitting in a recliner with his feet up. He had on his usual weekend outfit: khaki pants, a white T-shirt, and running shoes. Russ's hair is white. He enjoys telling people the white began to appear shortly after he and Rose were married, and by the time he was thirty-five, the transition was complete. Now, in his late forties, his hair is the only indication of aging. He works out regularly because he feels that law enforcement officers should be in top physical condition. There isn't an extra ounce of fat on his six-foot two-inch frame.

When I came into the room, he reached for the remote and turned off the TV.

"Leave it on," I said.

Russ shook his head. "I've decided I'm through with baseball. The free agency thing has ruined it. I've been a Cub fan my whole life. Even though they never won anything, I still went along with them. The players were like old friends. I figured they'd suffered like I did when they lost year after year. Now players move around so much, if I don't watch for a couple of weeks, one of them will have signed with another team. It's hard enough to watch the Cubs lose when I knew them. To watch a bunch of strangers get their butts kicked is more than I can take. Besides, Rose said there was something you wanted to talk about."

Just then, Rose came in with a pitcher of her ice tea, which is the best I've ever tasted. She puts in exactly the right amount of sugar and mint, which grows next to their garage. They're a lot of men who drink beer while watching a ball game on a Sunday afternoon, but not Russ. He drinks ice tea. I've never seen him touch alcohol in any form. It's not that there's any religious belief or philosophical reason for his abstinence. He doesn't care for the taste of alcoholic beverages and has no desire to experience the effect they have. Even though Russ doesn't drink himself, I've never heard him criticize anyone else for drinking except when it's resulted in a traffic accident or contributed to antisocial behavior.

I gave Russ the details of my meeting with the Richardsons on Friday and told him I was thinking about doing some investigating. He thought a bit and then said, "I don't see how it'd do any harm. We've done about all we can from our end and haven't gotten anywhere.

"Richardson calls me every couple of weeks and asks me if we've made any progress. I think he feels we haven't given the case enough attention. That irritates the hell out of me because we've done everything possible to find the killer. I want so bad to solve this one I've spent time on it when I should've been working on other things. I know losing a daughter like he did must be a terrible thing, and I've got to be patient, but I'm getting tired of listening to his complaints."

"What bothers me about getting involved is the possibility that I might do something that would mess up your investigation or violate some rule," I said.

"Don't worry about interfering with us. Right now we're just standing around scratching our heads. Any help we can get would be welcome. As far as breaking rules, that won't be a problem. You've got enough sense to know where to draw the line, and I don't know of any reason why a private citizen can't sniff around a little, but it was probably good that you refused to take any payment for your work from the Richardsons."

"What you say makes me feel more comfortable," I said. "Of course, if I get in trouble, I wouldn't let anyone know that you'd had knowledge of what I was doing."

"Good idea but not necessary because I'd deny it anyway,"

"What're your thoughts on the case at this point?" I asked, sipping from my glass.

"About all we have is a list of puzzling questions. Starting from the very beginning, things didn't seem to make sense. For example, how did the killer get the victim into his car? Everyone we interviewed said she was a smart girl, the kind who would've been careful. Besides that, when female students first arrive on campus, they get instructions on rules of safety. One obvious explanation is that she knew the person well enough to think there was no reason to be concerned."

"That would suggest it was a student or a campus employee she recognized," I said.

"Not necessarily. It might've been an old boyfriend or someone she knew from her hometown. Or suppose some guy pulled up in a car with stickers on the window from another college. He's young and maybe wearing a T-shirt with a college crest on it. He says he got a call from his girlfriend who's a student here. It's an emergency. She said she was going to quit school or commit suicide or something like that. He asks the victim to get in the car and take him to his girlfriend's dormitory. Unlikely, I know. I'm just trying to come up with some possible explanation."

"Do you think the killer might've met her outside of the car and forced her in?"

Russ shook his head. "It's doubtful. According to the reports we got from her friends, she worked out regularly and was in good physical condition. She wasn't very big, but still she probably would've been able to put up a good enough struggle to draw attention, and she was smart enough to have screamed for help. I suppose if she'd been in some deserted area maybe it could've happened that way, but there aren't many spots like that on the campus.

"Whitney left a note for her roommate saying she was going to a meeting. We never were able to find anybody who knew about a meeting that night. If she was planning to go to some kind of informal study session, you'd expect someone from the group would've contacted us. Are you familiar with the place where the body was found?"

"Only that it was on a road a short distance from the campus."

"It was in a shallow drainage ditch fifteen feet from the edge of the pavement. It could be easily seen by someone driving along the road coming from either direction. There was no question it was going to be found quickly. You'd expect the killer would hide the body in the woods or bury it in a shallow grave. That's what usually happens in this kind of case. It almost seems like the killer wanted the body to be found."

While he was talking, it was clear Russ had gone over the case in his mind many times.

"Then there was the lack of physical evidence. If she put up resistance, there might be skin samples under her fingernails or, in a sex crime like this, you'd expect to find some hair or semen on the body. Apparently, this guy wasn't into penetration. He got his kicks in other ways. There weren't any fiber samples or footprints either. When there's no physical evidence, you have to figure the guy was either very careful or very lucky."

"What's left for you to do now?" I asked.

"Just wait. There's a possibility we might arrest someone with knowledge of the crime who'd use it in a plea bargain, but that's not likely to happen because we can be pretty sure the murderer was alone when the crime was committed, and he's probably not the type to talk about it.

"The really nasty part of this thing is that the best hope we have for finding the killer is if he repeats. There's a chance he's killed before and a strong possibility he will again. The evidence that this thing was sexually motivated suggests he got a kick out of it, and probably sometime in the future, he's going to want more. I have a feeling he's moved on, and his next victim will be out of our territory."

"I suppose you've looked into similar murders around the country," I said.

"That was one of the first things we did. Nothing turned up at the time. We've had three reports since then. There was a killing in Kentucky that was similar in some respects—a sex motivated killing of a college student. It turned out the suspect they had in custody was at work on the day of the Richardson murder. In the past week or so, there were murders of young girls in Wisconsin and Iowa that were probably committed by the same guy. I don't think our man was involved. The crimes were basically different, involving violent abduction and rape."

I started to ask another question when, through the living room window, I saw Russ's daughter, Patti, cross the lawn in front of the house. She had a stuffed duffle bag over her shoulder. Russ and Rose have three children, a boy and two girls. Russ junior, the oldest, was a star athlete in high school who went to college on a baseball scholarship. After graduation, he took a job teaching social studies and coaching at the high school level. His baseball team reached the state finals in his second year as coach, something Russ was pretty pleased about. Their daughter Linda graduated from nursing school and went to New Mexico to work on an Indian reservation. Patti, the youngest, graduated from high school in the spring and would be starting her freshman year at the university. All of the children had inherited their mother's cheerful personality, but Patti got the largest dose. She was always relentlessly enthusiastic about whatever she did. Physically, she's a petite, very pretty version of Rose. When she came through the door and saw me, she dropped the duffle bag and flopped into a chair.

"Hi, Tom."

"Hello, Patti. In a few short days, you'll be a college student. How does it feel?"

"I'm excited. I can hardly wait."

"I stopped in today because I wanted to have a little talk with you before you start school."

"That's a fib. You came over to see Dad about something. Probably for some advice on what kind of tires to buy for your truck or how to adjust the carburetor. That's the kind of thing you two usually talk about."

"It's not. I came over with a warning for you. This year, if I find out you aren't studying hard enough, or partying too much, you're going to be in serious trouble with me."

"Oh, geeze," she said, rolling her eyes, "after eighteen years, I finally have the chance to get away from Dad's evil eye, and now you come along."

Russ groaned, but he was smiling.

"What's actually happened is that your dad has made me a deputy in charge of surveillance of a suspect by the name of Patti Merrick."

"You're trying to ruin my life, but it's not going to work. I have a question for you. When I see you on campus, do I call you Dr. Evers or Tom?"

"If you call me Dr. Evers, I won't answer."

"I'll try to remember that. Now, I have a warning for *you*. I've talked to some of my friends who've been in your classes. In spite of what they've told me, I'm planning to take all of the courses you teach."

"Okay, but I'll be especially hard on you."

"You treat me right, or I'll spread it around that you give good grades to girls who let you feel their bodies. I've got to go finish packing and practice being a college woman. See you around campus, Tom."

She grabbed the duffle bag and bounded up the stairs.

I watched her go, smiling fondly. "Russ, you're going to miss not having her around."

"I know. Life isn't going to be the same. When Patti came in, I was about to ask if you'd like to come downtown and go through the Richardson case folder."

"Wouldn't that violate regulations?"

"There's nothing to worry about. You've served as an expert witness and have consulted with us on several cases in the past. We'd probably have asked you to get involved in this case if a possible suspect had been identified . We'll keep it on an informal basis. I can arrange for you to go through the material in my office. Give me some notice before you come in."

We talked about truck tires and carburetor adjustments for a while before I left for home.

- 7 -

I pulled in the drive at three thirty. The sky had turned gray, and it was beginning to cool off. Beth was in the kitchen standing at the stove in deep concentration. When she heard the door open, she turned around. "I just finished preparing dinner. For appetizers we're having an assortment of cheeses and a marinade with artichoke hearts, black olives, and mushrooms. That'll be followed by coq au vin over noodles and fresh picked green beans with ham seasoning. When we're ready to eat, all I have to do is warm things up and cook the noodles. Let's go in the living room. I want to hear what Russ had to say."

"He said it was okay for me to do some investigating. In fact, I got the impression he liked the idea. I don't think he expects much from me, but he wants so badly to find the killer he might feel better if something was being done. After hearing how much time he's devoted to the case, I can't imagine I could add anything of significance."

Beth nodded.

"Patti bounced in when I was there. As you might imagine, she's excited about college."

"What did she talk about?"

"It's hard to summarize. You had to have been there. That kid has a special gift. Whenever I'm around her, I find myself having a good time. I've come to the conclusion she's in a different world, one that's more fun than the one we live in."

"I know what you mean," Beth said, as she stretched and yawned. "I'm feeling a little tired. I think I'll shower and take a nap. Would you like to join me?"

It was almost dark, and a heavy rain was pounding on the roof when we finally got around to dinner. It was still early when we finished eating it, but there didn't seem to be any way to improve on the day, so we went to bed.

I slept a full eight hours and was halfway through my morning run before the sun appeared on the horizon. I heard Beth moving around in the bedroom when I was getting out of the shower. Ten minutes later, she joined me in the kitchen. I stayed with her long enough to have a cup of coffee.

"My turn to cook tonight," I said, as I went out the door. Beth nodded in approval.

The campus was quiet at seven forty in the morning. A few upperclass students had already arrived. They're always eager to see their friends again and, in some cases, get out from under the supervision of their parents. The freshmen were due on Wednesday. By the end of the week, I could expect to be busy. I thought I'd better do some investigating while I still had some free time.

After checking my e-mail and finding that two committee meetings had been scheduled on Friday at the same time, I called Russ's number. He wasn't in his office. I left a message asking when I might be able to read the folder. He called back in twenty minutes and told me to come in during the lunch hour.

The city police department is located in a newly constructed building at the edge of town. It's a solid, windowless structure, which seemed suitable for the activities that went on inside. The first time I'd entered the building, I was impressed. The design and furnishings contributed to a pleasant, cheerful atmosphere. I'd been in dentists' offices that were far less attractive.

When I reached the front door, I met some of the office staff leaving for lunch. The uniformed officer behind the counter motioned for me to go on back to Russ's office. I recognized her from my previous visits to the department, but I couldn't remember her name. I wondered if females were more likely to be assigned desk duty than males.

Russ was on the phone. He waved me into his office and pointed to a heavy file folder on his desk. By the time I'd pulled up a chair, he'd finished talking. "Take all the time you need," he said. "I have a meeting to attend. If you finish before I'm back, put the folder in the bottom drawer of the file cabinet."

When he left, he closed the blind on the glass section of the door.

The folder contained reports of the officers who were first on the scene where the body was found, summaries of interviews, laboratory results, the findings of the medical examiner, and an envelope labeled photographs. I decided I'd save that until last—or maybe not even open it.

On the day of the murder, Whitney and two other students ordered a pizza about five o'clock. They ate in the dorm lounge. Whitney went back to her room a few minutes before six. No one saw her after that.

Whitney's roommate, Diane Jason, went to the library to do research on a paper early in the afternoon. Since there was no evening meal served in the dorm on Sunday, she ate some snacks from a vending machine in the library. She returned to the room at eleven thirty and went directly to bed. When she woke up at a quarter to eight the next morning, she assumed Whitney had studied in the library until it closed at midnight, and then had slipped out of the room quietly to go to her eight o'clock class.

According to the medical examiner's report, most of the injuries had been inflicted by an object such as a wooden club or a length of pipe. They covered a large area of the body, but the most severe were in the chest area and the upper thighs. The nose and front teeth had been broken. The pattern of the wounds suggested that the intent of the attacker was to maximize and prolong the suffering. The vagina had been penetrated by an object, probably the club or pipe used in the beating. There was no indication of penile penetration. The estimated time of death was between midnight and 3 a.m.

I opened the envelope containing photographs and removed the contents very cautiously. When I glanced at the color print on the top of the stack, I experienced a wave of nausea and quickly shoved the photos back into the envelope before returning it to the folder.

I was putting the folder into the file cabinet when Russ came through the door. "Did you learn anything?" he asked.

"More than I wanted to know. It was even worse than I thought."

"In my twenty-five years on the force, this one is as bad as I've ever seen. I've got another meeting. I'll talk to you later."

It had warmed up during the afternoon, and the pickup was parked in the sun. When I got in the cab, it felt like I was in a sauna. I ran into traffic, so it was a slow, hot trip back to the campus. The truck doesn't have air-conditioning.

Beth has told me I'm too cynical. She maintains that the modern world isn't as bad as I think it is. I've tried to interpret things in a more positive way, and have made some progress, but the time I'd spent with that folder set me back a long way.

As I inched along in traffic, it came to mind that animals rarely kill members of their own species. Nature films that show big horn sheep bashing their heads together or a pair of male lions snarling and biting and rolling in the dust give the false impression that one of the combatants is doomed. The violent confrontation is for the purpose of establishing dominance. It determines who'll have exclusive access to a group of females or have certain territorial rights. When the outcome of the battle is clear, the hostilities end. The victor has no desire to kill his adversary, even though, in all likelihood, he could. He's content with being in charge. The loser slinks off with no more than a variety of minor injuries, a bruised ego, and a more restricted sex life.

Humans have evolved to a level where they no longer share with other animals the obligation not to kill their own kind. Not only are they free to kill, but their highly developed central nervous system enables them to discover a remarkably large number of reasons to do so. Individually, they kill for material gain, power, and revenge. The neonates sometimes found in trash cans and dumpsters are testimony to the fact that murder can be a way to rid oneself of the burden of an unwanted child. Collectively, in the course of history, humans have killed to control territory and resources, to destroy those with differing religious beliefs, and, in some rare cases, merely for sport.

Of all the motivations for homicide, the most bizarre and distressing one for me is when it's for the purpose of sexual gratification. There is a grotesque irony in the fact that an instinctual desire, which insures the perpetuation of a species, can be satisfied by the destruction of a member of that species.

- 8 -

The air-conditioning in the psychology building contributed significantly to my comfort level, but I didn't expect it to do much for my mood. I stopped in the reception area to chat with Jean, who was back from vacation. She seemed a little depressed. I think the time away from work reminded her of how much more content she was in the role of full-time wife and mother.

I'd received several phone messages while I was out of the office. The only one of any importance was from Beth. She had a backlog of work after being away last week. It would probably be after eight before she got home.

I sat at my desk awhile trying to decide what to do in what was left of the afternoon. I could work on an article I was writing or spend time on the computer analyzing research data. It turned out to be neither of the above. I wasn't able get my mind off what I'd seen in the police file. I felt even more strongly about becoming involved.

I got out the notes I'd written at the station and looked through the list of people questioned by the police. According to the University Directory for the previous year, with a couple of exceptions, the students interviewed were seniors who would have graduated in the spring. They could only be reached by phone, if at all. No one in this group had been able to provide any significant information. I decided, for the time being, trying to reach them wouldn't be worth the effort.

One of the returning students was Diane Jason, Whitney's roommate. The police had interviewed her several times. She was first on the list I'd made at home of the individuals I definitely wanted to contact. I was frustrated because it would be later in the week before I could expect her to be back on campus.

The second name on my list was Julie Wood. Our psychology majors are required to write a thesis based on research they conduct during their senior year. The students work in pairs and the partners spend a great deal of time together. Julie had worked with Whitney. I knew from reading the police report that she

34

hadn't been contacted at the time of the murder. I had a feeling she might be able to provide some useful information about Whitney, and I was reasonably sure I could get in touch with her. I'd call her home. If she wasn't there, her family could tell me how to reach her.

Julie was highly attractive, immediately likeable, witty, and slightly irresponsible. I was concerned when she teamed up with Whitney because the two were so different. Julie's priorities were clear. She wanted to enjoy life to the fullest, and I'm sure she did. She had taken two courses with me and had gotten a C plus in both. I was convinced, after reading her exams, that she was intelligent enough to do far better work, but she wasn't interested in putting forth any extra effort.

Because Whitney was so dedicated to her studies, I imagined she could become very frustrated during the year with Julie's lack of motivation. It turned out there was no need to be apprehensive. I'd rarely supervised research partners who worked together so well. After a slow start, Julie showed an enthusiasm for the project I found to be remarkable.

Toward the end of the first semester, Julie made an appointment with me to discuss her plans after graduation. She wanted to get a graduate degree in social work. Three months earlier, I wouldn't have supported this decision, but her work in the seminar had been good enough that I encouraged her to apply. Later, she asked me to write letters of recommendation in support of her applications. In my letters, I said that Julie was a very intelligent, capable young woman who had the potential of becoming a first rate professional social worker. I also emphasized that she was a risk because she'd yet to consistently demonstrate the self-discipline and maturity necessary for success in a competitive graduate program. It turned out she'd been accepted on a conditional basis at a good university.

By the time I stopped at the grocery store and picked up some supplies for dinner, it was after six when I got home. After putting away the groceries, I went into my study and dug out a copy of a University Directory that would have a listing for Julie. The directory includes a student's campus address, phone number, and hometown address. It doesn't give the home phone number. I wasn't sure the phone company information service would be able to get me the number because I had nothing but a last name and a street address to give the operator. Fortunately, Julie was from a small town, and I got the number without difficulty.

I didn't want to interrupt a family dinner, so I waited an hour before putting in a call. Julie's mother answered. She told me Julie had gone back to school the day before and gave me her phone number. I reached Julie's answering machine. I gave my name and number and asked her to call when she got in.

The phone rang fifteen minutes later.

"Dr. Tom, I just got your message."

"Hang up, and I'll call you back. Students can't afford to pay for long distance calls."

When we were connected again, I said, "I want to ask you a few questions about Whitney, but first, tell me how things are going for you."

"I wasn't able to get a job in May, so I decided to enroll in summer school. I took two courses. The amount of work was awesome, but I got As in both. One of my instructors told me my term paper for the class was one of the best she'd read in a long time. I'm really looking forward to this semester. Besides the course work, I have a placement in a clinic for abused women and their children.

"When I met with my advisor this morning, she told me the staff thought I did excellent work this summer, and they were pleased to have me in the program. She said the admissions committee had some doubts about whether I should be admitted because of my overall grade point average. They decided to give me a chance after reading one of my letters of recommendation. She said usually recommendations tell about a student's strengths and don't mention any weaknesses. One of mine listed some weaknesses, so it carried a lot of weight. I knew it was yours. I didn't tell her you'd let me read it before it was sent."

"It's good to hear you're doing so well," I said, "but I'm not surprised. You remember what I kept telling you last year?"

"You said I had a large supply of brain cells that still hadn't been used. I've thought about that from time to time, and I think it's helped give me confidence."

"I'm pleased to hear that. Now, let's get back to the reason I called. Whitney's parents came to see me a few days ago. They're upset because the police haven't found her killer. They asked me to do some investigating. I doubt I'll be able to accomplish anything, but I decided to give it a try in memory of Whitney. I wanted to talk to you because you might be able to help."

"I'd like to, but I don't see how I could contribute anything."

"There's a possibility you can. I had the feeling last year that you and Whitney became good friends. I'm a little surprised the police didn't contact you during the investigation. I suppose it was because they had no way of knowing you'd spent so much time with Whitney in the period before she was murdered and might've been able to provide some valuable information. I want you to tell me all you know about Whitney and her life at school."

"Okay, I'll start from the beginning. I didn't know Whitney before we began working together on the seminar research project. You might say we traveled in different circles. After we were signed up as partners, I got scared. Whitney had the reputation as being one of the smartest girls, I mean women, on campus, and I wasn't what you'd call an outstanding student. I had visions of working thirty hours a week to keep up with her and having my senior year social life ruined, and I wondered if we'd get along personally. She seemed so serious, and being serious was something I hadn't practiced much."

"I was a little concerned myself when I learned you and Whitney would be research partners."

"The first thing we had to do was a computer search for articles relevant to our project. We decided we'd take turns at the terminal. Whitney started out and couldn't find what we needed. Then I tried and had the same problem. We went back and forth for maybe an hour and a half, getting more and more frustrated, and we couldn't find any of the library staff to help us. Finally, I took a break to go to the girls' room. When I came back, Whitney was stuffing things into her book bag. She said I could keep working if I wanted, but she was quitting for the night.

"I sat down at the terminal to give it one more try and saw that Whitney had typed a message on the screen in bold capitals expressing her frustration with the search process. It said—let me put it this way, there were some words in it I wouldn't have expected Whitney to use. I thought it was particularly well written, and I agreed totally. I deleted the message quickly, because I didn't want anyone to see it and think I'd written it. I left the library feeling that working with Whitney might be less of a problem than I'd expected."

"I was really pleased when I saw how well you and Whitney were getting along. You had more in common than I thought," I said.

"We did get along, and I owe a lot to Whitney. She thought the research was important, not just something to do so we could get a grade and pass the course. After awhile, I began to enjoy working on the project.

"I think I might've helped Whitney some, too. When I'd see her getting uptight, I'd try to lighten things up. For example, sometimes I'd talk her into going down to the bar for a beer after we finished a long night of work. She'd never done anything like that before, and it seemed to do her good."

"Did she date?" I asked. "She never mentioned much about her social life to me."

"She'd been going with Scott Griffin, a pre-med major, since her freshman year. Scott was a really nice looking guy who had a grade point average that was out of sight.

"At first, I thought he and Whitney were a perfect couple, but later on I began to have some doubts. When he'd come to pick her up sometimes, after we finished working on our research, I didn't think he treated her very well. He could be critical of what she was doing or how she looked, and he ordered her around. Besides that, I thought he was a bore. I wouldn't have put up with him for ten minutes.

"They broke up in the middle of February. I remember because we'd finished collecting our data and were ready to do the statistical analysis. I think they must've been having problems for quite a while before that. I had a feeling Whitney was depressed when she came back to campus at the beginning of the semester. It seemed to me that getting rid of Scott was the best thing that could've happened, but Whitney didn't see it that way. She was really upset. In fact, I ended up doing most of the work on the research project in the weeks before spring break. I didn't mind because Whitney had always done more than her share. Besides, I wanted to help in any way I could. I really felt sorry for her."

"I never saw that side of Whitney," I said. "When she was with me, she always seemed upbeat."

"I'm not surprised. Whitney was good at hiding her feelings. I guess you knew she stayed on campus over spring break?"

"Yes, she told me."

"It didn't make any sense to me. She'd been through a bad time, and I thought she needed to get away. I even invited her to come home with me for the week, but she said she couldn't leave because she'd gotten behind in her work, and there were some other things she had to take care of on campus."

"Did she talk about anybody she might've spent time with over the break?" I asked.

"No, she didn't. Sometimes I thought it was strange that we'd become so close during the year, and still she never talked much about what was going on in her life."

"Do you know if she left campus at any time during the week?"

"I got the impression she didn't, but I can't say for sure."

"Do you remember anything unusual that had been going on in her life earlier in the semester that might've been tied in with her murder in some way?"

"I can't think of anything in particular—though there was one thing that happened I thought was strange, but I'm sure it had nothing to do with Whitney's murder. A week after the memorial service, Scott Griffin called and wanted me to go to a party with him. I was shocked because it seemed like with Whitney gone, he thought it was all right to ask me for a date. I said some nasty things over the phone. The next day I started to call him to say I was sorry but didn't because I decided he should be the one to apologize."

"I agree with you; that was a strange thing for Scott to do. It strikes me as showing a lack of respect for the memory of Whitney."

"That's exactly the way I felt."

"You've told me a lot that I didn't know. It may help in the long run. If you remember anything else that might be important, give me a call."

"I will. I still think about Whitney and what happened to her, so I guess it's possible I might come up with something."

"I'd appreciate that, and come to see me if you're ever back on campus."

"You can count on it."

When I hung up the phone, I decided it was time to call the Richardsons. After four rings, the answering machine came on. I left a message telling them I intended to do some investigating into Whitney's death on a limited basis.

- 9 -

The next morning, it occurred to me that I should talk with Don Reynolds, the head of campus security, to let him know what I was planning to do. Also, I wanted to hear what he'd have to say about the case.

Don put in twenty-five years with the state police. By the end of his career, he'd worked his way up to a high level administrative position. He retired at fifty. A few months later, the university asked him if he'd consider taking charge of a reorganization of the campus security system. Under the previous head, the morale of the staff had fallen to a low level, and personal conflicts had impaired the functioning of the unit. Don agreed to come in for a year. He found he enjoyed the work and stayed on. In the three years since he'd taken over, the system had run smoothly, and he'd earned the respect of both students and faculty, which wasn't an easy thing to pull off.

I first met Don at the gym. He convinced me I ought to give handball a try. We've played once or twice a week ever since. Don is a natural athlete and keeps in top physical condition. Even though he's almost twenty years older than I am, there's no way I can keep up with him on the court.

After an hour of taking care of paperwork and answering e-mail messages, I headed across campus to the security office. From the entry area, I could see through the glass partition into Don's office. It was empty. Behind the counter, there was a pair of feet up on a desk. A newspaper hid the owner's face. I waited a minute or so and then asked if Don was going to be in. The paper lowered slowly, revealing the face of Rod Dudley, one of the security officers.

"He's on vacation. He'll be back in the office on Monday," Rod answered.

"Left you in charge?"

"Yeah. I guess he figured with no students around to cause trouble, I could handle the job. Should I tell Don you were looking for him?"

"Don't bother. I'll try to catch up with him next week."

When Don took over as director, he'd had to fill several staff vacancies. Rod was one of the first applicants. Even though he was young and had no experience in police work, Don felt he had potential and offered him a job. It turned out to be a good decision. Rod quickly gained the respect of his coworkers and always conducted himself in a professional manner. He got along well with the students, who affectionately called him Dudley Doright. Don often used him as a spokesperson for the department.

After Whitney's murder, Rod conducted a series of open meetings to inform the students of the increased security measures and the strategies they should use to insure their safety. I attended one of these and was impressed. Rod gave a highly organized presentation and dealt with the student questions effectively. I thought his performance had been superior to some of the lectures I'd attended given by distinguished scholars.

One of the things Rod had going for him, at least with the female students, was his remarkable good looks. He was a little over six feet tall with a muscular body, which he maintained through regular workouts in the weight room at the gym. He had a face like those guys who appear in adds for cigarettes or men's cologne. His blond hair came down to his shoulders. I figured he hadn't joined the state police, or some other law enforcement agency, because he'd have to change his hairstyle. Another possibility was that he wouldn't have access to the college women.

One night after a movie, Beth and I were eating pizza at a restaurant near the campus when Rod came in and sat at a nearby table. I pointed him out to Beth and asked her if she could understand why the female students found him so attractive. She just smiled and nodded.

The following Monday, classes started, and students began showing up at my door. There was the usual group of advisees who'd decided at the last minute to change their schedule, and those returning students who dropped by my office just to report on the details of their exciting summers.

Finally, mid-morning on Wednesday, things slowed down enough that I had a chance to call Don. I explained to him on the phone about my meeting with the Richardsons and asked if he could spend some time going over the case with me. He suggested we meet for lunch at the faculty cafeteria.

"We need to play some handball," he said, as we put down our trays on a table in a far corner of the dining area.

"That's right, and you can expect some strong competition this year," I said, as Don started in on the first of a group of plates that must've contained two thousand calories of food. Whenever I ate with Don, I was amazed he was able to keep his weight under 300 pounds.

"You talked to Russ?" Don asked.

"Yes, I did, and he gave me a detailed report of the police findings."

"As far as I can tell, he's conducted a first rate investigation, and he had the support of the state police. I wouldn't have done anything different. Russ is a good man. Some of the law enforcement people in a small city like ours aren't very good at handling this type of case. It's understandable because they don't have to deal with murders very often. When they do, the victim's been stabbed by his next door neighbor or shot by a guy he drinks beer with on Saturday night.

"I've gone over the case with Russ several times. I agree with his analysis up to a point. He tends to think the guy has moved on, but I'm not so sure. Suppose our friend has a preference for young women? He's demonstrated it in one case. Right in this area, he has a pool of several thousand potential victims, and he's shown he's clever enough to take advantage of the opportunities here. Why would he want to go anywhere else?"

"I take it you go along with Russ's theory that he'll probably kill again?"

"I do. We know from experience that individuals who commit this type of sex crime are likely to repeat. I'm concerned that no matter what precautions are taken, it may not be possible to stop him. I don't want to wish problems on anyone else, but I hope Russ is right about him moving on."

"If you had to develop a profile of the killer, what would it look like?"

"I've thought about that. This is entirely speculation, so don't quote me. He has a steady job and is probably a loner with few close friends. The people he works with and his neighbors think he's a normal guy who prefers to keep to himself. There's a good chance he's fairly intelligent. Age anywhere from early twenties to late thirties. He could be a student or even a member of the faculty."

"I've considered that possibility myself, but it's really hard for me to imagine someone connected to the campus would be capable of a crime like this," I said.

"I know, but in this business you have to keep an open mind. Before I took this job, my wife and I thought about moving to Florida. We went down one winter and stayed with an old friend from the state police who'd moved there after he retired. He lives near a university campus. He told me about an interesting case. A convicted serial killer reported that a faculty member from the university had helped him get his homosexual victims and participated in some of the murders. There was considerable evidence to support the allegation but not enough to bring charges."

"If the killer was a student or a faculty member the victim knew, it would explain how he managed to get her into the car," I said.

"That's right. It would solve one of the real puzzles in this case." Don looked at his watch. "I'm late for a meeting. Call me when you want to start playing handball."

"Before you go, can you give me any suggestions as to what I might do?"

"Russ's covered a lot of ground. At this point, there aren't any hard and fast rules on what direction the investigation should take. You're on your own."

I was on my way back to the psychology department when I heard someone shouting, "Thomas, hey, Thomas." It had to be Matt Donovan. He has a voice like no other. It reminds me of a base drum. I spotted him immediately as he was making his way through the parking lot across the street. You might say Matt stands out. He's six feet six inches tall, weighs 240 pounds, has a mop of red hair, and a full beard. Matt dresses pretty much the same way all the time. He had on his summer outfit of jeans, a T-shirt, and sandals. When the weather turned cold, he'd be wearing jeans, a plaid flannel shirt, and high-top basketball shoes.

"It's good to see you, Thomas," he called out, as he stepped in front of a slow-moving car. The driver looked like he was about to shout an obscenity but thought better of it when Matt smiled at him and waved a giant hand.

"How's Northern Michigan's Henry David Thoreau?" I asked.

"I'm fine, but I must point out the errors in your literary reference. Henry lived in quiet solitude in a ten by fifteen-foot cabin on Walden Pond, which he built with his own hands—not in a large log house with a wife, three children, two cats, and a dog. And, as I recall, there are no black flies in eastern Massachusetts."

I ignored the lecture. "Did you have a good summer?"

"Yes, I did."

"Does that mean you finished the book?"

"I mailed a completed draft to the publisher last week."

"How's Rachel?" I asked.

"Just fine. She loves it up north because she has more time to spend with the kids and to practice her cello."

I thought about Rachel and shook my head. "Matt, I've never been able to understand how you managed to talk such an intelligent, talented, beautiful woman into marriage."

Matt smiled. "Thomas, one thing we have in common is that we both have wives we don't deserve."

I smiled. "You're absolutely right, and we have to work hard at keeping them from realizing it."

"Now tell me how your summer went. Were you able to get away at all?"

"The prosecutor's office was too busy for Beth to take much time off, but we managed to have a good summer staying close to home."

I told Matt about the Richardson visit and that I intended to do some investigating. I was curious as to how he'd respond. I've great respect for his judgment, and he's the kind of person who says exactly what he thinks.

When I finished, he frowned. "What did Beth have to say?"

"She went along with it."

"It must be all right then. We've got to get together soon so you can bring me up to date on what those barbarians in the administration building are planning to spring on us this year, and we have to talk about basketball. This year we're going to be the intramural champs. Rachel will be calling to invite you to dinner as soon as we get settled. She'll want to see Beth."

Matt is one of the more interesting people I know. The males in his family worked in the steel mills for generations. He'd have probably gone the same route if he hadn't been offered a football scholarship to attend college. Soon after he arrived on the campus, he developed a taste for literature. He came to view football as a job that provided him with a free education. Rachel mentioned to Beth once that Matt had been drafted by the pros. He'd accepted a graduate fellowship instead. By the time he was in his early thirties, he'd published a highly acclaimed book in the field of nineteenth century American literature.

Matt's teaching style is unusual. The reading lists for his classes are impossibly long. His exams would challenge a doctoral candidate, and he gives very few As and Bs. If students give a weak answer when called on in class, or have failed to read the assignment, they can expect to be chastised. Under those conditions, you'd assume students would sign up for a course with Matt only as a last resort.

But in fact, Matt is such a popular teacher, the enrollment limits for his classes are reached during the first few hours of the registration period. Students typically have to wait for two or three semesters before they're fortunate enough to get into a class where they'll be overworked, receive a low grade, and run the risk of being embarrassed in front of their peers. Why do they do it? Matt is a master teacher who has the ability to get students excited about reading great literature. They understand he's demanding because he wants them to make full use of their abilities.

One of my advisees told me of his experience with Matt, which I think was typical. "After I was in the course for a week, I was afraid I couldn't handle the pressure. I wanted out. By the time it was over, I could hardly believe how much I'd accomplished. It was by far the best experience I've had at school." I tried not to think about the fact that the student had taken two of my courses.

- 10 -

I'd hoped to arrange a meeting with Diane Jason sometime during the week, but each time I started to call her, there was an interruption. Finally, late Friday afternoon, I found myself alone in my office with no one in the reception area waiting to see me.

I called the university switchboard and asked for Diane's phone number. The operator informed me the that new listings had not yet been entered into the computer, and she had no idea when they might be available. Next I tried calling the dorm where Diane and Whitney had lived the year before. The receptionist said there was no Diane Jason on the list of current residents. I called two other residence halls with no success. After my last call, I wondered what would happen if Diane needed to be contacted in case of a family emergency.

It wasn't until the following Tuesday that I was able to get a phone number for Diane. I finally reached her just before leaving for the day. When I identified myself, she remembered that Whitney had been my teaching assistant and had been working with me on her senior thesis. I explained briefly why I was calling. She seemed eager to help. It turned out it would be Friday before there was a time when we were both free.

Diane arrived at my office promptly at three o'clock. She was tall and quite thin. She had sharp facial features and deep-set, large, brown eyes. Her dark brown hair, which was pulled back in a ponytail, hung down to her shoulders.

"We've met before?" I asked, as she settled into a chair.

Diane nodded.

I had to think for a moment. "It was the time Whitney ended up in the health center with a bad case of the flu. She sent you over with the papers she'd been grading for me. I apologize for not remembering. As I told you on the phone, I've decided to do some investigating into Whitney's death. It's nothing official, but I've mentioned it to the police. I have a good friend on the force. Even if I don't

44

come up with anything, I'll feel better if I give it a try." I didn't see any reason to bring up my conversation with the Richardsons.

"I understand," she said.

"I want to find out as much as possible about Whitney in the time before her death. Occasionally, Whitney spoke of you, and it sounded as though you were fairly close."

"Yes, we were."

"How long had you roomed together?"

"Two years." She hesitated. "Almost two years. In my freshman year, I had problems with my roommate. She partied a lot and did very little schoolwork. She'd stay up late at night and sleep most of the day. Our room was always a mess. She thought I was stupid because I studied so much.

"Whitney was a sophomore on my floor in the dorm. I talked with her about the problem. The same thing had happened to her when she was a freshman. Toward the end of the second semester, Whitney asked me if I'd like to room with her the next year. Her roommate was a graduating senior. I jumped at the chance."

"It sounds as though it worked out all right."

"Yes, definitely. We were both away from the room most of the time. Whitney studied in the library with her boyfriend, Scott Griffin, and she was very active in campus activities. I'm a double major in physics and chemistry, so I spend a lot of time in the lab. When we were in the room together, we respected each other's need for quiet.

"If I was stressed out studying for an exam and a little irritable, Whitney would be patient with me, and I did my best to be understanding when she was under pressure. I considered her one of my closest friends. We kept in touch over the summer, and she came to visit for a week at my house before we came back to school."

"I understand she'd gone with Scott for a long time, and that they broke up before she died."

Diane nodded. "They started dating during their freshman year. I'm not really sure what happened between them, but right after the start of the second semester, I got the feeling things weren't going well. Not long after that, Whitney told me she and Scott had broken up. Maybe I shouldn't say this, but sometimes I wondered if their relationship was a good one."

"Any particular reason?"

"Nothing specific. It just seemed to me that sometimes he didn't give her the respect she deserved."

"How did Whitney react to the breakup?"

"It was really sad to watch. At first, she cried a lot. I'd wake up at night and see her sitting at the desk quietly sobbing. After awhile, she seemed to be pulling herself together, but I think she was covering up quite a bit. I know she was having trouble getting her work done. You knew Julie Wood, her research partner?"

I nodded.

"She was great. I'm pretty sure she did most of the work on the project for several weeks."

"I talked with Julie on the phone. She mentioned that."

"What made it even harder for Whitney was that her parents were so upset about it. I was in the room several times when she was on the phone with them. They must've kept asking what had happened because during every call, she'd tell them that it just didn't work out, or it wasn't her fault. I got the impression they'd wanted her to marry Scott. Maybe I can see why parents would think he'd be a good deal. He was nice looking, intelligent, and very ambitious. Still, to put that much pressure on Whitney didn't seem fair. I think they were hard on Whitney all along. She talked to them on the phone at least once a week, and I got the feeling she didn't look forward to the call."

"When I first talked with Whitney about changing her major to psychology, she seemed concerned about what her father would think. She never said anything about how he reacted."

"I know when Whitney told him she was dropping out of pre-med he said he'd pay for medical school but not for graduate school in psychology. I couldn't imagine how a father could say that. My parents have sacrificed so my brother and I could get a good education. I came to college intending to go into medicine, just like Whitney. My mom and dad were excited about my choice, but when I decided to change majors, I knew it'd be all right with them. My dad told me to do what I thought I'd enjoy.

"You probably know Whitney stayed on campus over spring break?"

I nodded.

"It might've been because she didn't want to face her parents. I invited to her to come home with me, but she said she had to stay here and get caught up on some work."

"Did Whitney tell you how she spent her time during the break?"

"When I got back to campus, I asked her how the week went. She didn't seem to want to talk about it, so I figured it wasn't a particularly good time for her. But I was pleased that she seemed to be in a little better mood. I remember thinking that maybe she was finally beginning to get over the breakup with Scott."

"Was there anything unusual that happened during the week after spring break, or did Whitney act differently in any way?"

"I didn't notice anything except what I told you about her feeling a little better."

"I've read the police file. You told them that on the Sunday Whitney disappeared, you spent most of the day in the library, so you didn't know what she did or if she met with anybody."

"That's right. We were in the room together for a while in the morning. She never mentioned anything about what she planned to do that day."

"Can you think of anything out of the ordinary that happened before spring break?"

"There was only one thing I can think of, and it wasn't all that unusual. Not too long after Whitney broke up with Scott, she began getting calls from other guys asking for dates. She always refused. Then she started getting calls from Charlie . . . I can't remember his last name. She kept saying no. He was really nice looking and very popular, but he didn't have a very good reputation. I was a little surprised when Whitney finally agreed to go out with him. He wasn't her type. Maybe it was because he was so persistent, or she just needed to do something to get her mind off the breakup with Scott.

"They went to a big annual party at his fraternity house. The kind of thing where everyone wears a costume. The evening didn't turn out well, and Whitney was back in the room about eleven. She was very upset and angry. Charlie had been drinking even before he picked her up. At the party, he got really drunk and forced her into his room. He tried to take off her clothes, and she really had to struggle to get away. The next day, she did her best to laugh about it. She said they ought to change the name of the fraternity to Delta Rho, the date rape house.

"Sunday evening, Charlie called Whitney. He apologized and asked her if she'd go out with him again. Of course, she refused, but that didn't stop him. He began calling every day. It was over a week before he finally gave up."

I couldn't remember anything in the police file about Whitney dating in the weeks before she was killed. "Did you mention that when you talked with them?"

"I guess I didn't," she said, after thinking for a moment. "I was so upset I may have left out some things. I'm sorry if I made a mistake."

"Don't worry. I'm sure you told them everything that was important. Do you know what fraternity Charlie was in?"

"I don't remember. There's a woman in the dorm who dated him for a while. She'd know. I think he was a graduating senior, so it isn't likely he's on campus now. I can check if you want."

"Why don't you see what you can find out and call me?"

"I will. I really want to help if I can."

"You already have. Thanks for coming in to see me."

During our conversation, I'd come to realize that Diane was a very talented and interesting young woman. It aroused my curiosity about her future plans.

"Before you leave, I want to ask you something else. You're a science major. What're you planning to do after graduation?"

"Hopefully, graduate school in physics. After that, I'll probably try to get a research position somewhere. I'd like to teach at a university, but I don't think I'd be a very good teacher. Even thinking about speaking before a group of people scares me."

"Diane, a career in teaching can be very rewarding. It's a little early for you to give up the idea."

"I suppose I should think about it," she said, as she got up to leave.

- 11 -

Things were quiet in the psychology building at seven thirty on Monday morning. The campus doesn't come alive until a little later when drowsy students begin to make their way toward eight o'clock classes and office doors are unlocked by early arriving, conscientious secretaries. I'd just begun to go over the lecture notes for my first class of the morning when the phone rang. Wrong number, I thought. No one ever calls at that hour.

"Tom Evers," I said, as I picked up the receiver.

"Dr. Evers, this is Diane. I was hoping to catch you before I left for class. I have an eight o'clock and won't be back to my room until late. Charlie's last name is Rutledge. He lived at the Sigma Gamma Delta house last year. He didn't have enough credits to graduate, so he's taking courses this semester and living off-campus. I have to run. Let me know if I can do anything more."

I hung up, thinking that Diane always handed in assignments on time.

I'd learned from experience that the best time to call a fraternity house was during the noon hour. Most of the students would be there for lunch and someone was likely to be near the phone.

At twelve thirty, I dialed the fraternity house number. It took six rings before there was a voice on the other end.

"Sigma Gamma Delta, this is John, good afternoon."

"John, it's important for me to get in touch with one of your brothers, Charles Rutledge. I understand he's living in town this semester. Could you give me his phone number?"

"I'll try, sir. Please hold on."

John neglected to push the mute button so the caller on the line couldn't hear.

"There's someone on the phone who wants Rutledge's phone number. Anybody got it?"

Pause.

49

"I know he doesn't want us to give it out. But the hell with that. I'm sick of trying to cover for him."

Pause.

"No, it's a male."

Pause.

John laughed. "It couldn't be the police. They have his number in more ways than one."

Pause.

"That sounds okay."

John came back on the line. "Sir, we can't seem to find Charlie's number, but he moved into an apartment with Dick Gannon. You might try calling there."

"Thanks for your help, John," I said. I hung up feeling that John had provided me with more information than he'd intended.

I checked the phone book and found a listing for Richard Gannon. Charlie seemed to be the type who'd be home during the day and out at night, so I dialed the number.

After four rings, an answering machine recording came on. "You've reached party land. If this is a female, you can count on us to satisfy your every need. Leave your name and number and we'll get back to you."

My two calls made me wonder if I was going to be able to get Charlie to come to my office. I decided on a strategy. Over the phone, I wouldn't reveal my purpose in wanting to see him hoping he'd think that if he refused my request, he could end up in trouble of some kind.

Before leaving at the end of the day, I tried another call. This time a male answered.

"This is Dr. Evers. I'd like to speak to Charles Rutledge," I said, trying to sound as serious as I could.

"You're talking to him now."

"Charles, it's important for me to meet with you as soon as possible. I'd like you to come to see me in my office—tomorrow would be preferable."

"What's this about?"

"It's not something I can discuss over the phone."

There was a long pause before he said, "I guess I could be there at three."

"I'll see you then. My office is in Coomer Hall, room 218C."

We both hung up without saying anything more. I'd have to wait until the next afternoon to see if my strategy worked.

It was twenty minutes after three when Charlie showed up at my office door. He had on baggy, oversized tan shorts and a white oxford cloth dress shirt with wide, pink stripes. It was unbuttoned down to a point just above his navel, revealing a mat of hair on his chest. His high top basketball shoes were untied, the laces dragged on the floor. I'd have to take Diane's word that he was nice looking. To me, he looked slimy, but I might've been slightly prejudiced by that time.

I motioned toward a chair. Charlie slouched down in it with his legs stretched out, pointing toward my desk. I had the impression he'd purposely kept me waiting. I decided I could play that same game, so I shuffled papers on my desk for a minute or two.

"I'm working with the police on the investigation of the Whitney Richardson murder case. It's come to our attention that you dated Whitney during the period before she was killed."

Charlie had been caught off guard. He shifted in the chair and seemed to lose his composure for an instant. As he repositioned himself, I imagined he was trying to decide what the safest response would be.

"I dated her one time." He paused to construct his story. "I took her to a party at the fraternity house."

"You dated her only once. Why was that?"

"The night didn't go well. We got separated at the party. I was talking to some people and she wandered off. I looked for her, but she'd disappeared somewhere. I thought maybe she wasn't feeling well and went into one of the rooms upstairs to lay down."

"Did you look upstairs?"

"At a party like that, you don't go barging into rooms," Charlie said in a tone of voice that suggested he was appalled at my lack of sophistication.

"What happened when you found her?"

"I never did. When it was getting late, I got worried. I looked around some more and then asked a few of the girls if they knew where she was at. One of them told me she'd seen her leave quite a bit earlier. Just before that, she saw her getting sick in the bathroom. She must've had too much to drink."

"Did you try to get in touch with her?"

"No. If she went back to the dorm drunk, I didn't want to embarrass her by calling, and she could've passed out from what this other girl said."

"Did you have any contact with her after that night?"

"Yeah, I called her the next day to see if she was okay. I even asked her if she wanted to go out for a Coke or something. She said she didn't. I think she couldn't face me because she was embarrassed about what happened at the party."

"Was that the last time you talked to her?"

"I called a couple of more times. I felt a little sorry for her. I didn't ask her for a date or anything like that. I could tell by the way she acted on the phone she would've liked to go out with me again, but I wasn't interested. She went with some pre-med nerd for a long time. She was pretty socially immature and didn't know how to act when she was with a guy."

"Did you have any contact with her the week after spring break?"

"Oh, no. I hadn't even talked to her in over a month."

At this point, I'd had about all I could take of Charlie, but before he left my office, I wanted to plant the idea that he might be a suspect in the case. He deserved to sweat a little.

"Where were you the night of the murder?"

Charles answered quickly. "Drinking beer with friends."

"Do you remember who these friends were?"

"Not exactly. Every Sunday night a bunch of us at the fraternity would get a few cases of beer. You know, to get ready for the week."

I decided to squeeze a little harder. "Could you come up with their names if you had to?"

"Most of them graduated, but there might be one or two that are still around."

"I've no further questions at this time, but you can expect to be contacted by the police, and they'll want to examine your relationship with Whitney in considerably greater depth than we have today." Of course, I wasn't at all sure that was true.

Charlie left considerably less arrogant and self assured than when he'd arrived. I imagined him dealing with the stress of the afternoon by picking up a cold six pack of beer on his way home.

As I made notes on the interview, I realized Charlie had never referred to Whitney by name. I wondered if that was of any significance.

After work, Beth usually spent forty minutes in the exercise room we'd set up in the basement. I was surprised when I got home to find her in the kitchen preparing dinner.

"Are you finished with your workout already?" I asked.

"I wasn't in the mood for strenuous physical activity, so I decided to take the day off and spend the time cooking."

I sat at the kitchen table while she worked and told her about my interview with Charlie.

"Do you think he's part of the puzzle?" Beth asked.

"I have no idea, but I want to see what else I can find out about him."

- 12 -

The next morning, Beth and I overslept. For some reason, we'd neglected to set the alarm. I ran only three miles instead of the usual five and still didn't get to my office until a little past eight thirty. One of the advantages of being a faculty member is not having to punch a clock. Because of that, some outsiders think we don't work very hard. Based on my personal observations, I'm convinced most academics devote at least as much time to their job as the majority of the workers in this country.

I checked for phone messages. There was one from Diane asking me to call. She'd be in her room until she left for a nine o'clock class. If I didn't catch her before then, she'd try to reach me later in the day. I picked up the phone quickly and dialed her number. I was curious why she'd call so soon after we'd talked. She answered after the first ring.

"This is Tom," I said. "Why such an early call?"

"I wanted to know if you'd be interested in talking with the woman who gave me Charlie's name and told me the fraternity he belonged to. She dated him off and on for quite a while."

"I certainly would."

"I thought you might. When I asked her about Charlie, she didn't go into any detail but said enough to give me the impression she'd had a bad experience with him. It's possible she could give you some important information. I know her well enough to feel comfortable about asking her if she'd be willing to come and see you."

"I'd appreciate that, but I wouldn't want any pressure put on her. Try this approach. Explain to her that I'm doing some unofficial investigating into Whitney's murder. Tell her that anything she might reveal to me will be entirely confidential, and I don't need to know her name. If she's willing to talk, have her

53

come to my office and say, 'Diane sent me.' The rest of the week, I won't schedule anything after four o'clock."

"I'll probably see her in the dining hall at lunch. I can check with her then and get back to you as soon as I have an answer. I've also done a little more investigating. I thought of another woman who dated Charlie. We were in a seminar together last semester. I called her yesterday. She lives in a sorority. When I mentioned Charlie's name, she cut me off immediately. It was obvious she didn't want to talk about him. If it's all right with you, I'll keep trying to find other people who might have something to say about Charlie."

"That could be worthwhile. But remember, you're still a student. I assume you have enough to keep you busy. Make sure you give your studies top priority."

"I just want to do everything I can to help. I can handle my assignments."

"Diane, I really appreciate what you have done so far."

"Dr. Evers, just call me Archie."

It took me a moment to figure out what she meant. "Okay, but only under the condition that you call me Mr. Wolfe."

"It's a deal. I'll talk to you later."

It might've appeared that Diane was being flippant with that Nero Wolfe reference. However, I knew her well enough to recognize that she was simply trying to insert some comic relief into a very grim and serious issue.

I had a brown bag lunch committee meeting, which lasted until one thirty. There was a phone message for me when I got back to my office. "Mr. Wolfe, this is Archie. She'll be at your office today at four."

I kept the afternoon free so I could work on the statistical analyses of some research data. As usual, I was mesmerized by the computer screen and lost track of time. I was brought out of my trance when someone appeared at my door and said, in a very soft voice, "I think Diane told you I'd be coming to see you."

She was above average in height with a full figure and narrow waist. Heavy makeup and hair which seemed to have lost its vitality from relentless bleaching tended to detract from her natural good looks. The outfit she was wearing—a simple blouse, fashion jeans, and stylish boots—had obviously been selected with care. She had a knack for choosing clothes, and she wore them well.

"Yes, she did. Please sit down," I said, as I got up from my chair in front of the computer and closed the door.

She was clearly uncomfortable, so I tried to be reassuring. "Thanks for coming. I realize it wasn't an easy thing for you to do. I know Diane has explained why I wanted to see you. I'm trying to find out more about the circumstances surrounding Whitney Richardson's murder. The reason for that is I knew Whitney well and thought highly of her. I'd like to see the killer apprehended. The police are aware I've become involved. Because I'm a private citizen and working in an unofficial capacity, I'm free to choose what information I share with them. I can guarantee our conversation will be entirely confidential. For that matter, no one will know we've talked. Diane didn't tell me your name, and there's no reason for me to know it.

"Recently, I found out that Charlie Rutledge dated Whitney before she was killed. I assure you, I'm not betraying any confidences when I tell you I've talked with him. I got the feeling in our conversation that he wasn't entirely straightforward with me. I'd like to get a better understanding of Charlie. I don't mean to imply that he's a suspect. I just want to find out more about Whitney's life before the murder."

I worried that I might have revealed too much to a person I didn't know. I had taken the risk because I felt it was the best way to get her to talk openly.

"I understand." Again, she spoke softly. There was a gentleness in her manner I found engaging.

In clinical practice, psychologists use several types of interviewing techniques depending on the purpose of the interview. Specific questions can provide the necessary information in some cases. The problem with this is that the patient may fall into a pattern of giving a brief answer and then wait for the next question. That may limit the amount of information elicited. Another strategy is to start off with more general questions, which allows the patient greater freedom in responding. Follow-up inquiries are used to encourage the patient to clarify and elaborate on these responses. Even though I wasn't conducting a clinical interview, the same rules applied. I decided on the second approach.

"I'm interested in the type of relationship you had with Charlie."

After a pause, she said, "I'm not sure where to start."

"You might tell me how you met and go from there." My comment seemed to give her the direction she needed.

"It was the beginning of the fall semester last year. We were in the same section of Intro to Sociology. He came in late the first day and took the seat next to me. I don't know why, but in every class I take, I always sit in the last row. At the end of the lecture on Friday of the first week, we walked out of class together. He asked me if I'd like to go out with him on Saturday. His fraternity had a pig roast the first weekend of the semester on a farm on North River Road. I'd heard about it. It sounded like fun, and I thought Charlie was a really cute guy.

"We had a good time at the pig roast. He asked me out the next weekend, and we dated until the end of January. It wasn't like we were going steady or pinned or anything like that. I know he went out with other girls, and I dated some other guys."

At this point, I realized I wasn't going to have to probe for information. The young woman sitting across the desk from me needed to talk. She wouldn't have come to see me if that wasn't the case, and I suspected she was about to tell me things she hadn't shared with anyone.

"I really liked going out with Charlie. He was fun to be with. Everybody knew him, and he could always find the good parties. He drank a lot and that caused some problems. When he was drunk, he could be critical and even mean. After we'd been seeing each other for a couple of months, he began to change. He was always, you might say, sexually aggressive, but it got worse. If I didn't do what he wanted, he'd twist my arm or hit me. I had to hide the bruises or tell people I'd bumped into something. At first, he'd apologize and blame it on being drunk, and he'd be nice for a while, but it would happen again. Finally, he wouldn't even say he was sorry."

She was silent for a moment. I wondered if she was beginning to feel she'd talked too freely. It was time for me to assure her that it was all right to continue.

"I imagine there have been times when you've wondered why you continued seeing Charlie."

She nodded, and tears began to collect in the corners of her eyes.

"I can understand how it might be hard to think about what happened," I said gently.

She took a deep breath and wiped her eyes with a tissue from her purse. "I finally did break it off. I was such a fool not to do it earlier."

There was another silence. It appeared she had won the battle with the tears. I waited without saying anything. She was quiet for so long I assumed she had reached the point where she wouldn't be comfortable telling me anything more. I was about to bring the meeting to an end when she began to talk again.

"There was this party at his fraternity." The tears returned. "He was drunk when he picked me up. A few minutes after we got to the house, he said we were going up to his room where he had a bottle of vodka. In the condition he was in, I didn't want to be alone with him, so I said I wanted to stay downstairs. That made him angry. He grabbed me by the arm so hard it hurt and pulled me up the stairs and into his room. Then he seemed to lose it. He threw me down on the bed and began beating me with his fists and calling me a slut and things like that. I was too terrified to fight him off. Later, he passed out, and I was able to leave without him knowing. That was the last time I saw him."

She sat motionless. She'd experienced what therapists refer to as a catharsis. A demon had been exorcized from her body. It left her emotionally and physically depleted.

"The things you went through when you were dating Charlie can be very damaging to one's feelings of self worth, and it's all too easy to blame yourself for what happened. I'm sure it must have been a very difficult time."

She nodded, as the tears slid down her cheeks. "It's been hard—really hard."

"I think you should consider getting some professional counseling. There's a person I'd like you to see. She's a friend of mine who has a private practice in town. It's important to her to help women who've had experiences similar to yours, so she doesn't charge them a fee." I wrote Janet Bryant's phone number and office address on a sheet of computer paper and handed it across the desk.

"Thank you, Dr. Evers," she said, as she carefully folded the paper and put it into her purse.

"Dr. Bryant is a very understanding person. I hope you'll get in touch with her. What you've told me this afternoon has been helpful. I don't have any other questions."

She got up from her chair and paused for moment. "My name is Jenny Lambert."

"Nice meeting you, Jenny. Thanks for coming to see me."

She nodded and walked out of my office.

Psychological and physical abuse of women occur in all segments of our society. There's no reason to expect that college women are immune. Nevertheless, when I come in contact with a case like Jenny's, I find it particularly disturbing. It reminds me that on the campus, as well as everywhere else, for every woman who reports abuse, we can be sure there are many more who remain silent. Just as Jenny had done for so long.

Out of curiosity, before leaving the office, I dialed Charlie's number. The machine informed me that there wasn't anyone available to answer the phone, and I was asked to leave my name and number. The change Charlie'd made in the message put me in a little better mood.

- 13 -

When I got home, there was a phone message from Beth. Busy day. She hoped to be home by seven thirty. Since I had nothing to do for a couple of hours, I decided to work on preparing the exams I had scheduled for my classes the next week.

I went into my study and turned on the computer. After looking at a blank green screen for twenty minutes, I gave up. Intelligent humans operate on the assumption that they're in control of their thoughts and actions. It would be absurd to think otherwise. Of course, this is the ultimate self-deception. If we had total control, there'd be few overweight people and excessive drinkers, only an occasional smoker, and students would seldom get failing grades. I knew I should be working on exams, but I couldn't direct my thoughts away from the investigation.

I opened my investigation file and began entering a summary of the work I'd done on the case, including the notes I'd made downtown and those from the interviews. I made a printout and reviewed what I'd written. It seemed I might've made some progress. Julie had given me more detailed information about Whitney's life in the months before the murder than the police had been able to obtain from the people they had interviewed. And Diane had told me about someone in Whitney's life before her death who was capable of violence that the police hadn't contacted.

I thought about what I might do next. Even though Charlie was obviously a disturbed individual, it was hard to imagine that a guy who had taken Whitney to a fraternity party, weeks before she was murdered, could be in any way connected to the crime. In spite of this, I wondered if it might be worthwhile calling Russ and Don Reynolds to see if their departments had had any contact with him. I'd just started on the exams when I heard Beth's car pull in the driveway. The exams would have to wait.

While we were eating a late dinner of leftovers, I told Beth about my interview with Jenny. She looked very serious and asked several questions. When she went off to bed shortly after we'd finished eating, I went back to my study. I felt guilty enough about spending time on the investigation, so I worked until after midnight preparing exams.

The next morning, I woke up to a heavy rain. Even though I look forward to my morning workout, sometimes it's a relief to have an excuse to take a day off. I lingered over a second cup of coffee and still arrived at my office a half-hour earlier than usual. I'd just sat down at my desk when the phone rang. It had to be Archie.

"Good morning, Mr. Wolfe. I didn't expect you to be in this early. I was going to leave a message. I wanted to let you know—I found two more women who've dated Charlie. Neither of them were willing to talk much about their experiences, even with me, but both agreed it'd be all right to tell you that Charlie had battered them physically. I thought you might want to know."

"Yes, and that adds to the information Jenny gave me yesterday. Oh, I should tell you she volunteered her name. I never asked."

"Don't worry, I already knew. Jenny came to my room last night and told me about her talk with you. She felt good about it."

I was relieved. "Archie, you've done a first rate job. I'm sorry to have to tell you this, but you're fired. It's time for you to get back to being a full-time student again."

"You can't fire me," she said emphatically.

"Why not?"

"Because I quit."

"That's the problem with the younger generation. They're always trying to avoid work."

"It's not our fault. It's the result of being raised by overindulgent parents who didn't set limits on our behavior and gave us credit cards before we were old enough to get a driver's license. We expect the world to be handed to us on a plastic tray." She laughed. "If I can do anything more, call me. And would you let me know about any developments that you're free to talk about?"

"I will. Before you hang up, I want to give you some advice. Not exactly advice, just a suggestion. You mentioned at our first meeting that you might be interested in a career in academics. I've a feeling you could become a fine teacher. When you get to graduate school, think about volunteering to teach an introductory course in physics. I know you said you'd be too frightened to do it, but you should keep in mind that most people are a little nervous when they face their first class. I was terrified."

"You said that just to give me some encouragement."

"That's right. I did. But it happens to be true."

"Thanks for the suggestion, Dr. Evers."

"Dr. Evers?"

"You forgot, I don't work for you anymore. I've got to run to class. Goodbye."

"Goodbye, Diane."

One of the reasons it's so enjoyable to work with college students is that most of them are able to laugh and have fun. On alumni weekends, I see graduates strolling around campus looking so grim. I sometimes wonder if there isn't some unwritten rule that on graduation day you have to begin taking life seriously. It seems to me the world would be a better place if we, as adults, could take a lesson from the students and lighten up a little.

I left my ten o'clock class feeling unhappy with myself. Every morning, I spend time going over my lectures for the day. Recently, I'd become so preoccupied with the investigation I hadn't been doing that, and it was having an effect on my performance. I made up my mind not to do any more work on the case for a while. Then I decided that contacting Don and Russ to see if they had any information on Charlie wouldn't take much time. Anyway, I had to call Don about starting handball.

The secretary at the security office asked who was calling before putting me through to Don. "Tom, I know what you want. A week ago, I did something to my back. I'd rather not talk about how it happened. I went to see the athletic trainer for the varsity teams. He gave me some exercises to do and told me my back should better in a couple of weeks if I don't aggravate it again."

"Handball was one reason I called. The other was to ask a favor. I ran across a student who dated Whitney Richardson in the period before the murder. He's a little strange. I was hoping you could check to see if your department has had any contact with him."

"I can try. The problem is we don't operate like the usual law enforcement agency. Since there's no prosecution involved, we don't keep much in the way of records. Mostly we write tickets for parking violations and unauthorized vehicles on campus, or go to fraternity houses and tell them to turn down the stereo. When there's an incident involving alcohol abuse or vandalism, we try to settle it as quietly as possible. Most of the time, it's a student with a clean record who's finished off the better part of a bottle of vodka or a couple of six packs and has done something stupid. We don't want some minor violation to go into a student's record. If it's anything more serious, the student affairs office, or the student court, may become involved. In those cases, there's a file. Give me the name and I'll talk to the guys and see what I can find out."

"His name is Charles Rutledge. He was supposed to graduate in June but didn't make it. He's living out in town and taking courses this semester. By the way, Don, how did you hurt your back?"

The line went dead.

Next, I called Russ. With him, I went into detail about my contact with Charlie and told him there was evidence that he had physically abused several women.

"I want to follow up on this. I'll get back to you as soon as I can."

Russ's response to my call added some to that growing feeling of accomplishment, and I had to remind myself again that I hadn't been meeting my responsibilities to the university. I went out to the reception area and told Jean I was going to close the door to my office and hide. If any students came looking for me, she was to make an appointment for them for the next day.

I worked through the lunch hour and the rest of the afternoon without interruption. By the time I left my office at half past five, the exams were ready, and I was caught up on the paperwork that had been lying on my desk for several days.

When I walked in the back door, I could hear the shower running. Beth must have just finished her workout. A few minutes later, she came out of the bathroom in an oversized terry robe with a towel wrapped around her head. "I'll be with you as soon as I get dressed. You could pour me a glass of wine while you're waiting. I've got some good news."

"What kind of news?" I asked.

"You'll have to wait until I'm dressed."

I poured the wine and a Molson Ale for me and went into the living room. Beth appeared a few minutes later wearing jeans and one of my sweatshirts and settled into the sofa.

"Okay, let me hear the news."

"Rachel called and asked us to dinner Saturday night."

"Best news I've heard in quite a while," I said. Rachel's meals are works of art. Course after course of exotic dishes served with style.

"Let's cook together and take the evening off. No work, only fun," Beth suggested.

"That sounds good to me."

"Before we start on dinner, I want to tell you about a new case I'll be working on. I first heard about it a couple of weeks ago, and it sounded interesting. Today, it was assigned to me, and I got filled in on the details."

"It sounds like you think it's an important one."

Beth nodded. "Last spring, an eighth grade girl in a Jefferson County middle school told her mother that the principal took her into a room next to his office and did bad things. The girl's parents talked it over and decided not to do anything about it immediately because they might be accused of bringing false charges. They instructed their daughter to tell them if it happened again. A few days later, the girl reported another incident.

"At that point, the parents decided to contact some families whose children were attending the middle school. When several mothers questioned their daughters, three other girls admitted to having similar experiences with the principal. In each case, the girls hadn't told anyone because they were afraid of what might happen if they did."

By the tone of Beth's voice, I sensed how deeply she felt about the case.

"When the word got around the small community, two high school girls came forward on their own and reported that they'd been sexually abused by the principal. Now it appears that there's a college woman who may be willing to testify about an experience she had the year the principal was hired. No one has talked to her yet.

"All of the victims identified so far tell roughly the same story. The principal invited the girl into his office on some pretense. Maybe he wanted her to be a hall monitor or something like that. After talking to the girl awhile, he said he wanted to show her something in a storage room that adjoins his office. Once in there, he closed the door and began to fondle her. Then he unzipped his pants and instructed her to stroke him."

I shook my head. "This type of thing is so traumatic for a young girl."

"As a woman, I don't need that explained to me," Beth said, as she paused to take a sip of wine. When she picked up the glass, her hand was shaking.

"After he finished with the girl, he told her that if she mentioned to anyone what had happened, her parents and her classmates would find out she'd done something bad, and she'd probably be expelled from school. It isn't surprising his victims kept quiet for so long." Beth shook her head. "I suspect there are many more who've had the same experience. I doubt they'll ever say anything about it, and I wouldn't blame them."

"What do you know about this guy?" I asked.

"He's in his mid-forties and married. Fortunately, he has no children. Apparently, he's quite an impressive man. Intelligent, nice looking, and very charming. He was hired seven years ago and has performed well in the job. The teachers have liked working with him because he was very supportive and encouraged innovative teaching. He also introduced some important new programs into the curriculum. The students and their parents thought highly of him."

"Talented but sick. Not all that unusual," I observed.

"Before coming to the Jefferson County middle school, he was principal in a large suburban high school. He told the search committee he was tired of the job pressure and the fast pace of life in a metropolitan area. You've got to wonder what the real reason was for his leaving."

"Why is he being tried in our county?"

"The defense asked for a change of venue because there was concern he might not receive a fair trial in the local court. I'm pleased about having the opportunity to prosecute this guy. I want to make sure he spends a lot of time in the state prison where the only opportunity for sex will be with his fellow inmates, and he'll learn first hand how if feels to be a victim."

"Now, that's an interesting thought. It sounds to me like a suitable punishment. By the way, your mentioning victims reminded me that Diane called this morning to tell me she'd talked with two other women who admitted they'd been physically abused by Charlie."

"So, Jenny wasn't an isolated case? He's a repeat offender?"

"We can be sure of that. After hearing that from Diane, I called Don and Russ and told them about Charlie. They're going to check to see if their departments have had any contact with him."

"Did Russ think he might be important in the case?" Beth asked.

"Based on the way he responded, I got the impression he did. Now, let's get to work on dinner. I'm hungry."

We got such a late start on the meal preparation that we had to settle for a Reuben sandwich with a side of potato chips and a dill pickle.

- 14 -

We went to the Donovans' house in Beth's car. I drove. Beth wore a navy blue corduroy skirt and a light blue, cotton, V-neck sweater over a white turtle neck. I had on my best pair of slacks, a tattersall shirt, and loafers I'd polished especially for the occasion. It was about as dressed up as I get, except for those university functions where a jacket and tie are required.

Matt opened the door when we arrived. The only time he wears anything but jeans is when he and Rachel entertain or go out socially. He looked quite respectable but a little uncomfortable in gray slacks with a sharp crease in them, a blue dress shirt, and size fourteen black shoes.

Rachel was in the kitchen with the children, who were finishing their meal. She feeds them early when there are guests for dinner so the adults can have the entire evening to themselves. She came into the living room looking elegant in a simple dress made of material in what appeared to be a southwestern Native American pattern. Beth told me later that Rachel had designed the dress and made it herself.

After a minute or two, Rachel and Beth went back into the kitchen. The Donovan children are Beth's favorites. I knew she was eager to see them. Matt followed along and returned with a Molson Ale for me and a glass, which I was certain contained Bushmills Irish whiskey. In his younger days, Matt regularly consumed relatively large amounts of alcohol. Shortly after he and Rachel began seeing each other, she severely rationed his intake. I've never seen him have more than a couple beers on the way from work or a drink or two before dinner.

Matt asked how my investigation was progressing. He seemed to be particularly interested, so I went into detail describing what I'd been doing.

"I knew Whitney and her boyfriend, Scott Griffin. They were in my Nineteenth Century American Novel course first semester last year. I thought about them after the murder. In my mind, they were an odd couple."

"In what way?" I asked. Matt got to know the students in his classes better than most teachers on the campus.

"I was impressed with Whitney's performance on the first exam. She had a talent for intuitive analysis, and she expressed her ideas in a clear and concise manner. It was obvious she appreciated fine literature. I gave her a B+, which is as good a grade as I give early in the semester. "Scott wrote well and had some good ideas. The problem was, they weren't his own. He'd obviously done some reading in literary history and criticism to prepare for the exam. I gave him a C+ for good expression and a diligent effort.

"When I got back to my office after handing back the exams, he was waiting for me. He demanded to know why he'd received such a terrible grade. I told him he'd included some excellent interpretations in his essays, but they were second hand. I explained that I wanted students to develop a skill in literary analysis, so they could experience the joy that can come from reading great books. I told him that on the next exam, I wanted to read *his* ideas."

"What did he say?" I asked.

Matt swirled the ice around in his glass and took a drink. "My explanation only made him more angry. He seemed to have difficulty controlling himself. I wondered what he'd have said if he weren't talking to a college professor. On the rest of the exams, he took my advice and actually did some very nice work, but it was just for the grade. He had no real interest in literature." Matt shook his head. "Not the most satisfying student."

"Do you think he could become violent?" I asked.

"It's hard for me to say. I don't know much about that sort of thing, but I suspect the woman he marries ought to be careful not to make him too angry. If you're asking if I think he would be capable of murder—no, I don't.

"By the way, if somewhere along the way in your investigation you think I could be of some help, I'd be happy to volunteer. Of course, you realize I'm basically a nonviolent person."

"I don't intend to get that deeply involved in this thing, but I'll keep it in mind," I said, smiling. "But about that nonviolent stuff. I've been playing basketball with you for a number of years, and I've noticed on occasion you can become somewhat aggressive."

"That reminds me. I want to start team practice for the intramural league early this year. I'll be calling you in a couple of weeks."

"Matt, I've been telling you all along that I'm not interested in playing anymore. I come out of each game feeling like I've been in a street fight. Those referees we get are sadists. Besides, we're not competitive. Last season we lost more than half our games, and I'm a bad loser."

"Don't make a hasty decision. Jerry will be back from sabbatical, and we have a superstar joining the team."

When I took a drink of Molson, I must've looked skeptical.

"I'm serious. We have a first year graduate student in the English department. His name is James Whittington. He played ball for a small college and took them to the Division III finals two years in a row. I'm sure he could have played for an ACC or Big Ten school, but he wasn't recruited because he was too small. He graduated from high school at seventeen and wasn't full grown. After enrolling in college, he grew three inches and gained twenty pounds. You have to see him play. He can do it all.

"Funny thing," Matt added, as he sipped some Bushmills. "He didn't mention on his application that he'd played ball. I learned all this after he got here."

"Let me guess. You didn't say anything on your application to grad school about having played football."

"I may have omitted that. Some of those narrow-minded academics think most jocks are semi-illiterate. James is as good a student as he is an athlete. He's already published some poetry."

Before we could talk any more basketball, Beth and Rachel joined us, and from then on the conversation was at a higher level. We sat around talking for an hour or so before dinner. The meal was indescribable—a course of cold fish and cheeses, followed by soup, and finally some sort of lamb dish with wonderfully seasoned vegetables. Beth and Matt had a delicious looking chocolate dessert. I couldn't manage to eat any more, and Rachel also abstained. We finished with coffee and a choice of liqueurs in the living room. The evening's conversation was equal to the food. It was after eleven when we got home.

Sunday is a family time for many couples our age. For that reason, it isn't always a good day for Beth and me. It can be particularly hard after spending an evening with Matt and Rachel and their handsome, well-behaved children because it reminds us that our life didn't turn out according to plan. When we'd paid off our education loans and accumulated enough savings to make a down payment on a house, we looked forward to starting a family. After three years of trying all the strategies that seemed reasonable, it became clear we weren't going to be able to have children. Even though we've come to accept that, there'll always be an emptiness in our life. We never talk about it. We realized long ago that there was nothing more to say.

I spent most of the day working on the vehicles—changing oil, rotating tires, and tuning things up. None of what I did was necessary. Beth picked the last of the vegetables and cleared the garden, so it would be ready for spring planting. We spent the evening talking about projects around the house that would keep us busy during the winter months.

- 15 -

While driving to campus on Monday morning, I thought about Matt's experience with Whitney's boyfriend. I considered trying to contact him but decided it wouldn't be worth the effort. When the police questioned him at the time of the murder, he said he hadn't seen Whitney since the breakup and claimed to know nothing about her life in the weeks before her death. Based on what I'd learned about the end of their relationship, there was no reason to suspect he wasn't telling the truth.

Russ called a few minutes after I arrived at my office. "I have a report on Rutledge. The department had two contacts with him in the last year, both alcohol related. Last November, he was stopped for doing fifty in a school zone. The arresting officer smelled alcohol on his breath and gave him a breathalyser test. His BAL was .09. He escaped with a traffic violation."

"Speeding in a school zone under the influence of alcohol sounds pretty serious to me," I said. "Charlie got off easy."

"There was another arrest last May at about the time the semester ended at the university. I got a laugh out of this one. Have you met Mary Sawyer?"

"Not that I remember."

"She's been with us for about two years. A tall blond with the kind of looks that make her stand out in a crowd. Mary pulled Rutledge's vehicle over after observing him cross the center line and run a stop sign. It was late in the afternoon. Rutledge was obviously drunk. He took a look at Mary and started making lewd comments. Maybe he thought he could charm his way out of a ticket. When he got out of the car, he grabbed Mary and started to rub her breasts. That was a mistake. Mary's a lot tougher than she looks. She kneed him in the groin and gave him a chop to the side of the head. He fell face down against the bumper and ended up pretty bloody. Mary barely managed to get him into the squad car before he passed out."

"I think I like Mary," I said. "There ought to be more women like her in law enforcement."

"When Rutledge woke up the next morning in jail and discovered the facial bruises and blood stains on his clothes, he was furious. He began screaming obscenities and threatened to sue the department for police brutality. Joe Higgins, who has a sense of humor, was at the desk. He walked back into the cell area and told Rutledge he wanted him to talk it over with the arresting officer who'd just come on duty and was in the building. I guess you can imagine Rutledge's reaction when he saw who'd done the damage. He never said another word before being released. The DWI cost him his driver's license for six months. We decided not to charge him with anything else."

"Russ, it sounds like your department is getting soft on crime."

"I guess we should've gone a little further in that case, but we try to go easy on college students. I don't know what to think about Rutledge at this point. We can be sure he drinks a lot. He starts early in the day, and he loses control. I'm going to assign one of the guys to do some more investigating."

"Thanks for the call. Don Reynolds is checking with his staff to see if they've had any contact with Rutledge."

"I'll get in touch with Don later. I'd like to know what he finds out. One more thing. Could I borrow your pickup this weekend? I'm putting a new roof on my garage, and I have to haul the old shingles out to the landfill."

"Sure, and if I can get free, I'll be over to help. Some honest physical labor might do me some good. I'll call you later on in the week."

That afternoon, I looked out my office window and saw Russ's daughter Patti talking with Rod Dudley. Patti was gesturing with both hands, and Rod was smiling. When they parted, Patti reached over and touched Rod's arm.

A few minutes later, she appeared at my door. "Tom, I need some advice."

"Come in and sit down. I've had a lot of practice doing that, and I'm very good at it. Unfortunately, most people don't pay much attention to what I tell them."

"I bet that's the truth."

"I want to warn you now—I'll give the same advice you'd get from your parents."

"They wouldn't be able to help. It's a campus thing. What I want to know is if I should go through sorority rush."

"That is a tough one. I don't know what to say."

"Come on, Tom, tell me what I should do."

"Okay, let's start with the advantages. If a sorority asks you to join, the members think you'll fit into the group. That means you'll make a lot of friends quickly without trying very hard. You can expect to have an active social life because ordinarily there are more parties, dances, and that sort of thing in the fraternities and sororities than in the dorms. Best of all, you can wear sweatshirts with Greek letters on them."

She frowned. "I know it's hard for you, but try your best to be serious. Now give me the bad news."

"Some people feel that the Greek living units are snobbish and elitist. Also, there's the perception that fraternities and sororities tend to place too much emphasis on the social. All the organized social activities and obligations take away from study time. Frankly, most faculty feel that way."

Patti made a face. "This is good to know. The problem is, it makes the decision even harder."

"My advice is to go through rush because after you've done that, you'll know if a sorority is right for you."

"That makes sense," Patti said.

I nodded. "Oh, I looked out my office window a little while ago and saw Rod Dudley talking to you. I knew you'd get into trouble sooner or later."

Patti rolled her eyes. "Tom, it's too bad you were born without a sense of humor. I met Rod a few weeks ago when we were having a problem in the dorm."

"What kind of a problem?" I asked.

"Earlier in the semester, I noticed things were missing from my room. I didn't think much about it because I'm not very neat, but it turned out the same thing was happening to other girls in our section of the dorm. Most of us don't bother to lock our rooms when we leave for a little while, so we decided someone must be stealing from us."

"I suspect the stolen articles weren't very valuable," I said.

"That's right. Mostly they were personal things like hairbrushes, bath towels, and bottles of shampoo. Sometimes a blouse or sweatshirt might disappear, but never anything that could be sold to make money. How did you know?"

"Petty theft in living units isn't all that unusual. I've been involved in several cases. Last year, the president of a sorority came to see me because the house was having a similar problem. It was one of the pledges who was doing the stealing. She thought a psychologist might be able to give advice on how to handle the situation."

"We thought some creep was sneaking into the dorm and coming into our rooms. We were scared because of the murder last spring, so we called the campus security."

"That was the right thing to do."

"Rod came to the dorm and met with a group of us. Like you, he had experience with this type of thing before and said it was usually someone in the living unit who was doing the stealing. He told us he was pretty sure we had nothing to be afraid of but to be sure and lock our doors and call him if we noticed anything suspicious."

"I think you got very good advice," I said.

"Rod was really nice. He asked us our names. When he heard mine was Merrick, he guessed who my father was. After the meeting, he came up to me and said I should be proud of Dad because he was such a good police officer and how everyone respected him. That made me feel good."

"So now you and Rod are friends?"

"Sort of. Whenever I run into him on campus, he stops to talk."

"I understand some of the women on the campus think he's good looking."

"Are you kidding? Everyone thinks he's gorgeous. Most of the girls I know would give anything to date him."

"How about you?" I asked.

"Rod's a little too old for me, and anyway, I've been dating this really cute guy." Patti looked at the wall clock. "I'm supposed to meet him in a few minutes. I've got to run." She jumped out of her chair and waved goodbye. "Thanks for the advice. See you around campus."

"I can hardly wait," I said, but Patti was out the door so fast I don't think she heard me.

After Patti left, a steady stream of students stopped by my office to talk about one thing or another. A few minutes after the last one left, the phone rang. It was Don Reynolds.

"I have some information for you about Rutledge. Our staff has had several run-ins with him. Always alcohol related." That sounded familiar. Those were the same words Russ had used.

"One night, he got a ladder and tried to climb through the second story window of a sorority house into the room where the women slept. Also some vandalism, like removing signs from the parking lot at two in the morning or throwing rotten fruit at the main entrance to the University Administration Building. The worst was last winter. You remember that racial incident at one of the fraternities?"

"I remember it all too well," I said. Someone had invited several black students to a party at a fraternity on campus, which was notorious for its heavy drinking. Sometime after midnight, a fight broke out. Two black students were badly beaten. One had been left with injuries which required hospitalization. Don wasn't at the scene, but his firm action later probably prevented some serious repercussions.

"Rod and Pete were on duty that night. You know the story. The fraternity was put on probation. No individuals were disciplined, though I personally thought several should've been. Rod suspected that Rutledge was largely responsible for setting the thing off. He even made some racist statements after our guys arrived. I'm not sure how all this fits into the Richardson murder, but one thing we do know, Rutledge is no model citizen."

Before hanging up, Don filled me in on some of the things that went on during the night of the fight, which had been kept from the public. The depth of the anger toward the blacks displayed by the white students left me both outraged and depressed. I drove home thinking that when this type of thing can occur on a university campus, the higher education system is failing in a very fundamental way.

- 16 -

Late Friday afternoon, I was in my office grading exams when the phone rang. The male caller began talking without a greeting. "Dr. Evers, this is David Richardson. My wife and I are going to the homecoming game tomorrow. We'd like to get together with you sometime when we're on campus. At your convenience, of course."

I thought it was presumptuous of David Richardson to ask for an appointment with me again on such short notice, but I did my best not to show the irritation I felt. "When will you be arriving?"

"We plan to be there at ten o'clock. A morning meeting would be best for us. We'll be going to the game, and there are several social events we'll be attending later in the day."

I thought about Russ's garage roof. "Tomorrow is a busy day for me, but I may be able to rearrange my schedule. I can let you know within an hour."

Mr. Richardson gave me his number and hung up the phone without saying anything more.

I knew there was nothing to keep me from seeing the Richardsons. I didn't agree immediately because the request came so late, and I didn't particularly care for David Richardson's attitude over the phone. At the very least, he might've thanked me for trying to set up a meeting time. Besides that, what I'd learned about his treatment of Whitney made me less sympathetic. In fact, I'd begun to develop a dislike for the man.

I thought about calling back and saying I wouldn't be available. Working with Russ on his roof seemed to be a better way to spend a Saturday morning.

By the time I got around to making the call, I'd cooled down, and I realized I hadn't contacted the Richardsons since they'd come to see me with their request, which was inconsiderate on my part. Also, because I'd come to like Joan Richardson, I felt some obligation to her.

Mr. Richardson picked up the phone after one ring. "This is David Richardson."

"I'll be able to meet with you at ten," I said.

"We'll be there, and thanks for making time in your schedule to see us."

"I'll see you in the morning," I said and hung up.

I tried to reach Russ at his office to tell him about the change of plans. He'd already left for the day. I dialed his home number and left a message on the answering machine saying I was going to be tied up in the morning, so I'd be dropping off the pickup at his house on the way home from work. Then I called Beth and explained the situation.

Russ was on the garage roof when I pulled in the driveway. I told him about the call from David Richardson. I said I'd be over to help with the roofing as soon as I could get away. We were speculating about the reason for the Richardsons' visit when Beth arrived.

Rose asked Beth to come over in the afternoon, so they could prepare a dinner together for their big, strong men who would've been working so hard all day. There was something about that suggestion that Beth and Rose found terribly amusing. After some discussion, it was decided that Rose would pick up Beth at our house after lunch.

We woke up on Saturday to a beautiful October morning. Fine weather for a football game or roofing a garage. Since I'd be working with Russ, I decided not to run. Beth and I drank coffee and talked until it was time for me to leave for campus. I dressed in khaki slacks, a sport shirt, and loafers for the meeting with the Richardsons. I grabbed an old pair of jeans, a T-shirt with the university crest on it, and worn out basketball shoes for later in the day.

The Richardsons appeared at my office door at exactly ten o'clock. They looked like the ideal homecoming couple. Good looking, tastefully dressed, and obviously successful. People to be envied by less prosperous alums.

By the time we'd gone through the polite greetings and commented on the beautiful weather, the animosity I'd felt toward David Richardson had mostly disappeared. In spite of appearances, the Richardsons were sad individuals.

I was surprised when Joan Richardson was the one who spoke first. "David and I are anxious to know if you've made any progress." It was obvious she was eager to hear about what had been happening. I was relieved that there was nothing in her statement, or her manner, to suggest that she was irritated with me for my failure to give them a report of my activities.

I began by apologizing for not keeping in touch. I told them I'd conferred with the police and they'd allowed me access to the case files. I talked about the interviews with students, being careful not to mention names or to reveal anything I'd learned from them. In order not to raise their hopes, I emphasized that I hadn't been successful in uncovering any additional information that would help in identifying the killer.

When I finished, neither of the Richardsons spoke. It was clear they were disappointed.

Joan Richardson finally broke the silence. "It's obvious you've devoted considerable time to the investigation."

There was a pause, as though she was giving her husband an opportunity to speak. When he didn't respond, she continued. "Of course, David and I were hoping that you'd have more to tell us. But be assured, we're very grateful for what you've done. We're convinced you're our only hope if Whitney's murderer is going to be found. Is it possible for you to let us know what your next step will be?"

The question caught me off guard because I had no further plans. "I seem to have exhausted all possible leads. I'm not sure there is anything more I can do."

I think what I said next was because Joan Richardson looked so disappointed at the suggestion that I might not continue with the investigation. "There's one more thing I've considered and that's contacting Scott Griffin. He was questioned by the police, but it's conceivable, at the time, he may've inadvertently failed to report some significant information. That would be understandable, because it was an extremely stressful time for everyone involved."

Joan Richardson looked over at her husband and made eye contact for an instant. Then she looked back at me and started to say something. Before she could get the words out, her husband interrupted. It was the first time he'd spoken since our original greetings.

"As you know, Scott and Whitney were very close. Something happened between them. We were very disappointed at the time. He's a very impressive young man. Joan and I felt that he and Whitney could've had a bright future together. I'm sure he gave a very detailed report to the police. It seems highly unlikely he could tell you anything that would help in finding the killer."

Immediately, Joan Richardson expressed her disagreement. "I think it would be worthwhile for you to talk to Scott." In spite of the fact that she spoke softly, it was clear she felt strongly about the issue. David Richardson looked pained. He obviously wasn't pleased with what his wife had said, but he remained silent.

I was tempted to ask what they knew about the relationship between Whitney and Scott, but I was certain I wouldn't be successful in getting any more information so I didn't bother. Since there seemed to be nothing more to discuss, I decided to bring the meeting to a close. I assured the Richardsons that I'd follow up on any new leads that might come up and keep them informed. I avoided mentioning anything about Scott. I anticipated one of them asking me if I intended to contact him, but neither of them did.

I thought about the meeting as I drove across town. I was puzzled that Joan Richardson had taken charge, and I couldn't understand the disagreement over whether I should talk to Scott. I saw the two interacting in a way I wouldn't have expected based on their behavior when I'd first met with them.

Russ was taking a break for lunch when I arrived. After changing my clothes, I had a sandwich with him and reported on my conversation with the Richardsons. I thought he might offer some insightful observations. Instead, he just shrugged and said, "Let's do some roofing."

I took two loads of shingles to the landfill and worked the rest of the afternoon on the roof. Russ had done a lot on his own, so by five o'clock, the job was finished. We washed up and joined Rose and Beth on the patio. Russ and I didn't mind much being waited on with samples of the large spread of food they'd prepared. We were both near exhaustion from our labors. By the time the steaks were done it was very cool, so we ate inside.

I looked over at Russ after we'd finished eating. He looked like he was struggling to keep his eyes open, and I think he was in better shape than I was. Beth suggested we leave, so I'd be in good enough condition to drive the pickup. I had no problem getting to sleep that night.

After breakfast in the morning, Beth and I took a third cup of coffee into the living room, and I gave her a report of my meeting with the Richardsons.

Beth said, "I get the impression from what you've told me that finding Whitney's killer is less important to David Richardson now than when you talked with him earlier."

"I came to the same conclusion."

"On the other hand, Joan Richardson is obviously very much interested in your pursuing the investigation."

"That was certainly clear."

"I can't make any sense out of their reactions when you told them you'd considered contacting Whitney's boyfriend. Joan Richardson thought it would be a good idea, but her husband was against it?"

I nodded my head. "I've no doubt about that. Not only what he said but the way he said it convinced me he didn't want me to talk to Scott."

"If he were sincerely interested in the murderer being apprehended, you'd expect him to be in favor of anything that offered a remote chance of providing additional clues. Did you get any hint as to why he felt the way he did?"

"No, but his attitude aroused my suspicion that there might be something important involved."

"You know what? I think you ought to get in touch with Scott."

"I agree. I'm going to try and locate him. If it turns out that I don't uncover anything of significance, I think it'll be time for me to give up my career as an investigator."

75

- 17 -

The week turned out to be a particularly busy one. On Thursday afternoon, I was finally able to clear my desk, and there were no appointments on my calendar for the rest of the day. I looked at the clock. It was a few minutes after three. Time to do a little detective work.

I called the alumni office. A polite young woman, who identified herself as Melissa, answered the phone. I informed Melissa that my name was Tom, and that I was a faculty member who wanted to get in touch with a recent graduate named Scott Griffin. I asked if someone in the alumni office might be able to provide me with his address and phone number. Melissa said she'd be happy to do that. She took my number and said she'd get back to me in a few minutes. A half-hour later, when I'd begun to wonder what had happened to Melissa, she called and told me she'd gone through the records and couldn't find any information on Scott Griffin. She went so far as to ask another person in the office to help in the search and apologized for not being able to provide me with the information I'd requested. Before hanging up, I thanked Melissa for all she had done.

I was puzzled. The alumni office doesn't lose many graduates. They're too valuable. Each year, during fund-raising drives, they're asked to give money to their alma mater. I'm always amazed at the large number who make pledges. In some cases, they can even be convinced to include the institution in their will. The addresses of many alumni are lost as time passes but usually not in the first year after graduation. It occurred to me that for some reason, Scott didn't want his address on file.

Another way to locate Scott would be to call his parents. I couldn't think of any reason why they'd be hesitant in telling me how I might contact him.

I got Scott's home address from the University Directory for the year before. He was from a small city in the northeastern part of the state. The long distance information operator could find no listing for a Griffin at the address I gave her. Either the Griffins had an unlisted number or they'd moved in the past year.

Who might know where Scott was? Most likely there would be friends of his still on campus who might've kept in touch. Unfortunately, I had no way of finding them. I was packing my briefcase getting ready to head home when I remembered that Scott had applied to medical school. That could possibly help me track him down.

Roger Secrest, a biologist on the faculty, has a reduced teaching load so he can serve as counselor to the dozens of pre-med students on campus. In addition to advising students on the courses they should take, Roger helps many of them with their applications to medical schools. He has a fantastic memory, and he's a meticulous record keeper. There was a fair chance he'd know where Scott went to medical school.

I dialed Roger's number. I knew that he normally spent every minute he could in the lab, which is quite a distance from his office. I hoped he'd hear the phone.

After a dozen rings, Roger came on the line. "Biology, this is Secrest."

I could tell by the sound of his voice that he didn't appreciate being interrupted.

"Roger, this is Tom. I need some information from you."

"I'm surprised to hear from you at this hour. It's rumored on campus that psychologists are rarely in their offices after three o'clock."

"Absolutely true. We take turns staying until five so if someone from the president's office happens to call, we're covered."

"If you need information, you've contacted the right person. I'm a human encyclopedia."

I laughed. "Your humility always impresses me, Roger. I need to get in touch with a pre-med who graduated last spring. The alumni office has no record on him. I thought you might know where he went to med school. His name is Scott Griffin."

"I remember Scott. Excellent grades and good scores on the Medical School Admissions Test. I haven't cleaned out my files from last year. Let me check to see what I have on him."

I could tell Roger considered finding Scott a challenge. He'd do his best to get the information. I'd hardly hung up the phone when he called back.

"I found my notes on Griffin. He applied to a dozen schools. Three high prestige schools in the east and one on the west coast turned him down. He was accepted at the rest. He came in to get my advice on which one to choose. I told him what I knew about their programs and rated them on prestige. I saw him a couple of days later. He told me he'd sent refusal letters to all but three schools. He said he wanted to take more time before making his final decision. I remember

I was a little puzzled by his choices. The schools were not particularly high in prestige, and I was fairly sure money wasn't a factor.

"I always ask my advisees to let me know what school they'll be attending. Sometimes students who are applying like to talk to grads who are enrolled in a program they're interested in. Scott never did, and I wasn't particularly surprised. He was always pretty cool and, in my opinion, a little arrogant. The kind who'd feel no obligation to come in and let me know what he'd decided."

"Based on what I know about him, that doesn't surprise me either. Do you know the three schools?"

"That's a tough one. I might be able to figure it out. Give me a little more time. By the way, I was going to call you. Our intramural basketball team had a meeting yesterday. We're planning to begin practice soon. You know, we almost won the championship last year. This year we think we can get the job done if we can find a point guard. That group you're playing with now is more like a circus act than a basketball team. A redheaded gorilla and his dancing clowns. We thought you might be interested in playing on a championship quality squad. It might be a while before you could break into the starting lineup because we have a sophisticated offense that takes time to learn, but I think eventually you could pick it up."

"Sophisticated offense? You've got to be kidding. Around the gym, you guys are referred to as the Keystone Kops of the intramural league."

"Yeah, I know. Some of these faculty types hate to lose. They take out their frustrations by criticizing the winners. You'll have to let us know in a week or so. We can't afford to keep the offer open too long. We've got a couple of younger guys who're interested. They're a little quicker than you and are better ball handlers, but you've got the advantage of experience."

"Roger, as usual, it's been fun talking to you, and I appreciate your help. It's late and I'm hungry, so I'm going to hang up and go home. Any further discussion about my playing for the Kops will have to be done through my agent."

"Fair enough. I'm sure you'll come around sooner or later."

After I hung up the phone, I shook my head and smiled. Roger is one of those characters you find on the faculty that make teaching at a university so interesting. Underlying his abrasive exterior is a very nice guy, who would be pleased to do a favor for a colleague. He goes out of his way to help students who are having problems and, in spite of his gruff manner, he is a very popular teacher.

When I arrived at the office the next morning, there was a phone message waiting for me. Roger named three universities and hung up.

A nine o'clock lecture and meetings with students scheduled for later in the morning kept me from trying to track down Scott until the lunch hour. Calls to long distance information in the cities where the medical schools were located failed to produce results. There were no listings for a Scott Griffin. Either he hadn't enrolled in one of the universities that Roger had given me or he had an unlisted phone. It could be a genetically transmitted trait.

I called information again and got the number of the main switchboard at the first university on my list. I dialed the number. I explained to the operator that I was trying to get in touch with a first year medical student. She said that information wasn't available to her, but she could transfer my call to the switchboard at the medical school. The second operator couldn't find a number for a Scott Griffin, which meant he wasn't currently enrolled as a student.

On my second try, I asked information for the number of the medical school rather than the one for the main university switchboard. This time I spoke with a very businesslike woman who quickly provided me with Scott's phone number and address. I hung up feeling quite good about my skill as an investigator.

I doubted Scott would be home during the day, but I dialed the number anyway. The answering machine confirmed that I had, in fact, reached the apartment of Scott Griffin, who at the time was unable to come to the phone.

Beth was in the kitchen when I got home. It was her turn to cook. While she was busy preparing dinner, I went to my computer and reviewed the notes I'd made on the police interview with Scott. A couple of things struck me. Deborah Field, the officer who'd questioned Scott, commented in her report that he'd refused to talk about his relationship and breakup with Whitney. Because he wasn't particularly cooperative, she speculated that he might've had more information about the case than he was willing to reveal. She suggested another contact could be worthwhile. There was no record of any further interviews.

I tried Scott's number after we finished eating. The first time I'd called, his answering machine came on after the fourth ring. I didn't want to give him the idea that someone was trying to reach him, so when there was no answer after three rings, I hung up. There was no answer to a second call I made just before the late news.

I started calling again each hour, beginning at nine thirty the next morning, figuring I might catch him at home on a Saturday. Finally, at three, a male answered.

"Is this Scott?" I asked.

"Yes, it is." He sounded puzzled when he heard an unfamiliar voice.

"This is Tom Evers. Whitney Richardson was my teaching assistant, and I supervised her senior thesis research. She may have mentioned my name to you." Of course she had, but there was no response from Scott. I was beginning to feel the interview wasn't going well.

"As I'm sure you know, the killer still hasn't been found. Whitney's parents contacted me and asked if I'd be willing to conduct an informal investigation. They thought I might be able to come up with something that could help in the solution of the case. I agreed and have been contacting people who were associated with Whitney in the time before her death."

I imagined that Scott was trying to figure out how I'd managed to track him down. I didn't bother explaining. I wanted to keep talking so he wouldn't have the opportunity to give me a reason he needed to hang up. If he did, I doubted I'd have another chance at him.

I'd decided earlier to mention that the Richardsons suggested I contact him. I was curious to see if it would produce any reaction. I thought it was possible that the mention of their name might make him more willing to be open with me.

"In a recent conversation I had with the Richardsons, they encouraged me to talk with you."

Scott had apparently recovered from the surprise of my call, because he interrupted me before I could say anything more. "I told the police everything I know," he said, emphasizing the word everything. "I have nothing more to say."

"I'm not working for the police. Whitney's parents asked me to become involved, and I'm trying to do what I can to help." My feeble attempt to keep the conversation going failed. The phone went dead before I could say anything more.

Even though I'd anticipated that Scott might not be willing to answer questions, the abruptness of his response, and the rudeness, surprised me. I told myself not to read too much into that, but it did tend to support Deborah Field's suspicion that Scott was holding back.

I went down the hall to Beth's study to suggest we go out to dinner at our favorite Italian restaurant. She was working at the computer. "I have a proposal for you," I said.

No response. I tried again. "Want to hear my proposal?"

Still, no response. A third try. "Let's go to Dominic's for dinner tonight."

"I'd love to," she said immediately, without turning around.

"For a while there, I didn't think I was going to be able to make contact."

"You said the right thing," she said, as she turned to face me. "Why don't we leave a little early and stop at Raders for a drink on the way?"

"That sounds like a good idea," I said.

Raders was a bar downtown across from the courthouse. It opened in the early 1900s and has always been owned by the same family. Each new generation has carefully kept the original structure intact. It's a fine bar and a valuable antique.

"I might order the same thing I had last time, the chicken sausage marsala."

"Is it possible you'd already thought about going out before I suggested it?"

"It never occurred to me. But it's certainly a great idea. I might even get dressed up a little. Now go away so I can get some work done."

When we go out to dinner, Beth takes an extraordinary amount of time getting ready. I suspect the preparation is an enjoyable part of her evening. We finally arrived at Raders at six thirty. Mike, the bartender, delivered Beth a glass of Chardonnay without asking for our order. He chatted with Beth a little before turning to me. I decided on a draft Guinness Stout.

In the next hour, Beth had a second glass of wine, and I had another Stout. We really didn't have much chance to talk because Beth's colleagues and acquaintances kept stopping by to chat. They alluded to things I knew nothing about. I tried hard not to feel insignificant.

At the restaurant, Dominic greeted us personally and, as usual, chided us for not coming to see him more regularly. During the dinner, I told Beth about my phone conversation with Scott.

Her reaction was similar to mine. She thought he was holding something back.

"Do you think it would be worthwhile for me to drive down to the medical school tomorrow and try to catch him at his apartment?" I asked.

"Yes, I do. It seems like a long shot, but there's that remote possibility you might turn up something significant. I probably won't be finished working on this case that's coming up next week until the middle of the afternoon. You can go if you promise to be back by then."

- 18 -

The next morning at six, I slipped out of bed quietly so I wouldn't wake Beth. Twenty minutes later, I got into the pickup with a thermos of coffee and a bagel spread with cream cheese.

The sun was coming up when I pulled onto the interstate highway that would take me to the city where the medical school was located. Everyone raves about sunsets, but a sunrise can be at least as beautiful, even though you don't hear much about them. I guess there aren't as many people who are up in time to see the sunrise, and when they are, they're not in the mood to reflect on the wonders of nature. On this October morning, the colors were too spectacular to ignore.

The traffic was light. To be out on the road this early on a Sunday one must have something important to accomplish. That made me reflect on the absurdity of my trip. Here I was, an unsophisticated academic, trying to solve a crime when I should've been spending time grading student exams or writing a research article.

I drove through miles of flat prairie. There were fields of corn which were being harvested by giant combines. The harvesting of soybeans, the other major crop grown in the area, was complete, leaving a brown stubble that looked like a badly maintained lawn after a long dry spell. It was the kind of landscape that contributes to the impression that the Midwest is a boring and unexciting place.

I thought about the migrants who began settling the prairie a hundred and eighty years before. To them, it must've been a land of beauty because its rich, black topsoil, adequate rainfall, and hardwood forests could provide them with the essentials of a good life—a reliable source of food and a warm home. They didn't have the need for spectacular scenery to find fulfillment in their lives.

An hour into my trip, I was able to pick up a National Public Radio station that entertained me until I reached the suburbs of the city where the medical school was located. The program, which originated in Canada, was about an increase in drug related crimes in the province of Ontario. In a perverted sort of way, it was

82

therapeutic to learn that our neighbors to the north were having to deal with the same sort of problems we were facing.

I had no difficulty finding the campus. I had attended several meetings there. I pulled into a nearly empty parking lot and walked to the university cafeteria where I could get more coffee and find someone who could give me directions to Scott's address.

At a quarter past nine, less than a third of the tables were occupied. I poured a cup of coffee from the urn and paid a cashier who wasn't quite awake. Five students, three males and two females, sat at a long table in the middle of the room. Judging from their age and appearance, I was sure they were graduate students who couldn't afford the luxury of a day away from their studies. I joined them.

"Hi, my name is Tom," I said, setting my coffee down on the table. "I need some help in finding an address." My question produced looks of mild curiosity from the group. "I want to get in touch with a student I knew as an undergraduate. He's a first year med student. I wonder if you could give me directions to where he lives." I read off Scott's address.

Three of the group began to answer at the same time. They all smiled at that and then nodded to one of the women to take over. She gave me detailed instructions that were so complicated I had to write them on a paper napkin.

One of the group asked me where I taught. When they learned that I'd driven a hundred and sixty miles on a Sunday morning, they wanted to know the purpose of my trip. When I told them it was to deal with a personal problem of some urgency that I wasn't free to discuss, they politely changed the subject. There was talk of long hours of work, financial problems, and concern about the future.

Their conversation reminded me of when Beth and I were first married and working on our graduate degrees. We'd dealt with the same problems these students were experiencing. We looked forward to the time we could afford to live in something better than a two-room apartment furnished with shabby furniture and would be able to buy anything we wanted at the grocery store without having to think about what it cost.

We'd reached that point some time ago, and our life has become more secure and comfortable. Occasionally, however, we look back and wonder if that simpler existence didn't have rewards and satisfactions we'd failed to appreciate at the time. Now it seems we spend far too much time in trivial activities like shopping for things we don't need and running senseless errands.

I finished my coffee and thanked the students for their help. When I got up from the table, one of the men asked me to stop by sometime when I could stay longer and talk. I was honest when I said I'd enjoy that.

With the directions the students gave me, I had no difficulty in finding the apartment complex where Scott lived. It was some distance from the medical school and nicer than you'd expect to find occupied by students. The landscaping and well-tended grass area suggested it might be the kind of place that would attract young couples and singles with successful careers in business or the professions who'd reached the point where they could afford to live reasonably well. I guessed that for Scott to be able to live in such relative luxury, his family must've been providing him with considerable financial support.

Each entry served four apartments. Scott's was on the second floor. I knocked. No sound. Maybe he'd already left for the day. I was about to leave when the door opened. Scott had on jeans with a rip in one knee and a sweatshirt with the medical school crest brilliantly displayed across the chest. It suggested he'd severed ties with his alma mater.

"I'm Tom Evers. I called yesterday. It's important that we talk. Can I come in?"

Before Scott could refuse, I crossed the threshold.

The room was large. On the left were sliding doors that opened onto a deck. To the right there was a dining area and a small kitchen. A hall across from the entry door must've led to the bedroom and bath area. There was a leather sofa with pharmacy lamps at either end and two comfortable looking wicker chairs. On one wall there was a large screen TV, an elaborate stereo system, and shelves filled with books. Along a second wall there was a long table, which served as a desk. At one end there was a computer. The walls were decorated with framed posters.

I was impressed. Scott was a man, if I could use that term, of taste. I went over to one of the chairs and sat down. I wanted to make it clear that I intended to stay.

Scott continued to stand by the door. I think he was hoping I'd get up and leave. Finally, he made his way to the center of the room and sat on the sofa at the opposite end from the chair I had chosen.

"Scott, I'm not here because I think you are in any way involved in Whitney's death. It's simply that I want to learn all I can about what was going on in her life before she died. I know the police questioned you at length. I'm asking you to go over it with me again. You and Whitney were close for a long period of time. I was hoping you'd want to do all you could to help find her killer."

- 19 -

Scott was facing the sliding doors, staring at something outside. He remained silent. That shouldn't have surprised me. In my phone conversation, he'd made it clear he wasn't willing to talk about Whitney or reveal anything he might know about her life in the weeks before she was killed.

In my eagerness to extract information, I'd put pressure on Scott by suggesting that, because of his relationship with Whitney, he was somehow obligated to tell me what he knew. There was no way that approach was going to work. As a therapist, I should've kept in mind that individuals are most likely to talk with someone they believe will be sympathetic, understanding, and not judgmental. When I confronted Scott, I'd developed a picture of him based on the reports of others. Because of this preconceived idea of the kind of person he was, I'd acted in a manner that wasn't wise if I expected to obtain information from him, and it was unfair. I was irritated with myself.

"Scott, I want to apologize for forcing my way into your apartment and for what I said. My rudeness, and my lack of respect for your privacy, simply resulted from the fact that I'd developed a great deal of affection for Whitney. Her death, and the manner in which she died, left me deeply troubled. When the Richardsons asked me to become involved, I realized I might feel better if I could make some kind of contribution to the discovery of her killer. I haven't been able to accomplish that, so my earlier reaction grew out of frustration.

"I know last year must've been an extremely difficult one for you. There's always stress associated with being a senior and having to plan for the future. Added to that were the problems with Whitney. I know nothing of the details of your relationship with her, but I'm aware that for a period of almost three years, you and Whitney spent a great deal of time together. No matter what the reason for the breakup might have been, or who was responsible, it had to be very difficult for both of you."

85

As I talked, I began to feel differently about Scott. He couldn't have been as bad as I'd imagined. Whitney was a sensible, mature, young woman. Her attraction to Scott had to have been based on more than his good looks and superior intelligence.

I assumed there was no hope of convincing Scott to talk because I was sure he'd never tell me anything about the past year, but I felt the need to say more. It was the therapist coming out in me. This was a young man who had faced a serious trauma. Because he gave the impression of being cool and aloof, it was unlikely he elicited much sympathy from those around him. Also, I suspected he was the kind who would feel uncomfortable talking about his feelings with others. These factors could make the events of the previous year even more difficult for him to deal with. He deserved at least a small dose of understanding.

"Whitney's murder had to have been a terrible thing for you, even though you were no longer together. I have the feeling you must've felt deeply about it. Then there was the questioning by the police. They probably weren't too gentle with you. Most likely, in the early stages of their investigation, they considered you as a possible suspect, which, of course, was absurd."

I stood up. "I'm sorry about the way I acted earlier. I won't keep you from your work any longer."

When I started toward the door, Scott gave a slight shrug and motioned for me to sit down. He started to say something and then stopped. I looked out the sliding doors and waited. For the first time, I noticed that the apartment was adjacent to a golf course. Two golfers were studying a green so intensely they could've been playing the final hole of the Masters at Augusta. I was trying to think of something to say to break the tension that had been building when Scott finally spoke.

"It was the worst fucking time of my life. In the last couple of weeks of the semester, I reached the point where I didn't think I could take anymore. Like you said, I think the police thought I might be the murderer. Some asshole policewoman kept asking me all these questions. She wanted to know everything about Whitney and me. How often I saw her. What we did together. Who our friends were. Even though I did my best to answer her questions, I got the impression she thought I was withholding something. What really got to me was that bitch even asked me about the kind of sex Whitney and I had. That pissed me off so much I could hardly talk. Can you imagine anyone asking about . . . "

By this time, there were tears in Scott's eyes and his lips trembled. It was clear that he was deeply angry. I sensed he was still struggling with powerful feelings of loss and grief.

"I can see why you might be furious."

Scott gave no sign that he'd heard me.

"Then there was the way people on campus treated me. They seemed to blame me for what happened. It was like they thought Whitney would've been alive if we hadn't broken up. They had the idea that I'd dumped her—and that somehow made me responsible for the murder. They didn't have a clue as to what went on between me and Whitney. They were blaming the wrong person if they thought I'd wanted to end it."

That surprised me. I'd assumed, like everyone else who knew the couple, that Whitney had wanted to continue the relationship and had been the victim of Scott's rejection.

Scott paused again. This time, I broke the silence. I wanted to know more about the relationship, and why it might've gone bad, but I was afraid to ask any specific questions for fear Scott would withdraw. I decided to raise the issue indirectly with the hope that he might want to talk about what happened.

"The fact that you and Whitney were together for such a long time tells me you were very important to each other. I can imagine you discussing your educational goals, career plans, and possibly even marriage. The end of a relationship like that between two intelligent, sensitive people isn't something that happens overnight."

Scott took a deep breath. "We began talking about our life together not long after we started dating. Whitney was in pre-med. We thought we could attend the same medical school and we'd get married sometime, even though we didn't make any specific plans."

I got the impression Scott was almost eager to talk about his relationship with Whitney. "When did things start to go wrong?"

Scott shrugged. "I'm not exactly sure. Maybe it was never quite the same for us after she changed her major to psychology. We'd talked a lot about our careers in medicine, what kind of practices we'd have and that sort of thing. When she got into psychology, we had less in common. It seemed like we weren't as close as we had been. In spite of this, we got along well. Whitney was a beautiful person.

"Then, at the beginning of our senior year last year, things got more complicated. Whitney was excited about graduate school in psychology and began thinking about where she would apply. I was surprised that it was more difficult to get accepted to graduate school in psychology than to medical school. Whitney made a list of universities she was interested in, and I checked out their medical schools. It became clear there was a good chance we wouldn't be going to the same university.

"I suggested to Whitney that she get a job in the area where I'd be in med school, and she could begin her graduate work when I was finished. That was a big mistake. Whitney got really upset and refused to talk to me for a few days. After that, we spent a lot of time arguing, something we'd never done before.

"During the first part of the spring semester, it got really bad. I was willing to try to work things out, but Whitney told me she couldn't take it any longer and it was over between us."

"Can you think of any reason why Whitney chose to break off the relationship at that particular time?" I asked.

Scott had been leaning back with his legs stretched out in a relaxed position. He immediately pulled himself up so that he was sitting upright on the edge of the sofa. He planted his feet on the floor. His hands rested on his knees as though he was about to stand up.

My question had obviously raised an issue Scott wasn't prepared to talk about. I suspected he realized he'd revealed a great deal about himself to someone who was almost a complete stranger, and now that stranger was asking him to tell even more. For individuals like Scott, letting someone into their private world can make them feel weak and vulnerable.

At this point, Scott began to behave as if I were no longer welcome. Since there was no point in prolonging my visit, I thanked him for talking with me and wished him the best in medical school.

As I started to open the door to leave, I turned and asked him to come and see me if he ever returned to campus. He surprised me by saying he was intending to come back for a visit sometime before the academic year was over, and that he might call me.

- 20 -

A bank of heavy, dark clouds had formed off to the west while I was inside the apartment building. It looked as though I'd run into a storm before I reached home. As I drove through the campus on my way back to the highway, I went over the time I'd spent with Scott. My early image of him had changed considerably. He'd been described to me by several people as being an arrogant, egotistical, and often unpleasant person. His behavior in my phone contact with him had been consistent with those descriptions. During the meeting, I saw a gentler, more humble side to Scott's personality, which helped me understand how Whitney could be attracted to him.

Whitney had been responsible for the breakup. I couldn't help wondering why, after they'd been together so long, she chose to end the relationship when she did. Was there something else going on at the time? Scott's response when I'd asked him seemed to suggest there might've been. If I'd been more patient during the interview and not interrupted Scott's report with such a direct question, he might've gone on talking. I'd started the meeting out badly and ended it the same way. It was an embarrassingly inept performance on my part, and I was disturbed to think I might've missed a chance to discover some significant information.

By the time I reached the city limits, it had begun to rain. No more combines in the fields. The farmers wouldn't be able to begin harvest again until the soil dried out. Most people would find a forced day or two off from work a welcome gift. Not the men and women who operate the combines. They can't have peace until the crops are safely stored in the grain bins. Every day out of the field during harvest is quiet agony. Some capricious act of nature, even as late as harvest time, could cost them a year's profits and result in bankruptcy. Farmers don't enjoy the benefits of a tenure system that guarantees academics job security even if their performance is below standard.

I don't like to drive. In fact, I consider every minute I spend in a motor vehicle a waste of time, even when I'm in my beloved pickup. Driving in the rain on the way home from what seemed to be an unproductive morning made this trip particularly unpleasant. Somewhere along the way, I realized I was hungry. The bagel hadn't been designed to keep a growing man satisfied for all the hours I'd spent on the road. I considered stopping at a fast food restaurant with a drive-through, but I decided I wasn't *that* hungry.

I hoped the storm might pass before I got home. It didn't work out that way. When I pulled in the drive, it was raining harder, and the sky was darker than when I'd left the city. Though it was still early afternoon, there were lights on in the house.

Beth didn't hear me come in the back door. I could picture her sitting at her desk, completely absorbed in the preparation for an upcoming case. I called out a greeting. I'd gotten as far as the living room when she emerged from the door of her study. She was smiling. "How did it go?"

"It wasn't an overwhelming success. Later, I want to give you the details for your expert analysis. Now I need something to eat and a nap."

"That's good, because I have some more to do before I can sit down and talk."

The refrigerator wasn't particularly well stocked. I had to settle for a cheese sandwich and a few stale potato chips. It wasn't much of a lunch, but it tasted pretty good. As my grandmother used to say, "Hunger never knew bad bread."

After finishing eating, I stretched out on the sofa and went to sleep almost immediately. I dreamed about a big, fat, bacon cheeseburger that those fast food restaurants advertise.

When I finally regained consciousness, it took me a while to figure out where I was. I glanced at the clock on the VCR. It was ten after four. I'd slept nearly two hours. Beth heard me stirring and came out of her study.

"Why didn't you wake me up? I missed most of the afternoon."

"You were sleeping so soundly I thought you needed the rest."

"Why don't you brew a pot of tea? Make it strong. I need a dose of caffeine. I'll start a fire in the wood stove. It's getting cool in here."

I'd just lighted the fire when Beth returned with the tea. "Tell me about your trip. I want to know if you found out anything that might be important."

I went through the entire morning, including the stop at the campus cafeteria, and did my best to give a complete description of the interview with Scott.

"I'm impressed with how you were able to get Scott to tell you so much. I thought there was a good possibility he might not talk to you at all."

"I was a little surprised myself. Unfortunately, I can't see that I learned anything of significance. I want your reaction."

Beth thought for a moment. "Scott's behavior during the interview was certainly interesting. The description of his relationship with Whitney intrigues me, but the fact that Whitney dropped him surprises me less than it did you. I can imagine what happened. Whitney wasn't quite as strong and self sufficient as it appeared on the surface. As a timid and slightly insecure freshman, it's understandable how she could be attracted to Scott. He was, by all reports, a very nice looking guy, and in case you didn't know, that's important to women. He was highly intelligent, which is something women also find attractive, and apparently very confident. We might expect she was charmed, and maybe even awed. I'm sure his confidence gave her a feeling of security. She could've come to rely on him quite heavily."

"If she'd become that dependent upon him, something important must have happened to cause the breakup," I said.

"I can imagine as she matured and grew stronger, those traits which initially made Scott so attractive were less important to her. His domineering ways undoubtedly became a source of irritation. A critical time was when she discovered herself in a position where she might have to postpone her education because Scott felt his career took priority over hers. Probably, she realized that his priorities might dictate how they managed their life later on. I suspect she began to wonder if he was worth that kind of sacrifice."

"Your analysis makes sense. Going to graduate school was very important to Whitney. The prospect of having to delay it would've been hard for her to accept," I said.

Beth nodded. "Even though they were having problems, it's surprising Whitney didn't try harder to work things out. Since Scott didn't want the relationship to end, we can assume he would've been willing to consider some sort of compromise. I share your suspicion that there was something more that contributed to the final breakup. I wonder if it could be a significant piece of the puzzle?"

"Scott's response when I asked him about it suggests to me it must be a sensitive issue. I can't help thinking I might've been more skillful in my questioning. On the other hand, it was probably the type of thing he'd be unwilling to reveal under any conditions. It might be interesting to know exactly what went on, but it's hard to imagine how a problem in a relationship between two college students could be related to a murder that occurred weeks later."

"I see your point," Beth said.

I asked Beth how her preparation for the trial was going. By the time she went over what she'd been doing, it was too late for any elaborate dinner preparation, so we warmed up some leftovers and ate on trays by the stove in the living room.

After dinner, Beth curled up on the sofa with the Sunday paper. While I sat watching the fire, I went over in my mind the events of the last few weeks.

Beth put down the last section of the paper and looked over at me. "You've been quiet. I bet you've been thinking about the investigation?"

"You're right. And I've made a decision. My career as a criminal investigator has come to an end. There is nothing more I can do. It was insane of me to get involved in the first place. There was no chance I'd ever be able to solve the case. The whole thing was just a waste of time."

Beth smiled. "Although I agree it's time for you to retire, I'm not sure I'll go along with the idea that it was a waste of time. There was always a possibility you might've come up with something important, and I think you enjoyed the hunt."

I smiled at her. "You're right. In a strange way, I did enjoy it. But it's over now."

Later that night in bed, before falling asleep, I thought about what it would be like to become a full-time faculty member again without the distractions of the past two months. It felt good. I had no idea how brief my retirement would be.

- 21 -

I woke up to the sound of Beth in the shower. On trial days, she's always up early. Through the bedroom window, I saw that the ground was covered with the first frost of the season. I checked the thermometer before starting my run. It was thirty-four degrees. Cold enough that I'd need to wear sweats. It reminded me that in a few weeks, I'd be moving my workout into the university gymnasium. Some of my colleagues run outside all winter but not me. I'm not that tough.

When I got back to the house, Beth was finishing breakfast. I poured a cup of coffee and joined her at the table. She wasn't very talkative. Her mind was somewhere off in the courtroom. I wished her luck as she headed out the door. I got a nod in return.

I drove through a deserted campus. It was still early. I pulled into the parking space only a few steps from the side entrance to the psychology building. Even though I run five miles every morning and don't mind walking, it irritates me when I have to park the pickup any distance from my office. The day was off to a good start.

On my way to class, I filled a coffee cup from the thermos I'd brought from home. The students are accustomed to seeing me sip coffee during my lecture. I encourage them to bring something to drink if they'd like. I do this because I think it produces a more relaxed, informal atmosphere in the classroom. In consideration of the custodial staff, there's a firm rule that no cups are left behind when we leave.

The morning went well. The students were particularly responsive. They asked excellent questions, and we had a good discussion of the material. I walked up the stairs to my office after my eleven o'clock class feeling pleased and a little irritated with myself. Because I'd been so caught up in the investigation in the past weeks, I'd neglected my teaching responsibilities.

The department reception area was deserted. Jean always took a long lunch hour on Mondays to get her hair done. Before she left, she'd put a note on my office door. I was to call Russ Merrick. There was a phone number. It wasn't the one for the police station. I wondered why Russ would want me to contact him away from his office. A terrible thought came to mind as I was dialing. I drummed my fingers on the desk while I waited.

Russ answered after six or seven rings. "Merrick speaking."

"Russ, this is Tom. I have a feeling you're going tell me something I don't want to hear."

"You guessed it. He struck again. We got the call at nine thirty-six this morning. A retired couple heading south in an RV stopped for breakfast at that little park by the river. The small one in a wooded area with a half a dozen picnic tables."

"I know the place," I said.

"When they finished their meal, the wife got out of the RV to put some trash in a container. She noticed the body at the edge of the parking area. It was obvious the killer made no attempt to conceal it.

"I was one of the first on the scene. The victim was partially clothed and had been badly beaten. It looked familiar. I have no doubt it's the same guy."

I sighed and rubbed my forehead. "Do you know anything about the victim yet?"

"Nothing except what we've been able to observe here. It's a young, black female. I'm guessing late teens, maybe early twenties. College student age. Though it was hard to tell because of the condition the body was in, I think she was quite attractive. Our killer is showing signs of being partial to good looking young women."

"I got to you on the cell phone. You're at the scene now?"

"That's right. I can't talk any longer. I'll get back to you."

"Before you hang up, would it be all right if I came up there?"

"Why don't you wait until later? There's quite a bit of confusion here. We're doing our best to keep people out of the area."

"I understand."

Russ began talking to someone in the background and hung up. I ate the sandwich I'd brought from home and spent what was left of the lunch hour and the early part of the afternoon at the computer preparing the exams I'd be giving to my classes later in the week. Images of the scene at the roadside park kept me from focusing my attention on the task. By mid-afternoon, I decided it was going to be impossible to get anything more done, so I logged off.

Several hours had passed since I'd talked to Russ. I thought things might've quieted down at the crime scene, and I couldn't see how it would do any harm if I drove by and had a look. As I approached the park, I saw that the entire area had been closed off. An officer stationed at the entry signaled me to keep moving. I got a glimpse of several other uniformed figures in the woods surrounding the parking lot. They were obviously searching for clues. Russ was nowhere in sight.

I turned at the next crossroad and headed toward police headquarters. Ten minutes later, I pulled into the parking lot. The receptionist recognized me and guessed why I was there.

"Russ is in a meeting," she said, looking very serious.

"Do you have any idea when he might be free?"

"I don't expect the meeting to be over for quite a while. You can wait if you like. Or I could leave him a message that you were here."

I thought a moment. Russ would call me as soon as he could. "No thanks. I'll get in touch with him later."

There was no point in going back to the office, so I decided to go home. On the way, I remembered that when Beth was in a trial, I did all the cooking. Since I couldn't remember what was in the refrigerator, I thought I'd better stop for provisions.

Sometimes I lose control in a grocery store. After spending half an hour wandering through the aisles, I left with so much, I had to put some bags in the back of the truck. By the time I had all the groceries carried into the house and put away, it was a few minutes before six. It occurred to me that the murder would be covered on the local news. I'd just turned on the television when the phone rang. It was Russ.

"Sorry I didn't get back to you sooner. I had a message saying you'd stopped in. We have an identification. Her name is Cheryl Martin. A sophomore at the university. Twenty years old. So far, I've talked to her roommate and her boyfriend. I have the names of a few more students who I want to interview. I'm in the process of trying to contact them. I expect to be getting reports from a couple of the other people who are on the case as the evening goes on.

"How about this? We meet at the Downtown Deli at noon tomorrow. By then I should know more, and I can bring you up to date on what we have."

"That'll be fine with me. I have an eleven o'clock class so it'll be after twelve before I can meet you."

"Then let's make it twelve thirty," Russ said. He was beginning to talk faster. I knew he needed to get off the phone.

"See you then. And thanks for the call. I know you must be on the run."

"I sure am. We've got to get this bastard," he said and hung up the phone.

I caught most of the TV news coverage of the crime. It was clear the station had relatively little information. The two anchors described the discovery of the body. That was followed by a tape of an interview with the chief of police. He said the usual things. It was a terrible crime, and all the resources of the force would be directed toward solving the case. He avoided a direct answer when asked if he thought the killer was the same person who had murdered Whitney Richardson.

After the interview, the camera switched to a round, balding weatherman named Bob who always managed to give viewers the impression that his report was the most significant portion of the newscast, and that he had information not available to any other weather person. He was explaining in some detail why there was a good possibility of precipitation during the early morning hours when I heard the back door open.

"I'm home," Beth called out. By the sound of her voice, I knew she was tired. She came into the living room and dropped into one of our large, overstuffed chairs. "I didn't hear about the murder until court was adjourned at five. Nobody around the courthouse knew any details. What can you tell me?"

"When I was in class, Russ left a message for me to call him. I reached him at the murder site a little after twelve. Then he called here a little while ago."

Beth was frowning by the time I finished giving her a summary of Russ's reports. She shook her head slowly. "This is the worst. He's still out there, and if he isn't apprehended, I think we can be fairly sure he'll kill again."

"Unfortunately, I have to agree with you. It looks like he's enjoying what he does enough that it would be hard for him to give it up. He's got to be found. Russ offered to meet me for lunch tomorrow to fill me in on the details."

"Sounds like you've become an unofficial member of the city police force."

"Oh sure. Now, tell me about your day in court. How did it go?"

"We're into jury selection. That's always tough. Sometimes I think the make up of the jury in a case is more important than the actual evidence. I know it sounds pretty cynical, but often that's the way the system works."

"You don't have to worry much about losing this one, do you?"

"I guess not. If I can't get a guilty verdict in a case where the defendant has been selling drugs to kids right outside the school grounds, I'd better start thinking about starting a practice where I write wills and negotiate divorce settlements."

"Go change your clothes. I'll see if I can put together some sort of meal."

After I'd arranged some cold cuts and French bread on a platter, I got myself a Molson Ale out of the refrigerator and filled one of our magnum wine glasses, which ordinarily come out only when we're entertaining guests for dinner, with Chardonnay. Beth was showing the effects of a difficult day. I thought the extra wine would be good medicine.

Beth was sitting on the sofa in the living room with her feet up on the coffee table. "Tom, you know I won't be able to finish all that," she said, when she saw the size of the glass.

She didn't, but she came very close.

- 22 -

The next morning, I was wide awake before daylight. When the sun finally came up, I got out of bed and put on my running clothes. Just as I was leaving the house, it started to rain. I went back inside and took a shower. I was scrambling some eggs when Beth came into the kitchen in her pajamas. "Couldn't sleep?" she asked.

"Too many dreary thoughts running through my mind."

"I know what you mean. I had a few myself during the night."

"As soon as I finish eating, I'm going to leave for work."

"The campus may not be a very cheerful place today."

"I know. There are going to be quite a few frightened, upset students. I'll see you this evening."

The department was quiet when I arrived. I closed my office door because I didn't feel much like talking to anyone. If there were no interruptions, I could get the examinations ready I'd been working on the day before. My first class wasn't until eleven. A few minutes after eight, there was a gentle knock on the door. It was Jean.

"I'm sorry to bother you, Tom. I know when your door is closed you prefer not to be interrupted."

"It's okay. Come in and sit down."

"I heard on the morning news that she was a student. They didn't give any more information. Do you know anything about her?"

"I talked to Russ Merrick last night. Her name is Cheryl Martin, a sophomore. That's about all I can tell you."

"Do they think it's the same person that murdered Whitney?"

"All the evidence points that way."

"Tom, I can't believe this is happening. A killer on our campus."

"I have trouble dealing with it myself," I said.

97

Jean closed the door quietly when she left.

Students typically show up for eight and nine o'clock lectures in a mild state of lethargy. Most of them are up late and stay in bed as long as possible in the morning, so when they arrive, they're still half asleep. At eleven, you can expect them to be wide awake, and they're usually so full of talk sometimes it takes a little time at the beginning of class to get their attention. On this day, the tone was much different. Students arrived in groups of two or three, moving slowly. There were no smiles and little conversation except for an occasional whispered interchange. A few late arrivals were coming in the door and heading for their seats when a woman in the front row quietly asked, "Dr. Evers, how can a person do something like this?"

This was a question in part based on the commonly held misconception that psychologists are capable of explaining all human behavior. It suggested the students might benefit from an opportunity to talk about an event which had to be very traumatic for many of them. I decided it would be worthwhile spending some class time discussing what had occurred on Sunday night.

"Kathy, I'll wait until everyone is settled before responding to your question."

When the room was quiet, I began. "Not long ago, we learned that one of your fellow students had been brutally murdered. This is shocking in and of itself. The impact on us is even greater because it's the second killing in less than a year. Though we can't be absolutely sure at this point, it appears the crimes were committed by the same individual. One of your classmates just asked me what kind of person could do something like this. I'm unable to give you a complete answer, but there are some things we can conclude. We know this is a person who has needs that are fulfilled by committing an unthinkably horrible act. How these needs develop in a human being continues to be a mystery. Fortunately, they are extremely rare, but this is of little comfort because there is one of them among us. It is a very disturbing situation."

The fact that my short speech was entirely unplanned was obvious. Looking back, I realize that I offered the students little in the way of insight into what had happened. It quickly became clear, however, that what I'd said had an effect because, almost immediately after I finished, the students began talking. First came the questions which reflected feelings of apprehension and fear. "Will he do it again?" a woman in the back asked.

I nodded my head. "Yes, there is a good possibility he will if he isn't apprehended." No point in not facing the realities, I thought.

"Could he be someone at the university—a student or employee?" another student asked.

"Highly unlikely, but possible. Much of the time, these individuals can act like normal, law-abiding citizens."

I motioned to another woman in the back. "How long before he might strike again?"

"No way of knowing—days, weeks, months—hopefully never," I said.

After a few more minutes of questions, a woman student said that Cheryl's room was just down the hall from hers in the dorm. She considered Cheryl to be one of the nicest girls she knew. Several in the group nodded in agreement. Another commented that she was always so cheerful and friendly. Everyone liked her. Others described her contributions as a member of various campus organizations. She studied hard and got excellent grades. Those in the group who knew Cheryl personally, and many who had no direct contact with her, were experiencing sadness and a sense of loss.

Finally, the feeling of anger among the students began to surface. Mostly it was reflected in comments on the appropriate type of punishment for an individual who committed a crime of this type. Several of the "eye for an eye" suggestions were so brutal that I was slightly disturbed. A fraternity member, for example, reported that some of his brothers had held a meeting to discuss the formation of a vigilante committee. He described in graphic, R-rated detail some of the dreadful things they'd talked about doing to the culprit if they captured him before the police.

After a half-hour, the room became quiet.

"I think it's time we get back to thinking about psychology."

The students opened their notebooks and picked up their pens. In the remaining time, I did my best to interest them in the lecture material. I wasn't successful. Their thoughts were elsewhere.

At the end of class, several students, who I think were too timid to speak in front of the rest of the group, came to me with more questions about the crime. When the last one finally left the room, I realized I'd be late for my meeting with Russ.

When I arrived at the deli, Russ was sitting at a table by the big, plate glass window in the front. He saw me come in the door and waved me to the cafeteria style serving line. He looked serious.

"Sorry I'm late. Some students stayed after class. They wanted to talk about the murder."

"That's okay. I needed a few minutes of solitude. The last twenty-four hours have been hectic."

Russ went first through the line. He ordered roast beef and cheddar cheese on a bun, German potato salad, and a piece of cherry cheese cake. I chose pastrami on rye and coleslaw. I passed on dessert.

Back at the table, Russ picked at his potato salad. I knew him well enough not to ask questions. When he was ready, he'd give me the details in a very well organized report.

"Tom, this thing is a carbon copy of the Richardson killing. It's as though we're conducting the same investigation all over again. Just like the first time, the murder took place sometime late Sunday night or early Monday morning. The body was left where it would be easily discovered. Based on what I saw, I'd bet anything the medical examiner's findings will confirm that the nature of the injuries and cause of death were similar in both cases.

"I got to the roommate yesterday afternoon. Her name is Amy Price. She's a sharp girl. Apparently, she and Cheryl were very good friends. She was badly shaken up and had trouble talking, but she tried her best to help.

"Cheryl had a steady boyfriend, John Baxter. I saw him after I talked to Amy. It turned out he was in worse shape than Amy. Communicating with him was even more difficult. I was able to get some information out of him. I want to talk to him again later. I think he may be able to give us more when he calms down. Seems like a nice kid. I felt sorry for him.

"Tom, doing interviews like these are the worst part of my job," Russ said, shaking his head slowly. "Based on what the two of them were able to tell me, I managed to piece together what went on Sunday afternoon and evening. Amy told me that Cheryl left after lunch to meet John in the library. She gave me the impression that both Cheryl and John were serious students. They spent a lot of time studying together. John said Cheryl was already in the library when he got there at one o'clock. She must have gone there directly from the dorm. She wouldn't have had time to stop anywhere."

I pictured a happy young woman, who had only a few hours to live, going to meet her boyfriend. There was a sinking feeling in my stomach.

"According to John, he and Cheryl usually spent all day Sunday together. They would study in the library during the afternoon and eat dinner in the university cafeteria. John works at the desk in the library's late hours study room, which is open until 1 a.m. Cheryl would stay there with him until closing. Last Sunday was different. At four thirty, Cheryl said she was tired and went back to her room to take a nap. She told John she'd come to the library when he came on duty.

"It was a promise she would never keep," Russ said sadly. I wondered if he was thinking that he had a daughter living on the campus.

"When Cheryl arrived at the dorm, Amy was leaving to go over to her boyfriend's apartment. Amy ate dinner there and spent the evening. Cheryl called John at the library a few minutes after seven. He was sure of the time because he'd just started to work. She told him she'd gotten a message about a special meeting and didn't know how long it would last. She said if she didn't get away until late, she planned to go directly back to her room. John said even though it was unusual for a meeting to be called at the last minute, he didn't think too much about it because Cheryl was active in several student organizations and on a number of committees. When she didn't show up at the library, he assumed the meeting had been a long one.

"Amy arrived back at the dorm at midnight. She went straight to bed and slept soundly. I guess these kids must sleep a lot better than I do. When she woke up at seven and saw that Cheryl's bed hadn't been slept in, she called John. Of course, he had no idea where Cheryl was. He immediately went over to the girls' room. My guess is that neither Amy nor John could let themselves think about what could've happened. They called all of Cheryl's friends who might know where she was. No one knew anything. Finally, they faced up to the reality of the situation and contacted campus security. Even if they'd called the night before, it wouldn't have made one bit of difference."

While Russ was talking, it had started to rain. A flash of lightening and loud clap of thunder caused him to pause. I noticed that neither of us had eaten anything. Russ's report had taken away our interest in food.

"Amy reported something else that could be important. Earlier in the semester, Cheryl told her she'd noticed a strange looking man standing across the street from the dorm when she left for her afternoon class. She was sure he was following her to the classroom building. Amy thought this might have gone on for a couple of weeks. It sounds suspicious to me, so we're going to follow up on it."

Russ took a small bite of his sandwich and chewed it slowly.

"This morning I learned more about the similarities in the two cases," I said. "In my class, the students began asking questions about the crime. This led to a discussion that lasted a good part of the hour. Several members of the class knew Cheryl personally. Their description of her matched closely with what you heard from Amy and John. She was a hardworking, serious student who got excellent grades. They mentioned her involvement in campus activities. It was obvious that she was well liked and respected by the other students. What impressed me was that the students could have been describing Whitney Richardson."

Russ was quiet for a minute. He seemed to be processing what I'd just reported. "Both Whitney and Cheryl were attractive, intelligent, well-liked, active in campus organizations, and they got good grades. What could this mean? One possibility is that our killer is attracted to a particular type of victim. Also, this is the kind of student that stands out from the group. Or, to look at it in another way, the type that's easily identified."

"Which suggests he might be an insider," I said. "Someone who is familiar with the campus and knows about students. I find that a little hard to believe."

"I do, too. But it's a possibility we have to consider."

"By the way, I assume Whitney's boyfriend Scott was never a serious suspect. At this point, he has to be out of the picture. I mentioned to you that Mrs. Richardson thought it would be worthwhile for me to contact him. I found out that he's enrolled at the state medical school. When I called him, he refused to talk.

That made me curious, so I drove down early Sunday morning and.caught him at his apartment. It was pretty much a waste of time, though I did find out a little more about his relationship with Whitney."

"You're right when you say he was never a serious suspect. But in a case as strange as this, you have to keep an open mind."

"What do you think about Charlie Rutledge?" I asked.

"He has to be considered a possibility. My people have been so busy we haven't gotten around to him yet. That reminds me. Do you know where he's staying? The address in our file is the fraternity house where he lived last year. He must've moved from there. There's no listing for him in the phone book."

"I don't have his address, but the fraternity gave me the name of the guy he lives with. I think I still have it at my office. I'll call you later."

Russ looked at the clock on the wall over the door. It was one thirty, and we had finally finished our lunches. I hadn't even remembered eating.

"I've got work to do," Russ said, as he picked up his tray.

"So do I. Just one thing before you get away. Would it be all right if I did some investigating on this one? I know it's different than the Richardson case, but I'd like to see what I can do."

"It's okay with me, but it would be best if you held off until we've finished our work. We should be done by the end of the week. I'll let you know."

During the drive back to campus, I began thinking about how I might approach this new phase of my investigation.

- 23 -

The next day, I gave exams in two of my classes. I was so busy the rest of the week grading papers and attending meetings that there wasn't time to think about any investigating.

Beth called me late Thursday afternoon to tell me the jury had come in with a guilty decision after less than two hours of deliberation. She sounded relieved and tired. When Beth finished a trial, I could count on her not bringing work home for a few days. The pile of unfinished business on my desk was so high that I'd planned to spend most of the day on Saturday in my office. With the unexpected early end of the trial, I was determined to enjoy a free weekend with Beth. I worked until after midnight in my study at home and gave up running in the morning so I could get to campus early. A little after six on Friday, I drove out of the parking lot without my briefcase.

On Saturday, we watched two rented videos and picked up a pizza. After a late brunch on Sunday, Beth stretched out on the sofa with a book. When I tried to read, my attention wandered. My thoughts kept returning to the events of the past week. Finally, I gave up and went into my study and sat down at the computer. I opened up the investigation file I'd started weeks before. I entered in the details of the second murder that Russ had provided and what I'd learned about Cheryl from the students in my class.

When I finished, I reread the entire file. I was again struck by the similarity in the crimes. The choice of victims who were so much alike could hardly have been accidental. I was convinced that the killer, for some odd reason, had a preference for attractive, talented young women who had distinguished themselves academically and were involved in student activities.

My thoughts went back to the meeting I'd had with Russ at the deli and the consideration that someone with first-hand knowledge of the campus would have an easier time selecting victims who were so much alike. This could mean an employee of the university or a member of the student body. Don Reynolds had mentioned this possibility when I'd talked with him about Whitney's murder. I recalled his story about the time he'd visited a university in Florida where a professor was suspected of being involved in a series of sexually motivated murders.

The idea that the killer might be someone associated with the campus was difficult for me to accept. I also knew that some of the inhabitants of my own ivory tower were not always what they appeared to be. I'd learned this from a disturbing incident that occurred several years earlier.

When I joined the faculty fresh out of graduate school, there was a fourth-year doctoral student in psychology named Jonathon Reichart who sighed up for a seminar I was scheduled to teach. I was a little uneasy having Jonathon in the class. He was at least ten years older than I was and had the reputation of being extremely bright and knowledgeable. One of my colleagues explained to me that Jonathon received an MBA and had a highly successful career in business before deciding to apply to graduate school in psychology when he was in his mid-thirties. Because of his age and lack of academic training in psychology, some of the members of the admissions committee had reservations, but in spite of that, he was accepted. Any concerns about his ability and motivation turned out to be unfounded. He quickly won the respect of the faculty and was expected to make some substantial contributions in the field after he completed the work for his Ph.D.

It turned out there was no reason for me to be apprehensive about having Jonathon in my first graduate seminar. Almost immediately I developed a liking for him and a respect for his keen intelligence. I remembered thinking at the time that I'd feel fortunate if all my students in the future were as good as Jonathon.

Several weeks into the semester, Jonathon came to my office and asked if he could bring another student with him to class. He explained that he had become friends with a young graduate student in physics by the name of Jeremy Phillips. Jeremy had graduated from college at age eighteen. At the rate he was going, he would be receiving his Ph.D. before his twenty-second birthday. Jonathon explained that Jeremy was very much interested in the topic of the seminar and would do all the required reading. At first, I was skeptical, but I eventually agreed because I trusted Jonathon's recommendation. I was also intrigued by the prospect of having an obviously brilliant young student trained in another discipline become part of the group. My decision was the correct one. At first, Jeremy was self-consciousness about entering into the discussion. Once he overcame this, largely because the other students encouraged him to participate, his presence turned what I thought was a good seminar into a great one.

On the last day of final exam week, Jonathon and Jeremy spent the night celebrating the end of the semester, drinking beer at a local bar with several other graduate students. They left together a little before midnight. An hour later, there was a 911 call reporting a shooting at Jonathon's address. When the paramedics arrived at the apartment, they found Jeremy lying in the bedroom with a gunshot wound in the chest. He died in the emergency room at the hospital without gaining consciousness. Jonathon told the police that a handgun he'd been showing Jeremy had gone off accidently.

The information uncovered during the subsequent police investigation shocked everyone. It was determined that Jonathon had never received an advanced degree. In fact, there was no evidence that he'd ever been enrolled in a college or university. He had a record of numerous arrests, beginning in adolescence with acts of vandalism and car theft. Later, as an adult, he was charged with fraud and forgery. He'd served three prison terms. It was shortly after his release from the most recent one, which was for assault with a deadly weapon, that he submitted a falsified application to the graduate school supported by forged documents.

Jonathon was charged with manslaughter. The trial, which was moved to another county because of the possibility of local prejudice, resulted in an acquittal.

Those of us who knew Jonathon doubted that he was capable of intentionally killing another human being. On the other hand, it came as a shock to learn that an individual with his background, and apparent potential for violence, could go unnoticed by a relatively large number of faculty and students who had been closely associated with him for a period of several years.

I went to bed thinking that the range of possible suspects had broadened significantly.

- 24 -

Monday was the first day of registration week. During this period, faculty advisors meet individually with their advisees to work out a schedule of classes for the next semester. Because it isn't unusual for faculty members to advise as many as thirty students, this is a time consuming and hectic process. Unfortunately, there are a fair number of advisors who feel they can't spare the time for such an unimportant activity, so they instruct the students to choose whatever courses they want and take their registration card to the department secretary to be signed. These students often make bad choices and end up in academic difficulty.

The actual registration process begins on Wednesday morning and continues through Friday afternoon. Many of the popular courses reach their enrollment limit before the end of the registration period. This means students have to meet with their advisors again to revise their schedules. Often they feel frustrated when they are forced to enroll in classes that aren't of particular interest to them. With twenty advisees that semester, I had appointments with students every hour I wasn't in class or attending a meeting. Even if Russ had let me know that it was all right to go ahead with the new murder investigation, I would've been too busy to do anything.

I was in my office at two on Friday with a line of advisees outside the door who had run into problems during registration when Russ called. I told him I'd get back to him later. It was almost four when the last student left my office. The woman who answered the phone at the station informed me that Detective Merrick had left his office on an emergency fifteen minutes earlier.

After Beth and I finished dinner, I went to the phone and dialed Russ's number. Rose answered. She said Russ hadn't come home yet. I asked her to have him call me when he got in. Two hours later the phone rang. Russ began talking immediately. I could tell he wasn't in a particularly good mood.

"We've done about all we can on the case and haven't been able to come up with anything that would help us in identifying the killer. I talked to John Baxter again. He wasn't able to give me any additional information. We contacted several more students in the dorm. Nothing there either. It took a while to locate Rutledge. He moved since you talked to him. He's living over on the west side of town with a woman who works at the university in the accounting office. She must be ten years older. She's plain looking and overweight. I'm not sure what he sees in her, but I suppose it could be a free pad and some spending money.

"Rutledge says he never left the apartment on the day of the murder. The woman confirms that. I'm pretty sure she's terrified of him and would say anything he told her to.

"Rutledge is raw sewage. We have to consider him a suspect. He has a history of physically abusing women and based on that incident in the fraternity house, we know he's a racist. A black victim could be pretty exciting to this type of animal. If we could get access to his car, we might be able to find some physical evidence. Unfortunately, we don't have enough evidence to justify a search."

"Did you find out anything about the stalking?" I asked.

"So far it has been a dead end. We couldn't find anybody who knew about it besides Amy."

"What's next?"

"I suppose there's still an outside chance the killer might get drunk and let something slip or even brag about what he's done. In this type of situation, a reward might help. The Richardsons have money. Did they ever tell you they'd considered offering one?"

"They never mentioned it. I wonder why? It would be a logical thing to do."

"It's very simple. They aren't willing to spend any of their hard earned money to find the killer."

"They offered to pay me."

"If you'd begun to send them bills regularly, your investigation might've ended relatively quickly. Besides that, I bet Richardson was smart enough to guess you wouldn't take any payment for your work." Russ laughed. "He knows how dumb professors are."

"You're getting pretty cynical in your old age."

"Been in this business as long as I have, you can't avoid it. And it's a good thing. Cops that are cynical can do a better job. They suspect everyone and trust no one."

"Is it all right if I start nosing around a little?"

"That's the reason I called. It's okay for you to go ahead. I told the people in records that you might be in to read the file. You won't find much to go on, but at least you'll know who we contacted. In the chance you happen to run across anything that might be important, let me know. I want to get this thing settled as soon as possible. If you find something that helps us find the killer, understand you won't get any credit for it from the department."

"I can live with that. I realize how humiliating it could be if some dumb college professor upstaged the local police in this high profile investigation."

Russ laughed. "I'm glad you can understand the position we're in. I consider Amy and John to be the two most important informants in this case. In my opinion, they're fine kids. They did their best to cooperate. Even so, I think it would be worthwhile for you to spend some time with them. There could be some things they might reveal to you that they wouldn't tell me, a police detective. And John was still in pretty bad shape emotionally when I saw him a week ago. He was obviously having trouble talking about what had happened. Maybe by the time you get to him he'll have settled down and have more to tell.

"Before you hang up, Rose wants to talk to you—hold on."

In a minute, Rose came on the other extension, and I heard Russ hang up.

"Tom, have you seen Patti recently?"

"A few weeks ago, she came to my office to ask me some questions about sorority rush. That's the only time I've talked to her since she's been on campus. Why do you ask? Is there something wrong?"

"I hope not. We talk to her on the phone at least once a week, and she comes home for dinner every other Sunday. Recently, she's seemed to be a little preoccupied. I've been wondering if she might be under some kind of stress."

"The first year of college is a stressful time. I can't imagine that Patti is having any serious problems. She's a sensible young woman. You've been through the college thing with Russ junior and Linda. They did very well. I don't see why you can't expect the same from Patti."

"I think you may have noticed that Patti's a little different. She isn't as serious about things as they were."

"Yes, I have. But I don't see any reason why you should be concerned."

"Thanks for listening, Tom. Let us know if you find out anything."

"Of course I will."

When I hung up the phone, I went into the living room and found Beth stretched out on the sofa reading. She immediately put down her book. "What did Russ have to say?"

"He didn't have much to report. There hasn't been any progress in the investigation."

Beth didn't say anything.

"Tell me what's on your mind," I said.

"You could probably guess. You're thinking about getting involved again, and I'm very uneasy about it. I can understand the situation with Whitney. You knew her personally so her death was especially disturbing, and the Richardsons asked for your help. This case is equally as tragic, but you never had any contact with the woman. I know you're going to say that the same person did it, so essentially it's a continuation of the Richardson investigation, and I can't argue with that. I guess it comes down to this. I don't want you to be exposed to any danger. Now we know this is a serial killer, the kind of beast you stay away from if at all possible. You may not be the greatest, but you'd be difficult to replace."

"You're right. I should forget about the whole nasty mess. The problem is, I have a very hard time thinking about quitting. I'd only be trying to uncover some information that might help Russ find the killer. That's as far as I'd go. The rest would be up to the police. They get paid to do the dirty work." I thought for a moment. "How does this sound? I'll spend a little time on it. No more than two weeks. Then, no matter how things stand, I'll give it up."

"All right. I'll go along with that. But let me warn you. If you don't get out at the deadline, I'm filing for a divorce," she said, shaking her finger at me. "I know an excellent attorney. I'd claim spousal abuse, and you'd lose everything, including your reputation and an incredibly attractive and stimulating partner. Keep that in mind."

I smiled. "It's a deal. By the way, I find you to be particularly attractive when you're assertive. How would you like to join me in bed?"

"I've been waiting all evening for you to ask."

- 25 -

The weekend weather was beautiful. The changing leaves were at their peak. Beth and I took care of household chores on Saturday morning. The rest of the day, we hiked through the woods behind our house so we could get close to the display of fall colors.

On Sunday, while Beth was taking an early afternoon nap, I began thinking about what I could do in the next two weeks. Obviously, the first thing on my list would be to talk with Amy and John. How to make contact was a problem. Neither of them would have any idea who I was. It would be understandable if they were hesitant in coming to my office to talk about the murder. I decided it might help if I could get an introduction from a black student.

In recent years, blacks had been heavily recruited by the university's Office of Admissions in order to create a more diverse student body. As a result, the percentage of blacks in the entering freshman class increased steadily. It was expected that these students would be integrated into the general student body, but for complex reasons, things hadn't worked out that way. The black students on our campus had gradually developed a separate community. They had their own formal and informal social activities and had established black fraternities and sororities. Of course, this didn't mean black and white students never had contact with each other. Among the majority of the students there was a mutual acceptance, and the groups got along well. In fact, many close friendships developed between members of the two races.

Because the black students tended to stick together, I had the feeling it might not be too difficult to find one who knew both Amy and John. Unfortunately, only a few blacks had taken a course with me in recent semesters. Those who were enrolled in large, introductory psychology sections where there was little opportunity for personal contact with individual students.

A dozen or so names came to mind. I would be able to recognize them if we met on campus, and I could remember how well they did in the course, but there were only two I'd spent time with outside of class. One was a particularly talented woman who had decided to minor in psychology. I worked with her on a plan of study. She was a first semester junior at the time and would've graduated. There was a chance she might've enrolled in a graduate program. I checked the student directory. Her name wasn't listed.

The other student, Mark Breland, had taken introductory psychology with me in the spring semester of his freshman year. If he were still in school, he would've been a junior. Mark sat in the back row between two white giants who must have had a combined weight of at least a quarter of a ton. I assumed correctly that they were members of the football team. Mark was the only one of the three who attended class regularly. I rarely saw the other two after the first week of the semester, and predictably, they failed every exam. Mark did C+ work.

Two weeks before final exam week, Mark showed up at my office door with his right arm and shoulder in a cast. He had been injured on the last day of spring football practice. He asked if he could take an oral final exam. I knew from experience that oral exams were unpleasant, for both the teacher and the student, so I suggested he take an incomplete grade and fulfill the course requirement by writing three papers over the summer. He chose that option without hesitation.

When I'd done this before for students who hadn't been able to take the final for one reason or another, often it didn't turn out well. They tended to procrastinate and ended up having to write the papers after returning to campus. In order to complete the work from the last semester, they had less time to work on their current courses and problems arose. In an effort to prevent this from happening with Mark, I told him that if the papers weren't on my desk by the first day of the fall semester, I'd submit a failing grade to the registrar. Even with my ultimatum, I wondered if Mark would get the papers to me on time. Of course, I would've given him an extension if he hadn't met the deadline.

I was surprised when I arrived at my office on the day fall classes began to find an envelope on my desk containing the three papers. They were considerably better than most I'd received at the end of the summer vacation—good enough that I felt Mark deserved a B in the course.

Maybe it was Mark's manner—the aloofness, the suggestion of arrogance, or the way he inappropriately called me Doc—that made me wish there was another student I could contact. But I couldn't come up with another name. I checked the student directory. Mark was still on campus living in a fraternity.

The next day, during the lunch hour, I dialed the number of the fraternity house. The student on phone duty gave me the standard response to my request. "Please hold. I'll see if Mark is in." After waiting several minutes, I was ready to hang up when Mark picked up the phone. He sounded as though his afternoon nap had been interrupted.

I identified myself and told him that he might be in a position to do me a favor. I said it was something I couldn't discuss on the phone. I asked if he would he be willing to come to my office sometime and talk.

Ten minutes later, Mark was sitting across the desk from me, slouched in the chair with his legs stretched out. I began to doubt even more the wisdom in asking him for help.

I started the conversation by commenting on the papers he'd handed in the year before. I complimented him on getting them in on time and told him that they had been well written. I'm not sure he knew how to handle my comments. I suspected he'd never heard praise from a faculty member before.

When I asked about football, Mark seemed to become more comfortable. I was surprised how freely he talked. His injury had turned out to be quite severe. The doctors told him that if he continued to play, he would be risking permanent damage to his shoulder. He decided to quit the team. He described the relief he'd experienced in not having to attend exhausting practice sessions and in having more time for study.

As I listened to Mark go into unnecessary detail about his experiences in football and his new priorities, I began to wonder if there was anyone in his life he could confide in. My concern about asking him for help was greatly diminished.

It was some time before Mark finished talking about his life, and I was able to ask him if he'd had any contact with Cheryl, John, or Amy. He said John was a close friend, and he knew Cheryl. He'd been around Amy only a few times, when she was with Cheryl, so he didn't know her very well.

I explained briefly my work on the Richardson case, and that I was involved in the investigation of Cheryl's murder. "Would you be willing to work with me?" I asked.

Mark sat up in his chair and leaned forward. "Yeah, I would. What can I do?"

"You could start by telling me about Cheryl."

"Like, what do you want to know?"

"I want to understand what kind of a person she was. The things she liked to do. The people she associated with who might know something that could give us a clue as to what happened that night."

"I can do that. Cheryl was class. Beautiful, smart, and nice. I'll tell you something, Doc. I fell in love with that girl the first time I saw her. But, by that time, she and Big John were together. Anyway, I wouldn't have had a chance. I'm not serious enough, or maybe too wild would be a better way to say it.

"Cheryl didn't hang out much with the blacks on campus. It wasn't like she looked down on us or anything. I just think she didn't have the time. She studied a lot and was busy with all those committees she was on."

"Besides John, do you know of anyone she might've talked to about personal things?" I asked.

Mark shook his head. "I can't think of anyone."

"Tell me about John. First, how did he get that nickname?"

"I'm not exactly sure. He's not all that big. There's just something about him. He's different from the other dudes. He doesn't talk much, but when he does, people listen. That kind of guy; you know what I mean?"

"I think I do."

"Let me tell you something, so maybe you can understand Big John better. Did you play any sports when you were young?"

"Some," I said.

"With a lot of us blacks, sports are really important. Maybe the most important thing in the world. If you're good, you get respect from the brothers and sisters, and from other people, too. In high school, I was a star in football. People in the stands would cheer when I made a big play. It made me feel like I was accepted, or something like that.

"I was a good football player, but I liked to play basketball better. It was more fun. I was on my high school team. I would've given anything to play in college and maybe get one of those million dollar pro contracts. I wasn't good enough, so I ended up here on a football scholarship.

"Like in high school, after football season, I spent a lot of time in the gym playing basketball. That's where I met Big John. He'd come late at night to shoot baskets. Sometimes, we were there all alone when they turned out the lights. We got to teaming up in two on two games. We hardly ever lost. Not because I was so good. It was Big John. He's quick; he has the moves and a feeling for the game. If you get clear, he puts the ball in your hands. Sometimes, I couldn't figure how he did it.

"One afternoon, late, most everybody had gone to dinner. There was just enough guys left so we could have a full court five on five game. While we were playing, one of the assistant varsity coaches came in and sat on the bleacher seats. He stayed until we broke up. When we all headed to the locker room, he went over to Big John and started talking. They must've had a pretty long discussion because most of us were out of the shower and dressed by the time Big John came in.

"We were wondering what'd happened out there. Big John just said the coach was talking to him. We kept after him to find out what was going on. It turned out the coach asked Big John to come and work out with the varsity. He said they had an extra scholarship because one of the players had left school. I told Big John that was great and asked him when he was going to start practice. He said he wasn't going to do it."

Mark shook his head and frowned. "We couldn't believe what we'd heard. One of the guys told him he was out of his—uh—mind. Big John just shrugged and headed into the shower. I couldn't figure it out. First, I thought Big John was either stupid or crazy. Then I realized he wasn't either one. He was just smart. He knew he might be getting into something he didn't need, and he had the guts to say no."

"You respected that."

"Yeah, I did."

"John's a quiet person, even around friends?"

"That he is, Doc."

"The detective who questioned John after the murder is a friend of mine. He's a good cop and a nice guy with years of experience in interviewing people. He told me John was so upset it was hard to get much out of him. I need to talk with John. I figured if I asked him to come to my office and answer some questions about the murder, he'd probably refuse."

"You're right. I stopped at the apartment on Saturday. Big John was not talking—period. He was just staring at a game on TV. The place was a mess, his stuff was all around, like he might be packing to leave school. I asked him and he said he was thinking about it."

"You're a friend, somebody he trusts. Do you think there's a chance you might convince him to come and see me?"

Mark looked dubious. "I don't know, Doc. Sure I'd like to help you, but this could be tough. Maybe he's already left."

"Would you be willing to give it a try?"

"Yeah, I'll see what I can do."

"I need to talk to Amy, too. I'll need your help with her. She doesn't know me. I think she might feel uncomfortable talking about the murder with a complete stranger."

"Like I told you, I don't know Amy real well, so I wouldn't be able to help. But her and Cheryl got along good. They roomed together since they were freshmen. I figure she must be okay. I think she'd have no problem about talking to you."

Mark had been in my office for over an hour. It was time for me to get ready for my afternoon seminar. "Mark, even if you're not able to get John to talk with me, you've told me some things that may help in the investigation. I appreciate it."

"I'll see if I can get to Big John, Doc. Say I was able to pull it off—when are you here?"

Each semester, Jean makes a copy of the schedule of each member of the department that she refers to when someone calls for an appointment. I gave one to Mark.

"I'm on my way, Doc. Wish me luck."

I was headed back to the department after the seminar when I heard a female voice coming from behind me calling, "Dr. Evers." I turned and saw Patti bounding down the hall toward me.

With a frown on my face, I said, "Patti, we had an agreement that you'd call me Tom."

"I know, but I thought it might not be right when people are around."

"I'll overlook it this time, but I don't want it to happen again," I said, smiling.

"Okay, I'll remember."

"You look as though you're excited about something."

"I'm very excited."

"Let's go to my office where we can talk in private."

By the time Patti had settled into a chair, she was breathing normally.

"I took your advice and went through rush. I just got a bid from Theta Phi Alpha. I like all of the girls, and the house seems like it would be a really nice place to live. I can't wait to move in."

"I think you've made a good choice. The Theta Phis have a good reputation on campus, and when the grade point averages for the living units is published each year, their house is always near the top of the list."

Patti took a deep breath and exhaled. "I'm relieved to hear that. After those negative things you said about sororities, I thought you might not approve of me joining one."

"Well, I approve. I'm sure you'll be happy living in the sorority house, and I imagine you'll make some lifelong friends."

"Once, every semester, the members can invite their favorite professor to dinner at the house. I'd like to have you as my first guest. Will you come?"

"I'd be honored, but I'll come only if you promise to call me Tom while I'm there."

"I'll bet my sororities sisters will be impressed when I call a famous professor by his first name."

"Don't be sarcastic. Now, tell me how things are going in your classes. I know the activities involved in rush can be distracting."

Patti frowned. "I've gotten a little behind, but things are settling down so I'll have time to get some work done. I'm not to going to mess up because if I do, I'll have to face you, and I know how mean you can be."

"I can be very mean. Now get back to your room and study."

Patti stuck out her tongue at me when she went out the door."

- 26 -

I wanted to set up a meeting with Amy as soon as possible, so before leaving the office that afternoon, I dialed her number. There was no answer. Knowing that many students spend very little time in their room during the day, I decided my best chance of reaching her would be later in the evening. After Beth and I finished dinner, I began calling again. Finally, at ten o'clock, Amy picked up the phone. She sounded tired.

I gave my well-rehearsed explanation for calling. When Amy was slow to respond to my request for a meeting, I was afraid she was going to refuse. It turned out she had exams on the next two days and didn't want to take any time away from studying. We arranged to meet later in the week.

The next afternoon, I decided to go home early. It'd been a very busy day. I was tired, and I needed to run some errands. At quarter past four, I was locking my office door when the phone rang. I wasn't in the mood to talk with anyone. Then it occurred to me that Beth would occasionally call at this time of day, so I went back and answered it.

"Doc, John's willing to talk. He's dropping out of school, leaving in the morning. Can you stay around for a while?"

"I'll be here."

"I'll go to his apartment and walk him over to make sure he gets there."

After a half-hour of nervously shuffling papers on my desk, I heard voices in the waiting room. Mark stopped at the door. "Doc, this is John." He put his hand on John's shoulder as if to reassure him that everything would be all right. "I'll catch you later, bro." John's eyes followed Mark as he went down the hall toward the waiting room.

John was maybe an inch taller than Mark but not as solidly built, so he seemed smaller. It was obvious his nickname didn't come about because of his physical size. He settled slowly into the chair across from my desk. He sat with his back

116

straight, elbows on the chair arms, his hands touching. He picked at a knuckle with his thumb.

Depression comes in a package. When it's unwrapped, the same things are always there—painful emotion, a sense of futility, loss of motivation, and an inability to concentrate. Reach down deeper and you're likely to find disturbances in sleep and appetite. Frequently, at the bottom, there will be suicidal thoughts.

There was no question in my mind that sitting across the desk from me was a person whose depression package was a particularly heavy one. After what he'd been through, it was unfair of me to put him through another interview. I should've realized that earlier. Now it was too late to turn back.

"Mark explained why I wanted to see you?"

John nodded.

"I know you've talked with Detective Merrick on two occasions. He told me you were very cooperative and provided some important information. He and I decided it might be worthwhile to talk with you again. Occasionally, in this type of situation, after some time passes, people begin to remember other things which may be of help. Often, it's something that at first seemed unimportant. I'd like you to tell me what went on that Sunday."

"Where should I start?"

"At the point where you met Cheryl in the library."

Speaking quietly, with little show of emotion, John took me through Sunday and on into Monday until the time he and Amy contacted Campus Security. I let him go on without interruption. He reported the events almost exactly as he had in the earlier interviews. I learned nothing new.

I asked if he could remember anything Cheryl had said that might give some kind of clue. After thinking awhile, he shook his head, as if he were frustrated by not being able to come up with something.

I remembered from the notes in the file downtown that John had never mentioned the stalking. I wondered why. I was tempted to question him about it, but I held back. John wasn't the type to withhold information without good reason. It might've been something he didn't want to discuss. Or possibly he wasn't aware of the incident, though it seemed unlikely Cheryl wouldn't have told him about it.

As John recounted the events for me, it became clear that he and Cheryl had a very special relationship. It was certainly far deeper and more serious than the usual college romance. They seemed to be well suited to each other, and I imagined that if fate hadn't entered in, they would have spent the rest of their lives together. I began to understand why John was so devastated by Cheryl's death.

My colleagues on the faculty will often refer troubled students to me. The depressed ones, who make up the majority, typically think about dropping out of school. In their quiet desperation, they imagine that because their depression developed on campus, they can escape it by leaving. Unfortunately, the depression will follow them, and possibly become even more severe because of the feelings of failure aroused by quitting. Usually, I encourage these students to remain in school, at least for a while. Depression is an episodic condition, so ordinarily the depressed person will begin to feel better within a relatively short period of time. Only in cases where the depression has become so severe that the student is no longer able to attend class and complete assignments, or is a suicidal risk, do I recommend withdrawal.

When I heard that John was planning to drop out, my intention was to convince him to stay. During our meeting, I decided that wasn't the appropriate strategy. The best thing would be for him to get away from the campus, and the terrible memories associated with it, until the depression had lifted. However, before he left my office, I wanted to spend a little time talking with him about his problems.

"Mark said you're planning to leave school?"

"My father is taking a day off from work tomorrow. He's picking me up in the morning."

"I can understand how you've come to that decision. The memories here are more than you want to face. I suspect you haven't felt much like studying."

He nodded.

"Or even going to class."

Another nod.

"There's one thing that worries me about you going home." John looked puzzled. "If you leave, there is a chance you won't finish your education. This has happened with other students I've known who left school for one reason or another. From what I understand, you've worked hard and have done well here. To give this up would be tragic."

John looked away. He was obviously too deeply involved with his problems to be able to think about the future.

"I'd like you to promise yourself you'll be back in school before too long, here or somewhere else."

He nodded again.

I continued in an effort to provide some therapeutic first aid. "I'd like you to remind yourself over the coming weeks that the feelings you are experiencing, the depression and grief, are the normal reactions in a situation like this. It's important to understand that these feelings will decrease over time. When you begin to recover from the initial shock and horror, you can expect the healing process to begin. Eventually, you'll feel stronger, and you'll be able to get on with your life. I know this is hard to imagine, but I promise you, it will happen."

I didn't expect John to respond. I just hoped these ideas would be lodged somewhere in his memory bank. If he took them seriously, they could contribute to his recovery. Before he left my office, I wanted to make one additional point.

"Because Cheryl's death was such a great loss for you, the healing process will take time."

John said something very softly, as though he were talking to himself. It sounded like, "I lost more than Cheryl," but I couldn't be sure.

"I'm sorry, John, I didn't hear what you said."

"Oh, nothing . . . nothing."

I didn't feel comfortable in pressing him, and I doubted if he would have repeated what he had said anyway.

At that point, John leaned forward in his chair as though he was about to stand and looked at the clock on the wall. I wondered if the thought of something he couldn't reveal to me had made him even more uncomfortable.

"I know you have things to do," I said. "Thanks for coming to see me."

With one last nod, John moved toward the door. He appeared to be relieved that the ordeal in my office was over.

When I pulled in the driveway, I saw Beth looking out the front window. She was wondering why I was so late. I explained over dinner. Before going to bed, I sat down at the computer in my study and typed a summary of the interview with John for my investigation file. When I went over what I'd written, it seemed clear that nothing new had been discovered. I began to feel a sense of guilt again about asking John to go over the recent terrible events. It wasn't until much later that I realized the significance of John's mumbled comment. If I'd been perceptive enough to decipher its meaning at the time, much human suffering and tragedy might have been prevented.

- 27 -

On the afternoon of my appointment with Amy, I had to attend a meeting at the office of the Vice President of Finance to discuss the psychology department's budget proposal for the upcoming fiscal year. The meeting, which started at one o'clock, was still going on at three when Amy was due at my office. Since it is unwise to offend an administrator, especially when you are talking about the allocation of funds, I couldn't bring myself to leave early.

I finally left the administration building at three twenty, worried that Amy might not have waited for me. When I arrived at the department, Jean was busy at her computer. There was only one student in the usually busy reception area. She was sitting in a corner chair using a felt marker to highlight something in the textbook on her lap. She had on a bulky, gray sweater, faded jeans, and running shoes. I assumed she'd taken a test because she had on a baseball cap, which many female students wear on exam days when they don't take time to shower and style their hair. Sticking out from under the cap were strands of reddish brown curls.

I started across the room toward the hall that led to my office wondering if failing to show up on time had cost me the opportunity to talk with Amy. I was afraid I might have some difficulty getting her to agree to another meeting. As I passed Jean's desk, she looked up from her work. "Dr. Evers, this student had an appointment with you scheduled for three o'clock." Calling me Dr. Evers was Jean's way of expressing her displeasure with me for being late. She felt it was inconsiderate to make students wait.

When I turned to the student, she got up from her seat. "Hi, I'm Amy."

"Amy, thanks for waiting. I apologize for being late. I was at a meeting in the administration building that went overtime," I said, as we walked down the hall to my office.

Inside, Amy settled into an arm chair. She kept her book bag on her lap, which suggested she was uncomfortable and would be relieved if our meeting was a short one.

"I'm embarrassed that I didn't recognize you when I came in."

"You expected Cheryl's roommate to be black."

"Yes, I guess I did."

"Don't feel bad. On this campus, everybody seems to assume that whites only room with whites and blacks with blacks. It happened to Cheryl and me all the time until people got to know us. At first, it made me mad. Cheryl, who was the one who should've been upset, would just laugh about it, so I started doing the same thing."

I went through my speech again about how I was working with the police, and why it was important for me to see her. Maybe it was because Amy was so open with me that I went as far as to tell her I'd initially gotten involved in the investigation of Whitney's murder at the request of her parents. Amy listened intently. When I finished with my introduction, she put her book bag on the floor.

"I'd like you to start off by going over that Sunday for me. Tell me everything you can remember."

Amy nodded and took me through the day and the following morning. At one point, her eyes filled with tears. She paused to get a tissue out of her book bag. As with John, no new information came out.

"You and Cheryl roomed together when you were freshmen. Most students switch roommates after a year. You must've gotten along well."

My question brought a smile to Amy's face. "Yes, we did. We were good friends, but we almost didn't room together this year. In the spring semester, you have to request roommate assignments. Even though I wanted to stay with Cheryl, I never mentioned it to her because I assumed she'd want to room with one of her black friends. She never said anything to me either. Finally, on the day before we had to turn in our preferences, Cheryl asked me who I was going to room with. I told her I was going to ask for a single room. She thought all along I'd want to have one of my white friends as a roommate. We both felt a little stupid."

"Being so close, I imagine you talked about personal things with each other."

"Yes, we did pretty much. I always felt I could discuss a problem I might have with Cheryl, and I think she felt the same. Even so, I guess there are always some things you don't reveal, even to your closest friends. We respected each other's privacy."

"As you look back, can you think of anything Cheryl said that might give us a clue to what happened?"

"No. The detective asked me the same question. I've thought about it. I just can't come up with anything. You know about the stalking thing?"

121

"Yes, Detective Merrick told me about it. Could you go over it again for me?"

Amy shrugged. "There's really not much to tell. One day, Cheryl told me that some guy had been following her to her afternoon class. She said he would be waiting across the street when she left the dorm. I kidded around about it. I said it was probably because he was in love with her. She said she was pretty sure it wasn't a student because of the way he dressed, and he had tattoos all over his arms. That made me think it might be a little more serious."

"You told Detective Merrick this stalking lasted for some time."

"I'm not sure how long. Cheryl didn't know exactly when it started. I guess it took a while for her to realize what was going on. After she told me about it, I think the guy was around, off and on, for a couple more weeks."

"When this was going on, did Cheryl seem frightened?"

"Not really frightened. A little apprehensive maybe."

"I take it she didn't describe the person to you."

"Only that he had tattoos."

"Did you tell Detective Merrick about the tattoos?"

"No. I suppose he didn't ask me anything about the guy because I never saw him, and I didn't think about mentioning it. I guess maybe I should have," Amy said. The worried look on her face suggested she wanted me to reassure her that she hadn't made a mistake.

"Don't worry," I said. "In a time like this, you can't think of everything. And it's not likely the stalking had anything to do with Cheryl's murder." Amy sighed with relief.

"I talked with John. He gave the impression he and Cheryl had a very strong relationship. Do you know if Cheryl was involved with anyone else during the time you knew her?"

"Cheryl was really nice looking. I guess you would say she was beautiful. During the first weeks we were on campus last year—when we were freshman— she was getting calls all the time. She went out quite a lot. Her dates would usually take her to parties. Most of them were pretty wild—heavy drinking and that sort of thing. Cheryl was straight. She never touched alcohol. I know she didn't enjoy the parties much, so after a while she stopped dating.

"Later on in the semester, she began talking about John. He was in one of her classes. She liked him. He's really good looking, and he wasn't like most of the guys she dated. He was so timid. I think she finally ended up asking him for a date. After that, Cheryl never considered going out with anyone else."

"They must have been well-suited to each other."

"At first, I wasn't sure. They were so different. Cheryl was outgoing, and she loved to be around people. John is quiet and serious. Everyone likes him, but he's a loner. Then I realized that even though Cheryl seemed to be confident, she really wasn't. John is strong in his own way. She needed someone like him to lean on."

"Were you aware that they ever had any problems?"

"They got along very well, better than my boyfriend and me. Once in awhile they'd have a problem. When they did, Cheryl would take it hard. Last spring, Cheryl applied for a summer job in Chicago. The pay was good, and she hoped to make some contacts that would help her land a position after graduation. John thought they both should apply for a summer job on campus so they could be together. Cheryl ended up going to Chicago, and John went home for the summer. It turned out all right because they were able to see each other on weekends.

"Then a few weeks ago, Cheryl went through a period when she was pretty depressed. I figured the only thing that could've caused it was that she and John were having problems. I asked if I could help. She told me it was something personal she was going to have to work out by herself."

"Could it have been that Cheryl's depression was due to something besides her relationship with John?"

"It's possible. But there was another thing that made me think something might be going on between her and John. A couple of times recently, when Cheryl was out of the room, a guy called, asking for her. That hadn't happened in a long time. I wondered if he wanted to date her. He could've been trying for quite a while. Maybe John found out and was upset about it."

"I don't suppose you remember when these calls were made?"

Amy nodded. "Actually, I do. They both were on a Sunday. I know because Cheryl's and my schedules were the same every Sunday. Right after lunch, she'd leave to meet John in the library. They ate dinner in the cafeteria. John worked in the after hours room in the library, so Cheryl would study there until John got off at one A.M. She wouldn't get back to the room until late. I always stayed in the room until the middle of the afternoon when I'd go over to my boyfriend's apartment. Both calls came just before I left."

"Do you remember which Sundays?"

"Yes, on the two before Cheryl was killed."

"There was no call on that last Sunday?"

"Not that I know of, but there might've been. Cheryl came back to the room to take a nap. She said she'd had trouble sleeping the night before. It could be the guy called after I left."

"Are you sure it was the same person both times?"

"Yes. He sounded exactly the same."

"You thought it was a student?"

"I just assumed he was because I couldn't imagine who else would be calling Cheryl at that time of day."

"Do you think it's possible that it wasn't a student? Could it have been an older person?"

"He only said a few words, so I can't be sure. But I think I would have noticed if there was something different about the way he talked. He spoke quietly and was polite. I remember he thanked me both times."

"Did he ask you when he could reach her?"

"I think he did. I probably told him he might catch her later in the afternoon. Sometimes, like on that last day, Cheryl would come back to the room and take a nap."

"Did you tell Detective Merrick about these calls?"

Amy frowned and thought for a moment. "I can't remember. I was pretty upset when I talked to him."

"I have just one more question. Did Cheryl ever mention that someone named Charlie Rutledge tried to get a date with her?"

"No, but he could have. I doubt that Cheryl would bother telling me when she got a call from a guy."

"Amy, I really appreciate your coming in to talk. You've told me some things that could be important. And I want to apologize again for being late for our appointment.

"By the way," I said, as we both stood up, "you look as though you've been staying up late studying for those exams. I suggest you go back to your room and take a long nap."

Amy smiled. "Sounds like a good idea. The problem is, I might sleep through dinner time at the dorm."

"If you happen to think of anything else that might possibly help us, give me a call."

"I definitely will."

I walked in the back door just as Beth was bending over to put a casserole in the oven. She looked up and said, "I want to hear about your interview with Cheryl's roommate."

"It sounds like you may be getting caught up in the investigation," I said.

"Maybe, just a little."

We sat at the kitchen table drinking warmed over morning coffee while I reported on my meeting with Amy, including the embarrassing part where I'd assumed she was black.

"I think I like Amy," Beth said when I finished.

"She's a very interesting young woman. What do you think about the calls?"

"They must have been made by the killer to arrange a meeting with Cheryl. He couldn't get through to her on his first two attempts. Obviously, he was successful on the day of the murder."

"You sound as though you're fairly certain about that."

Beth nodded. "I am. It would be too much of a coincidence to think a guy was calling for a date on two Sunday afternoons. If he was really interested, he would have tried at another time during the week."

"Maybe he did and Amy didn't know about it. She said that Cheryl probably wouldn't tell her about calls she got from guys," I said.

"That's a possibility, but if he talked to Cheryl and she refused to go out on a date, why would he keep calling on Sundays?"

"I see your point. Amy thought it was a student."

"That's entirely understandable. She said she couldn't imagine anyone else calling at that time. I think it's just as likely he wasn't a student. His voice may have sounded as if he were of college age. But the male voice doesn't change that much during the early adult years. Even though you're well past thirty, over the phone, you could be mistaken for a twenty-year-old. Of course, in a face to face contact, you'd never pass for a college student."

"Was that some sort of comment on my appearance?" I asked, frowning intentionally.

Beth smiled. "Nope, just stating a fact. And don't get paranoid. I personally think you've become even more attractive as you've matured."

"Why did you smile when you said that?"

"I don't believe I did. Now let's get serious. I think we may have learned something about the killer from Amy's report. His manner of speaking and the way he expressed himself led her to believe he was a college student. Based on this, it's safe to assume the guy is reasonably intelligent and probably fairly well educated."

"Your analysis is convincing. I'm impressed. It raises an issue that's been in the back of my mind for a while now. Could the killer be a member of the faculty? Don Reynolds suggested that possibility when I talked with him about Whitney's murder. At first, I thought it was an absurd idea. Now, I'm not so sure. What's your feeling on this?"

"In my professional career, I've come in contact with some very weird situations. I think it's something that has to be considered."

"I wish you hadn't said that. It's a very disturbing thing to contemplate."

"I can understand how you feel. It bothers me, too."

- 28 -

I was in my office at noon with the door closed eating the lunch I'd brought from home when I thought about what Beth had said the night before—that she wouldn't rule out the possibility the killer might be a member of the faculty. Even though I was the one who had brought up the idea, I'd have probably dismissed it if she hadn't made that comment.

If the killer turned out to be a colleague, he'd most likely have had contact with the victims in the classroom. I decided I should try to find out if Whitney and Cheryl had taken any courses from the same instructors.

The Office of the Registrar is responsible for maintaining student academic records. Unfortunately, I knew that gaining access to the files I needed to examine might prove to be difficult. Two years earlier, the university registrar of thirty years retired. She was a dedicated administrator who ran a highly efficient office. Her staff liked and respected her. Things went so smoothly under her direction that faculty took things for granted. We didn't realize how important she was until we were faced with her replacement, a man imported from another university.

After only a few weeks in his new position, our registrar informed the faculty that the record keeping system and registration procedures were terribly outdated. He introduced major revisions that resulted in almost total chaos. His response to the problems he'd produced was to blame the faculty for their lack of cooperation. He informed us of this in a series of insulting memos.

The next day, when my afternoon seminar was over, I went directly to the Registrar's Office. Inside the double doors, there was a counter. Sitting at the desk on the other side, I saw Alice Murray, the receptionist. Alice was perfectly suited for her job. She liked working with students and always went out of her way to help them if they had problems with their registration. Even the most frustrated student usually left her presence in a better mood.

126

Several years ago, I'd worked with two colleagues on a research project designed to find out why some students with good potential encountered difficulty during their freshman year. Alice helped me with the part of the study that involved analyzing several years of student transcripts. She undertook this tedious job cheerfully and with such humor, I actually ended up having fun.

I barely got inside the door when Alice looked up and, with a mock scowl on her face, said, "Tom, I want to make it perfectly clear that I'm not the least bit interested in doing another transcript search with you."

"Come on, Alice, I don't think you minded at all getting away from the reception desk for a while. As a matter of fact, I'm here to see if I can get permission from Mr. Wagner to examine the records of some students. Do you suppose he might be able to spare some time to meet with a lowly faculty member?"

"I'll go back and put in a good word for you."

"Alice, you are such a dear."

Several minutes later, she returned. "Surprise. The master will see you."

"If I get his permission to go ahead, I'm looking forward to working with you again."

Alice rolled her eyes. "It must be my lucky day."

The door to the office was open. Wagner was sitting behind an executive style, mahogany desk that was bare except for a telephone and a folder he was examining. I glanced around the room. It was beautifully furnished.

One of my many irrational prejudices is that men who wear three piece suits shouldn't be university administrators. Even though they may be intelligent and dedicated, they never seem to understand, or appreciate, what goes on in the world of academics. As a result, they cause problems. Wagner's three piece suit was deep blue with gray pinstripes. The collar of his white shirt looked like it had been starched. Another bad sign.

I was encouraged when Wagner greeted me politely and motioned for me to sit down. I settled into a large, soft leather chair. "We haven't met before. My name is Thomas Evers. I teach in the psychology department."

I explained that I needed to examine the academic records of several students. This was a legitimate request because teaching faculty are allowed access to personal information about students. I was concerned that Wagner would want to know what my purpose was. There wasn't any need to worry. He didn't ask. He informed me that all members of his staff were working on some very important projects, placing emphasis on the word important. He told me the work load was lighter when summer school was in session. If I would come back then, there might be a possibility of someone being available to help me.

I apologized for taking up his valuable time and told him to have a nice day. As I passed Alice's desk, she looked up and mouthed, "He's a shit." I nodded in agreement.

According to university policy, academic records of students are considered to be confidential. Access to them is restricted to certain administrative offices and faculty. This is a wise policy. For example, it would be inappropriate for the media to obtain information about the academic performance of a graduate who was running for a high level political office.

As a member of the faculty, I could've demanded that Wagner allow me to see the transcripts of Whitney and Cheryl. This was not an option because it was likely I'd have to reveal the reason I was interested in examining them. Also, simply viewing the transcripts alone wouldn't have provided me with the information I needed. There are multiple sections of many of the courses offered at the university. For example, every semester my department offers four sections of introductory psychology, each taught by a different instructor. On the student's transcript is a list of the courses taken and the grades received. The identity of the instructor who taught the course the student was enrolled in isn't recorded.

The information I needed was stored on the computer that was used by the university administrative offices. With few exceptions, only the personnel in the Registrar's Office had access to the student record files. Without the cooperation of Wagner, there seemed to be no way I could find out the instructors who had both Whitney and Cheryl in their classes.

I was back in my office when it occurred to me that there might be another possibility for getting the information I needed. On the campus, there was an office called the Bureau of Research and Evaluation, which conducted studies designed to aid the faculty and administration in dealing with problems and setting policy. The director of the BRE was Jack Egan, a quiet, unassuming man in his mid-fifties. I had the greatest respect for Jack as a person and for the work he did. It was unfortunate he never seemed to get full credit for his contributions to the institution. Once, when we had been discussing a joint research project, Jack mentioned he could obtain data from the computer that contained the files of the Registrar's Office.

No matter how busy he might be, Jack would always take time out to meet with a colleague, so I didn't bother to call ahead. The BRE, for some unknown reason, was located in the basement of the Physics building. The secretary was away from her desk. I walked down a narrow hall to Jack's office. When he saw me, he smiled. "Tom, it's been awhile since we've had a visit from you. What's on your mind?"

"Jack, I'm here with an unusual request. Let me give you some background."

From past experience, I knew that anything you told Jack would be considered confidential. Because of this, I felt free to explain in detail how I'd become involved in the murder investigations. When I finished, I asked him if he could find out if the victims had taken courses from the same instructors. I didn't bother explaining why the information was important because I knew Jack would understand.

"Tom, I'll get on this right away. I'm pretty sure I can have a report to you by late tomorrow afternoon. Would that be soon enough?"

"Tomorrow afternoon? I was hoping you could get it to me as early as the end of next week."

"I wish I'd known that. I could've kept the results around for a few days and made the job look like it was really difficult."

When I thanked Jack, he gave a little shrug. I didn't mention that I was aware of the risk he was taking by entering the administrative data file as a favor for a faculty member. If someone found out, he could be in deep trouble. He knew I understood.

After I left the Physics building, I decided to stop by Campus Security and check in with Don Reynolds. I hadn't talked with him since Cheryl's murder. It was after five, but I knew Don often worked late.

The reception area was dark Don was in his office talking with someone. The person's back was to the door. It had to be Rod Dudley. He was the only one in security with long blond hair.

Don waved me in, and Rod turned toward me. "Hi Tom, how ya doing?" He got up from his chair and headed toward the door. "I have to go. I'll leave you guys alone."

"Don't let me interrupt an important conference."

"Rod and I were talking over some plans. We were just finishing."

After Rod left, Don said, "I bet I know why you're here. You want to know when I'll be up to playing handball."

"I am interested in getting started. It won't be long before it's too cold for me to run outside, so I'll have to start working out in the gym. I figure a game of handball with you is the equivalent to a five-mile run."

"This back problem won't go away. I began to have some pain when I bent over. It got steadily worse. I can't sleep, and I have to carry a pillow around with me so I can sit down. I finally went to a medical specialist. He told me it'll be a while before I can expect much improvement. He even suggested I may never be able to get involved in any strenuous physical activity."

"I'm sorry to hear that. Actually, the reason I stopped by was to talk about the second murder. Since this is obviously the work of the same guy, I decided to spend a little time on it. I'm interested in hearing about any ideas you might have."

"I haven't the slightest clue. Unfortunately, I was right when I said he'd probably stay in the area. He's shown that he likes it around here, and we have to assume he's going to do it again. The precautions we took before, the increased patrols and the education program, didn't help. It seems strange that intelligent young women wouldn't be extremely cautious. At this point, we have a pretty good idea that one was careless."

"Unfortunately, it seems like that must have been what happened," I said.

"I assume Russ has been sharing information with you. I haven't talked to him since he called me to check on Rutledge. Has he come up with anything new?"

"Not that I know of. He's pretty frustrated and isn't in the best mood. It's getting late, so I won't keep you any longer."

"Tom, before you go, I'd like your advice on something. When you came in, Rod and I were talking about having another round of meetings like the ones last spring to inform the freshmen women of the precautions they should take to insure their safety. Do you think that would be worthwhile?"

"Yes, I do. The students have a lot of respect for Rod. They take seriously what he tells them. It's possible that those presentations he made last year saved some lives. If you decide to go ahead with this, you might consider opening the meeting to the upperclass women. They might benefit from a refresher course."

"Good idea. I'll start making the arrangements."

- 29 -

The next morning, I left for campus earlier than usual. I needed to get caught up on some work before my morning classes. I got to the department at seven thirty and went through the dark reception area, not bothering to turn on the light. When I flipped the switch in the hallway leading to my office, I saw Mark leaning against the wall.

"I need to talk to you in private, Doc. I was hoping you'd come in early."

I unlocked the door and closed it when we were both inside. Mark settled into a chair.

"Say I knew something that might be important about Cheryl, but maybe there's reasons I can't let anyone know about it."

"Whatever you say in here is just between the two of us. If you don't want me to tell anyone else, I won't. I promise you that." Immediately, it occurred to me that I might have spoken too quickly. Perhaps Mark was about to give me information I'd have to reveal.

"It's not just me. There's other people involved. At first, they didn't want me to talk at all. I told them you were okay. You understand what I'm saying?"

"I think so."

"A while back, Cheryl saw someone following her around the campus."

"Let me tell you now. I heard about that from Amy. The police know about it, too."

"There's more that nobody knows but me and a few of the brothers. When I tell you what happened, you'll see why the brothers don't want somebody to find out. This dude kept after Cheryl till she got scared. She couldn't tell John because she was worried he might do something that would get him in trouble, so she came to me."

Mark shifted in his chair and hesitated a moment before continuing. I wondered if he was having second thoughts about confiding in me. "First thing I did was to hang around the dorm when Cheryl left for her class. Pretty soon, the dude showed up. Cheryl gave me the nod. He's kinda skinny, real short hair cut, and tattoos all up his arms. He had some tools hanging on a big belt, like he was working on maintenance. I stuck to him. He followed Cheryl to the building where her class was, and then he went into another building. I waited outside. After awhile, he came out and went around back and got in a van. On the door it said University Electrical Maintenance. I got real mad thinking about this weird dude paying attention to Cheryl."

"I can understand why you would feel so strongly," I said

"I talked it over with some of the brothers, and they got mad, too. We had to do something, so we got out the university phone book and found the number of Electrical Maintenance. One of the brothers called to find out where it was. He asked when the repairmen got off of work. The woman there said four thirty.

"The next day, three of us went over and waited. When Tattoos came out, we followed him to a pickup truck in the back of the parking lot. There was nobody else around. We told him what could happen if he didn't keep away from Cheryl. We didn't do anything real serious. We might have grabbed him some, not much you understand, just a little bit, so he heard what we were saying."

"What you told me could be important," I said, trying to think how I could use what Mark had told me. He must have read my mind.

"You see why you can't tell this, Doc?"

"I understand. It won't go out of this room, but I don't think you and your friends have anything to worry about."

"There is something to worry about. Suppose somebody finds out about a meeting some blacks had with a guy that works for the university, and he decides it's in his interest to complain. No matter how good a reason there is for the meeting, it's going to be trouble. The two brothers who were with me are on the football team. Scholarships are the only way they would be here. Lose them, and they're back on the streets. And me, too. You got to believe me, Doc," Mark pleaded.

"You're right. I wasn't thinking clearly. All of you would be in jeopardy."

I tried to think how we could get around the confidentiality thing. "You decided to tell me this because you thought it could be important, and I might be able to do something with it. Now we have to figure a way to use this information without causing problems for you and your friends.

"How does this sound? Suppose I meet with this guy. I don't have to let him know how I found out who he was. Cheryl's roommate or some other friend might have known about him and told me. I'm fairly sure I could have a talk without him guessing it was one of you, and even if he did, he probably wouldn't be too happy having other people learn about the meeting you had with him. It could be embarrassing. If it looks like he might've had something to do with the crime, I'll get back to you, and we can see where we go from there.

"Talk to your friends. Find out if this would be all right with them. I'll go along with whatever you decide. If they have a problem with it, we forget that we ever had this conversation."

Mark frowned. "I understand how it is, Doc. Let me have a discussion with the brothers. This is serious to them. They want the killer caught as much as anybody. I'll let you know."

At a quarter after four that afternoon, I was alone in my office when the phone rang. It was Jack Egan. "There are three faculty who've had both women in class. Statistically, that's about what you would expect given the number of undergraduate courses offered each semester. They are Sutter in biology, Williams in economics, and Perry in English. The courses were at the introductory level. Whitney took them two or three years ago. Cheryl was enrolled in Williams and Perry's classes this semester. She took the biology course second semester last year."

"Jack, I really appreciate this. If there is any way I can return the favor, let me know."

"As a matter of fact, there might be something coming up soon. I've just started on a project that will require some work from a number of faculty. You know how hard it can be to get that kind of cooperation. If I could get you and a few others who have some credibility to talk to your colleagues, it might be easier for me to get the help I need."

"I don't have a whole lot of influence around here, but I'd be willing to do what I can."

I had the feeling Jack was eager to talk about the project, so I asked him to describe it. He spent the next fifteen minutes going over the details, pausing occasionally to ask my advice on some aspect of the design.

After getting off the phone, I looked at the names I'd written on a scrap of paper. Ralph Sutter in biology. Late sixties, multiple by-pass surgery, unsteady on his feet. Even though he was a notoriously boring lecturer, Ralph's classes were filled every semester. There were good reasons for that. He gave the same exams year after year. They were available in the files of every living unit on campus. And Ralph didn't have any policy on class attendance. A student could meet the graduation requirement in science with almost no effort, which was an attractive option for many. When Ralph chose to continue teaching after the normal retirement age of sixty-five, his departmental colleagues and the Dean had to have been disappointed. Ralph was one of the highest paid faculty members on the campus. His salary was large enough that the university would have been able to hire two competent, young biologists to take his place.

Margaret Williams in economics. Early thirties, popular with students, respected by faculty, married to an historian. Because they weren't able to get faculty positions at the same university, Margaret and her husband saw each other only on weekends during the academic year. Ralph and Margaret obviously couldn't be considered suspects.

Rob Perry in English. Late forties, a good teacher. A bachelor who spent a great deal of time with students outside of class. It was generally assumed that Rob was gay, even though he'd never come out and said he was. At the very first faculty meeting I attended, Rob stood up and criticized a recent change in university policy. I'd never heard such strong words spoken in an open forum. A short time later, Rob wrote a letter to the editor of the school paper, which was of the same quality. As time passed, I learned to expect this from Rob. Though I've had difficulty accepting his style, I found myself almost always agreeing with what he had to say. I think many of the faculty members, including myself, relied on Rob to speak out on important issues. In my limited personal contact with Rob, he came on as a bit arrogant and pompous. It seemed to me he might be a little unstable, but certainly not capable of brutal murder.

While driving home, I remembered that it was my turn to do the cooking. Since it was Friday night, the meal had to be special.

The car was in the garage. Beth must've been able to get away from the office earlier than usual. I called out from the kitchen. No answer. I found her in the bathroom just as she was getting out of the shower.

"You're looking good," I said.

She smiled. "Stop leering at me and get out of here."

"I think I'll stay around and watch."

"No way, buddy."

"All right, I'll see you later."

I went to the kitchen, put a bottle of white wine in the refrigerator to chill, and began working on dinner.

- 30 -

On Saturday, we woke up to a cold rain. Beth decided we should have a substantial breakfast on such a dreary morning, so she fixed pancakes and sausages. I purposely avoided talking about the investigation. It was Beth who brought it up after we had finished eating and were in the living room finishing the last of the coffee. She knew Jack Egan was going to get me a list of the faculty who had both Whitney and Cheryl in class. She asked me if I'd heard from him. I told her the names Jack had given me. She knew all three and agreed they weren't likely suspects.

"I wasn't thinking straight when I decided to do this. It's impossible to imagine that a member of this faculty would be capable of murder."

"You never know. It could still turn out to be someone on the faculty or a university employee," Beth said.

"That may be closer to the truth." I told her about my conversation with Mark.

"The way Mark described this guy makes him look like a real possibility to me," Beth said. "No one has developed a profile in this case. That's for big city investigations. If there were one, I bet the electrician would fit it pretty well."

"I had the same feeling. But remember, we were speculating that the murderer is reasonably intelligent and has some education."

"Tom, don't talk like an academic snob. There's no reason to think a man who has a responsible technical job couldn't meet those qualifications."

"Of course, you're absolutely right. I was being unfairly biased. I think it's important to check this guy out. The problem is, I can't do anything until I get permission from Mark. He and his friends are understandably apprehensive. I have a strong feeling they won't want me to get involved. Of course, if they say no, it looks like that would be the end of it. I can't tell Russ, or anyone else, what I know."

Beth nodded in agreement "I can't imagine you breaking a confidence like that, but the fact that Mark came to you with the story suggests to me that he'd like you to follow up on it. There's a chance he may able to influence his friends."

"I wish I could share your optimism."

"There's something else we need to consider. Suppose the electrician did turn out to be the killer. If he gets the idea you're suspicious, you could be in danger."

"That's not something we need to worry about. It's unlikely I'll have the opportunity to talk with him."

I decided it would best to change the subject. We had an invitation to a party that evening, the first one of the year for us. As the colder weather sets in, people on campus start thinking about entertaining. From late October through the holidays, you could count on a busy social schedule.

"Even though it would be nice to see people tonight, I'd just as soon stay home by the fire and read," I said.

Beth smiled. "You're trying to change the subject."

"I was and it didn't work."

"Yes, it did, and I agree with you about the party. We always say when we're invited out that we don't want to go. Then we end up having a good time. I suspect it'll turn out the same way tonight."

"I have to go to my office today and get caught up on some work. It's going to take some time, so I'll take a lunch with me. I should be back early afternoon."

Beth talked about what she would wear to the party while I made my sandwich.

I wasn't in a good mood as I drove through driving rain to the campus. If I hadn't spent so much time on the investigation the past few days, I would've been able to take the weekend off. There was only a handful of cars in the parking lot, so I was able to park close to the door of the psychology building and avoid getting drenched.

The halls were deserted. On the floor inside my office there was a folded sheet of notebook paper that someone had slipped under the door. I was puzzled. Sometimes students will leave notes for me like this, but usually not after five o'clock on Friday or early Saturday morning. The message was brief. "Talk to the man."

I finished work on the exams early in the afternoon. When I got home, Beth was sitting at the kitchen table drinking a cup of tea and working on a crossword puzzle. I showed her the note.

"Mark is certainly a man of few words," she said.

"He writes exams and papers the same way. Always brief and to the point. Exam grading would go much faster if all students wrote the way Mark does."

"I assume you're going to contact the electrician."

"Yes, I am. I'll be cautious. There won't be any problems, and this is the last thing I plan to do. I promise you, my investigation will be over by the end of the week."

"I have a hunch that might change after you've talked to Tattoos."

I shrugged.

The dress for faculty parties can be best described as casual. It would be inappropriate for a man to come wearing a jacket and tie. The women dress up a little more, but informal is still the rule.

I put on a pair of corduroy slacks, a crew neck cotton sweater over a tattersall shirt, and the loafers I'd polished to go to dinner at the Donovans'. Beth wore a denim skirt, a navy cotton vest over a white blouse, and a pair of those slipper type shoes that look very uncomfortable to me.

We parted as soon as we arrived at the party. Beth ended up in a group of faculty wives, and I found some colleagues I hadn't talked with in weeks. It wasn't long before I saw Matt heading my way from the other side of the crowded room. At his size, it wasn't easy to get through. I could tell he had something on his mind.

"Tom, what have you been up to? I've been calling your office all week and got no answer."

"I've been busy. Why didn't you leave a message on my voice mail or send me an e-mail?"

"I don't trust that leave a message thing. I talk only to live human beings, and I have no idea what e-mail is, so how could I use it?"

I shook my head. "It's the communication method of the future. If you don't learn it soon, you'll end up a twenty-first century version of the dinosaur."

"That I can deal with. I wanted to let you know we're starting basketball practice next Thursday at three thirty. We have to get in shape. We're going to win the championship this year, and don't give me that line about retiring. Just be there."

Matt moved off without giving me a chance to tell him again I wasn't about to spend two nights a week all winter acting like an adolescent.

A little later, I saw Beth talking to Margaret Williams over in a far corner of the room. They were about the same age and seemed to share the same view of the world. Whenever they got together, they ended up in a serious conversation. I joined them. I'd decided not to contact the faculty Jack Egan had identified for me, but when I saw Margaret, the temptation was too great.

Beth was suspicious. "Margaret, I think Tom is going to want to talk with you privately. He's on a mission and a little out of control."

"Sounds interesting," Margaret said.

"There's no stopping him. I'll leave you two alone," Beth said, as she moved away.

I asked Margaret if she knew I was involved in the murder investigations. She didn't, so I explained.

When I told her she was one of the professors who had taught both victims, she asked the obvious. "Are you thinking that a member of the faculty might be the killer?"

"Not really, but I felt I needed to follow up on every possibility. The list was short and, as you can imagine, there were no likely suspects. I wasn't even going to talk to them. Then when I saw you were here . . . "

"How did you find out Whitney and Cheryl were enrolled in my classes?"

"A favor from a friend who has access to the administrative computer where the registrar's records are kept."

Margaret thought a minute. "Jack took a risk in doing that for you."

"You and Beth are just alike. You think you're so smart."

Margaret smiled. "Tom, you know we're smarter than the average male. Whitney took my introductory course several years ago. Cheryl was taking it this semester. Both were in large classes—sixty or seventy students. I remember Whitney because she did such outstanding work. I had no contact with her outside of class. I assumed she was taking the course as an elective."

Margaret took a sip of punch from the cup she was holding. "I talked with Cheryl on several occasions. She came up after class on the day I handed back the first quiz to schedule an appointment with me. She was interested in a career in business and trying to decide whether to major in management or economics. I'm sure you've learned she was a very talented young woman. We had two meetings early in the semester. I explained the opportunities there would be for her if she chose econ. She seemed to be leaning in our direction, and I was delighted. We arranged a third meeting to discuss a plan of study. I was surprised when she didn't show up and missed two classes that week. Later, she came in to apologize. She told me she hadn't been feeling well and had gotten behind in her work. We scheduled another appointment. It was for the Wednesday after she was killed."

I said, "Knowing how important your students are to you, I can imagine how you must have felt when you learned of Cheryl's murder."

Margaret sighed. "You know that we all appreciate having students like Cheryl in our classes and are able to get to know them personally."

I nodded.

"Her death, and the way she died, struck me as an unthinkable tragedy."

"Unthinkable is a perfect way to describe the fate of both Cheryl and Whitney," I said. "I assume Cheryl didn't say anything about her personal life that might give a clue as to what happened?"

"No, she didn't," Margaret said, shaking her head, "but I did have the feeling there was more to her missing the appointment and classes than she told me. Before that she'd been so upbeat and full of energy. When she came in to apologize, she looked tired and depressed."

I started to explain that there was a period when Cheryl and her boyfriend were having some problems when we were joined by two others. Margaret wished me good luck with my project. I left as she was explaining why her husband, Keith, wasn't at the party.

On the way home, I gave Beth a summary of my conversation with Margaret.

Beth thought for a moment. "It's interesting that both Margaret and Amy thought Cheryl was under some kind of stress in the period before she was killed. Do you think her mood could be tied in with the murder in some way?"

"I can't imagine how it could be. If she'd received any threats at the time, she certainly would've reported them. It must have been just an odd coincidence."

"You're probably right. On the other hand, I can't help wondering."

- 31 -

I finished my Monday morning run in near record time because I wanted to be on campus by seven thirty when the University Maintenance Plant offices opened.

In order to get the name of the electrician, I figured some deception would be necessary. I'd convinced myself that in an investigation, deception wasn't equivalent to lying. Those detectives in mystery novels did it all the time.

In the campus phone directory, there was a separate number listed for the electrical maintenance department. The woman who answered the phone told me her name was Emily. I identified myself as a member of the faculty. I said I'd talked to a university electrician about doing some wiring in a new addition to my house. He said he might be able to work for me on weekends. Unfortunately, I'd lost the paper I'd written his name and phone number on. I gave Emily Mark's description minus the tattoos.

"That would be Billy Wade," she said. "He's already left the shop. I could leave a message that you called."

It occurred to me that Billy might get suspicious if he found out someone was trying to get in touch with him. "Please don't bother. I'll stop by the shop some afternoon when he gets off work. What time would that be?"

"Four thirty, but you might want to be here a few minutes before that. Sometimes Billy leaves early."

I pulled into the lot behind the maintenance building at ten after four and parked in an area set aside for visitors that was close to the rear door. I got out of the truck and leaned against the front fender. A few minutes later, Billy came out of the electrical shop.

Mark's description had been accurate. Billy was wearing jeans and one of those short, western style denim jackets. He didn't look any different from the other maintenance staff I'd seen on the campus. Still, there seemed to be something menacing about him.

I caught up with him just as he was opening the door of a pickup truck that was of the same vintage as mine. His was battered and rusty, the kind that ordinarily has a gun rack showing through the back window. I couldn't see one as I approached.

"Billy Wade?" I asked.

He turned and looked at me. "That's right."

"I need to talk to you."

"About what?"

"It's too cold to talk out here. Come on over to my truck."

"If you need to talk, we do it here. I'm on my way home."

"This may take a while, and I'm not going to stand out in the wind."

He started to climb into his truck.

"It's about Cheryl Martin. You can talk to me in my truck now, or you can talk to the police later. Take your choice."

He closed the truck door and followed me across the parking lot.

Inside my pickup, he looked straight ahead at the brick wall of the maintenance building. I didn't say anything.

"Okay, what do you want to talk about?"

"You were following a student around the campus, and then she's murdered. I'd say you could be in serious trouble."

"Who said I was following some girl around?"

"Maybe a lot of people know. It's hard to keep that kind of thing a secret."

"It was those black bastards. You believe them? Nobody else would."

"I'm not sure what you're talking about. I want some answers from you."

"You're a professor, aren't you?"

"Yes, I am."

"What right have you got to ask me questions? All of you faculty think you're so fuckin' important. Above everyone else around here. I was in the School of Engineering for a year. I quit because I was sick of those asshole professors over there who lecture on all of that theoretical shit and don't know anything about the real world. Not one of them could handle my job for a day. They make three times what I do and only work nine months a year."

"Are you telling me you'd rather talk to the police?"

There was a pause. "Okay, ask the questions. Maybe I'll answer, maybe I won't."

"Why were you following Cheryl Martin around the campus?"

"I never followed anyone."

"Let's cut the bullshit. Why were you following her?"

"I'll tell you what happened. I was working on a wiring problem in her dorm. It was complicated, so I had to work overtime. The floor was deserted. Everyone was down in the dining room eating. This Cheryl, or whatever her name was, she came up the stairway and walked down the hall to the spot where I was working. When she got close, she smiled big and brushed against me. I just ignored it. Then the next day, I was outside the front door of the dorm when she came out. She gave me a long look."

"You got the idea she was coming on to you?"

"Sure she was."

"So you kept following her around?"

He scowled and rubbed the stubble of beard on his chin with a dirty hand. "If you think I was interested in some black girl, you're crazy. She was the one who was interested. When I didn't respond, she got pissed off. That's what really happened."

"Where were you the Sunday night she was killed?"

Billy looked at me and smiled as though he had finally gotten the upper hand. "The same place I am every night . . . Smokey's Tavern. I was there from seven until after midnight. You ask anybody. They'll tell you."

"All right, Billy. No more questions."

There was a look of surprise, and maybe some relief. He opened the door of the pickup and then hesitated. Without looking toward me, he asked, "Will the police find out about this?"

I reached for the ignition key and started the engine. Billy got out and slammed the door.

Driving home, I went over the interview. I'd wondered if a maintenance man could have a voice and manner on the phone that could be convincing. Even as angry as he had been during our talk, he was soft spoken. His grammar was acceptable, and there was no trace of the local regional accent. Over the phone, his speech probably wouldn't sound much different from that of the males Whitney and Cheryl associated with on campus. He might've passed for a student or even a member of the faculty.

Beth came up from downstairs as soon as I called out a greeting. "You finished with your workout?" I asked.

"No, but I want to know if you talked to the electrician."

I described our meeting, which had been short enough that I could give her an almost word for word account of the conversation.

"What do you think?" I asked.

"His attitude and the way he talked reminds me of some of the criminals I've prosecuted. When we first talked about him, I thought he could be a possible suspect. After what you've just told me, I'm convinced."

"You're coming from the legal perspective. As a psychologist, I'd have to agree. Billy has a good job and maybe some close friends. He could give the appearance of being an average, normal guy. But my brief contact with him leads me to believe he's a very troubled individual. The underlying hostility is obvious. I see him as having the potential for violence and even being capable of murder.

"Because the attacks on the victims had a strong sexual component to them, it's doubtful the killer has normal relationships with women. We don't know if Billy's married, or has a significant other, but when you consider the time he spends at Smokey's Tavern, it seems doubtful."

"Since you can't tell Russ about your talk with Wade, it's up to you to check his alibi."

"There's no other way to get it done," I said, as I got up to get the telephone directory.

I might have guessed. Smokey's Tavern wasn't listed in the yellow pages. The white pages gave an address on the south side of town. I could picture the area.

"Smokey's is on South 15th Street," I explained to Beth. "It must be down by the city water treatment plant in that area where there are a couple of abandoned warehouses and a grain elevator."

"I've driven through there occasionally on the way out of town," Beth said. "I don't remember a bar."

"I don't either. I'll check it out tomorrow. If Wade's alibi holds up, it looks like we're at a dead end."

"If it doesn't, you're going to have to be watching over your shoulder for a guy with tattoos and a short haircut."

"That's occurred to me. I intend to be very careful no matter what I find out at Smokey's. You understand that I'm basically a coward."

"I find that comforting. In fact, I've always had a deep respect for cowardice, particularly in men. Maybe that's one of the reasons I was attracted to you."

Beth went to her study after we finished eating dinner to prepare for a trial that would begin in a few days. I sat down at the computer and opened the investigation file. I typed in a summary of my talk with Billy. After that, I began thinking about how I would check his alibi.

The bartender at Smokey's might be able to tell me if Billy had been at the bar on the Sunday night of the murder. The first thing to do was to contact him, or her, though I couldn't imagine a place like Smokey's having a woman behind the bar. It was possible that Billy stopped in for a beer or two after work, and I remembered Emily, the secretary in electrical maintenance, said Billy sometimes left early. I decided to time my visit so I would be gone by four thirty.

- 32 -

You have to wonder about yourself when you give two lectures, talk to a half a dozen students who stop by your office, and attend a committee meeting—and all the time you keep thinking you can't wait to get to a bar in a rough neighborhood. That's what happened the next day. I locked my office door at a quarter after three. The reception area was empty. Jean was working at her computer. She looked up as I passed by her desk.

"If anyone needs to see me, I'll be in Smokey's Tavern the rest of the afternoon. I'm sure you know where it is, south side of town near the city water treatment plant."

Jean shook her head slowly and wrinkled her brow into a frown. "Tom, I've been worried about you lately. You've been acting strangely. Maybe you should think about getting into counseling or, better yet, take some medication."

I managed not to laugh. "You think I'm crazy, don't you?"

"I prefer to think of it as emotionally unstable. I'm worried about Beth. I only have to deal with you during work hours. She has to put up with you twenty-four hours a day. She's such a nice person. She shouldn't have to live with a nut case," Jean said, as she turned back to the computer screen.

Neither of us had noticed the two students who'd come into the room and must've overheard most of our conversation. I left wondering if Jean would try to explain to them that they shouldn't take what we said seriously.

There was a plastic bag in the pickup with a change of clothes I'd brought from home—a pair of well-worn jeans, a flannel shirt, and a pair of high-top leather shoes I wore when I worked in the garden. I wasn't familiar with the dress code at Smokey's, but I figured that outfit would blend in with the crowd better than the one I'd worn to campus. I went back into the building and changed in the men's room on the first floor. I slipped out when the hallway was deserted to avoid

144

meeting up with a student or one of my colleagues who might be curious about what I was wearing.

Smokey's Tavern was a large, single-story building surrounded by a gravel covered parking area. It was constructed of some kind of imitation logs, which were apparently intended to give it a rustic appearance. It looked cheap and shabby. A rusty pickup truck and a battered Buick were parked in front. The after work crowd hadn't arrived yet.

I pulled around to the back of the building. I wanted my pickup as far out of sight as possible in case Billy stopped in early, and I'd have to get away without him seeing me.

When I went in a side door, I was hit by the smell of stale beer and cooking fat. There was a long bar and a half a dozen booths along the opposite wall. At the far end of the room, there was an open area where there were four pool tables. I sat on a stool just inside the door, so if Billy happened to come in the front entrance, I might be able to slip out before he saw me.

The bartender was a large, fleshy man. I was sure that under the heavy layer of fat there was more than the average amount of muscle. I imagined he'd be able to break up a fight, or throw out a belligerent drunk, with little difficulty. One of the customers called him Curley. He was completely bald.

I looked down the bar. Lite beer seemed to be the preferred beverage, so that's what I ordered. I'm always amazed to see tough, blue collar types drinking a watered down, tasteless brew that has a lower alcohol content than regular beers. Dramatic testimony to the power of advertising.

I finished the bottle quickly. When Curley brought me the second, I made my move.

"You know Billy Wade?" I asked.

"Oh, yeah, I know Billy," Curley answered. I got the impression he was accustomed to chatting with customers. It was probably part of the job he enjoyed.

"Billy and I go way back. He used to be a regular here. Is he still coming in?"

Curley nodded.

"I took a job in Chicago a few years ago. Now I'm on the road about half the time. I stopped by here two weeks ago Sunday around eight o'clock. I was hoping to see Billy, but he wasn't here, and I couldn't wait around. You know if he came in that night?"

Curley stared at me.

"Curley, you wouldn't remember that. I'll be passing through on Sunday night in a couple of weeks. What are my chances of catching Billy?"

"Pretty good. On Sunday, a few of the guys who're good pool players show up to see who's the toughest. Like in that movie with Tom Cruise and Paul Newman. Between you and me, they're all full of shit."

I laughed the best I could. "Billy was always full of shit. We closed some bars on a lot of nights. I'd like to see him again."

Curley looked at the big clock on the wall behind the bar. Ten minutes fast. I suspected Smokey's might have violated the state liquor law a time or two, so it was important to get the lights out and the drunks on the streets at legal closing time. "Billy stops in sometimes after he gets off work. Why don't you hang around awhile."

"I've got to be in Cleveland tomorrow, so I have to hit the road. When you see Billy, don't mention I asked about him. I want to surprise the old son of a bitch. By the way, did Billy ever get married?"

"Are you kiddin'? No woman in her right mind would go near that guy."

Curley was a good bartender. As we talked, he kept an eye on a couple of customers at the other end of the bar. Both had bottles in front of them that were nearly empty. Curley got two Bud Lites out of the cooler and delivered them. The guys didn't look up when he picked up bills off the bar and went to the cash register.

I hadn't been in a bar like Smokey's since I worked on a laboring job after my junior year in college, so I didn't know if a tip for the bartender was the standard. I left a bill and a half full bottle of beer on the bar and went to the men's room, which was by the side door. I slipped out while Curley was getting a beer for a new arrival. If a tip was out of line, I figured he'd think I left in a hurry and forgot to pick up my change. I thought I saw Billy's pickup coming down the street as I pulled out of the parking lot, so I turned in the opposite direction.

I was home almost an hour before Beth arrived. She found me sitting in the kitchen with a half empty bottle of Molson on the table in front of me. "The day didn't go well, and you're worried. Pour me a glass of wine and get yourself another Molson. As soon as I get out of these clothes, I'll meet you in the living room. I want to hear about it."

Beth took a sip or two of wine while I told her about my talk with Curley.

"So, the bartender wasn't able to confirm that Billy was in the bar on the night of the murder?"

"That's right."

"I suppose there are other customers who might be able to provide Billy with an alibi," Beth said.

"That's a possibility, but I can't think of any way to get in touch with them."

"Now you're worried that you have information which could result in the arrest of a dangerous killer. Information you've promised not to reveal to anyone."

"Right again. What am I going to do, counselor?"

146

"That's a tough question. Let me think about it while I start dinner."

A little later, Beth came out of the kitchen with another Molson. "Drink this. It may help."

By the time we sat down to dinner, the alcohol in my bloodstream was having a significant effect. The problem seemed to be less important. "Did you ever notice that college professors can be somewhat arrogant and opinionated?" I asked.

"I have noticed that from time to time."

"And that they are overly impressed with their importance?"

"I think I know what you're referring to."

"Let me explain why they're like that. Of course, I'm not talking about me. I'm talking about most other professors."

"I understand."

"Faculty members spend twelve hours a week lecturing to one hundred or more intelligent young people who come to class with the assumption that professors are the final authority. They listen intently and write down what they hear in their notebooks. There are, of course, some bright students who recognize that professors are fallible. They never mention this because they suspect that if they did, they might be penalized when grades are assigned. How many working people can go on for weeks, or even years, without having their authority questioned? In your profession, someone is always maintaining you are wrong."

"There's no question about that."

"Because professors are so seldom challenged, they tend to overestimate their abilities and develop an exaggerated feeling of power. When I got involved in the murder investigation, I expected to be able to solve a crime that had baffled the experts. This, of course, was an absurd assumption based to a large extent on that professorial arrogance.

"When I left Smokey's, I was worried. Maybe I'd found a vicious killer I couldn't tell anyone about. Now I see how presumptuous it was for me to think that."

"So, you aren't concerned anymore. Wade couldn't be the killer."

"That's the way I see it."

"Nice try, professor, but it's not working. You're still worried."

"Sometimes I hate it when you understand me. Let me try to convince myself I don't have to break my promise to Mark and pass on what I know to Russ."

"I don't think you need to feel guilty. It's unlikely Wade is the killer, and even if you told Russ what you know about him, my feeling is that he couldn't do much with the information."

Beth stood up and stretched. "I had a bad morning with a monster judge. It wore me out. I think it's time for me to head off to bed."

"I'll join you in a little while. I still have some thinking to do."

147

I went into my study. I felt the need to record a summary of the day's activities in the investigation file. When I was finished, I couldn't resist reviewing the notes I'd made over the past weeks. I tried to think if there was anything more that could be done. I considered the possibility of contacting other students who knew Cheryl. That could be difficult and time consuming, and it probably wouldn't be worth the effort, since Russ and his staff had done such a thorough job. Then I thought about talking with Rob Perry. Why bother? He certainly couldn't be considered a suspect, and it was highly doubtful he'd be able to provide any information of value.

It was after midnight when I turned off the computer. Knowing that I'd made the last entry into the investigation file left me with a feeling of deep frustration for having failed on a mission I felt was so important.

- 33 -

I woke up to an empty bed. I found Beth in the kitchen dressed for work. She had just finished her breakfast. "I was awake early and slipped out of bed quietly. I have a busy day coming up and wanted to get an early start."

I looked at the clock. "You must have turned off the alarm when you got up."

"I could have. I don't remember. Sorry if I ruined your morning."

"You didn't. In fact, I'm happy about it. I got some extra sleep, and I have an excuse for not running."

"I have to go. See you tonight." She opened the door to leave and then turned and looked back. "And no more talk about murders."

Jean looked up from her desk when I walked into the reception area. "Little late this morning, Tom. Big night at Smokey's Tavern?"

"I had quite a time."

"Last night I mentioned to Les that you were going to Smokey's. He said to tell you to be careful. Things get pretty rough there at times."

Les, Jean's husband, had lived in the area all of his life and knew the city. "Thanks for the advice. I don't intend to go there again."

"By the way, Professor Donovan stopped by after you left yesterday. He asked me to be sure and remind you of basketball practice at three thirty today. He said he'd been trying to call you but got no answer. Doesn't he believe in leaving messages?"

"No. It's kind of a philosophical thing with Matt. He believes technology is partially responsible for the problems in modern society. Not using it is a way of protesting. He does his writing on an old-fashioned typewriter, and he doesn't have any credit cards."

Jean frowned. "I never thought of that before. It makes some sense."

"Next time you see Matt, ask him about it. He can be very convincing. When you talk to him again, remember to call him by his first name. He doesn't care for titles like doctor or professor."

"I'm beginning to like Matt," Jean said.

I was part way down the hall when I called back to Jean. "Did you explain to those students about our conversation yesterday afternoon?"

"I didn't even try," she said.

When I was unlocking my office door, the phone rang. It was Rod Dudley.

"What can I do for you, Rod?" I asked.

"Don and I are setting up another series of meetings with the female students to discuss safety precautions they should be taking. Don said he had talked it over with you."

"That's right," I said. "I told him I thought the presentations you made in the spring may have saved some lives."

"I'd like to think it made a difference," Rod said. "When Don and I were taking, I remembered that I saw you at one of the meetings. Since you have been involved in the case, I wondered if you would be interested in coming to the meetings with me. The presence of a professor might impress upon the students how important it is to be careful."

"What does Don think about it?" I asked.

"He likes the idea."

I felt complimented and was about to agree when I had some second thoughts. "Rod, that meeting I attended went very well. The students obviously took what you said seriously, and they felt comfortable asking questions. I can't imagine any way I could have made a significant contribution. You know I'd like to help, but I think you would be better off working alone."

"I understand," Rod said. "If you change your mind, give me a call. The first meeting is next week."

"I will," I said.

I was honest in telling Rod that I didn't think I could have been any help to him, but I could also imagine Beth's reaction if I told her I would be going to five or six evening meetings during the next couple of weeks.

A few minutes before three o'clock, I passed Jean's desk again on my way to the department storage room where the coffee pot was on all day. "Remember, you have to be at basketball practice in half an hour. Matt might be upset with me if you don't show up."

Since I'd retired from the game, there was no reason to go to the gym. Still, I thought I owed an explanation to the rest of the guys. After all, most of us had been playing together for three or four years.

There were three, side by side basketball courts in the recreational gym. At three twenty, several students were playing on the middle court. The other two courts were empty. I went into the locker room where I assumed the team members would be getting dressed for practice. It was deserted.

When I went back out in the gym to watch the game in progress, there was someone shooting baskets on one of the end courts. He was tall, maybe six-five, and trim. As I watched, he hit half a dozen jump shots in a row from outside the foul circle. When he finally missed, he picked up the long rebound, dribbled once, and slam dunked.

I tried to place him. He hadn't played on the varsity the previous year and the only black recruit in the freshman class was a six-foot guard. As I puzzled over the identity of the mystery player, the ball he was using rolled toward me. When I tossed it to him, I noticed he was wearing a T-shirt from a small college in the southern part of the state.

"You're James Whittington?"

"Yes, I am."

"Matt Donovan said you might be playing in the intramural league."

"I will be, and I'm looking forward to it."

"Sorry. I should have introduced myself. I'm Tom Evers."

James shook my hand. "Matt has talked about you. Are you going to play this year?"

"No, I've decided I'm getting a little too old for the game."

"I'm sorry to hear that. Matt thinks we have a good chance of winning the championship if you were on the team. Without you at point guard, he doesn't think we can do it."

"Matt told you that?"

"Just this morning he said he hoped you'd show up for practice today."

"Maybe I should work out with you guys today and see how it feels."

I was back out on the court with James when Matt and the rest of the team wandered in. Jerry, back from sabbatical, yelled over, "Hey Tom, are you so far out of shape you have to come to practice early?" I looked at the clock. It was ten minutes to four. I started to ask James what time practice was scheduled to start, but he was out of range, heading for the drinking fountain.

It was a typical practice. A lot of academic trash talk and some good laughs. With James on the court, we had the feeling the team would be competitive in the NBA.

I cornered Matt in the locker room after we had showered. "It was a set up, wasn't it? You told me that practice was at three thirty so James could work on me."

"Thomas, I find your accusation that I might've been a party to deception to be quite insulting."

"Why are you smiling?"

"Because I'm pleased that you'll be with the team this season."

I left the locker room muttering, "Redheaded gorilla."

Beth had started dinner preparation by the time I got home. "I'm a little late. Basketball practice started today. I didn't intend to, but I ended up working out with the guys. I enjoyed it. I know I said I was going to quit, but now I'm considering playing one more year." I paused. "Why are you smiling? Everybody is smiling at me today."

"Because you're amusing. I think you and Matt will be playing until the young guys get up the nerve to tell you that you're over the hill. Remember when Rachel and I went to that game a couple of years ago, when you two thought you were going to win the championship? We could hardly believe what we saw. Two thirty-plus, reasonably intelligent men out there shouting, pushing, shoving, and elbowing other players. Rachel and I were embarrassed."

"Matt and I noticed you two were doing a fair amount of clapping and cheering. Not exactly appropriate behavior for two highly intelligent, sophisticated, thirty-plus women."

"I don't recall Rachel and I acting like that, but if we did, it was to bolster your male egos."

"You always need to have the last word. Get to work on dinner, woman. I'm hungry."

Beth gave me one of her big smiles and made an obscene comment.

"That wasn't very ladylike," I said, as I moved quickly through the kitchen door before she could reply.

When we finished dinner, Beth brought out a battered, loose leaf notebook. I knew we were in for an evening of planning. She reminded me that it had been a long time since we'd entertained any of our friends. She already had a social calender set up for the rest of the semester.

The following weekend, we invited Rose and Russ to dinner. I brought Russ up to date on the investigating I'd done, leaving out the part about Billy Wade, and told him I didn't intend to do anything more. I got the impression he was hoping I might be able to come up with something important.

On the Saturday after Thanksgiving, the Donovans came to dinner, along with two other faculty couples. We finished off by hosting an open house at the end of final exam week in December, which has become sort of a tradition.

The holidays aren't a particularly happy time for us. We spend time with our families. While Beth enjoys seeing her nephews and nieces, she always returns home a little depressed because the visit reminds her of our life without children.

- 34 -

The students' holiday vacation runs through the first week in January. I look forward to the period following New Year's because I can count on working in my office without interruption. I use the time to prepare for the second semester. One afternoon, toward the end of the week, I was finishing the syllabus for one of my courses when the phone rang. It was Patti. She needed to talk. Twenty minutes later, she appeared at my office door. Her face was flushed. Obviously, she had been crying.

Her grades had just arrived in the mail. Russ was at work, and Rose had gone to the grocery. The results were not good: two D's, a C, and a C+. That would put her on academic probation, and if she didn't show significant improvement in the spring semester, she'd be dropped from school.

Patti talked for ten minutes. She told me her boyfriend wasn't into studying. She talked about too many parties, too many late nights, and too much beer. Throughout the monolog, she referred to herself in highly uncomplimentary terms, using harsh language.

When she seemed to run out of energy, she paused. "Tom, you have to help me."

I waited a bit before responding. "First, we have to rule out suicide."

The smile didn't match up well with her cheeks still wet with tears. "I knew if I came here you'd make me laugh. I don't want to laugh, and I know what you're doing. You're trying to tell me I'm taking this too seriously."

I nodded.

"Maybe I am, but I can't help it. Tell me what I should do."

"You're asking me how to tell your parents? First, remember they are very nice, understanding people."

153

"I know they are. That's why I'm having so much trouble. I can deal with this, but they shouldn't have to. My brother and sister didn't do anything to disappoint them like I have."

"Here's my advice. Tell them exactly what you've told me. No, on second thought, leave out some of the details and clean up your language."

Patty laughed. Some of the tension she'd bought with her had disappeared. She frowned. "Okay, I guess I can try."

"You have no choice. Your parents have to know what's been going on."

"I bet you think I'm really stupid."

"No, I don't think you're stupid. You are a very intelligent, sensible, young woman who did some stupid things."

Patti stood up and took a deep breath. "Here I go." She was halfway out the door when she stopped and turned around. "If Mom and Dad kick me out of the house, could I come and stay with you and Beth?"

"Are you good at cooking and house cleaning?"

"Not really."

"That's a problem, but we might consider it."

When I got to my office the next morning, there was a message. "Hi. This is Patti. I think everything is going to be all right. Thanks for listening."

A blizzard hit our part of the Midwest on the day before the second semester was scheduled to begin. Eighteen inches of snow fell in a twelve-hour period. Before the storm was over, there were four foot drifts in many areas. For the first time in anyone's recollection, the beginning of classes was delayed for two days.

That turned out to be only the beginning. For six weeks, we had bitter cold temperatures and record snowfall. I filled the back of my pickup with firewood for added weight and managed to get to campus every day. Most of the time, I had to take Beth to work because of the road conditions. In mid-February, the thermometer climbed into the forties, and the snow finally began to melt. The change in the weather greatly improved the mood of both students and faculty.

In spite of the inconvenience, Beth and I enjoyed the cold and snow. We spent weekends reading, warmed by the wood burning stove, and walked through the white, untouched snow in the woods around our house.

As a dedicated academic, I hate to admit that the high point of the winter was when we clinched the intramural basketball championship two weeks before the end of the season. Our only loss came when James missed a game because he had to go home to attend the funeral of his grandfather.

At the celebration in Jerry's Bar after the last game, we elected James honorary captain and gave him the trophy to keep. He seemed to be enjoying himself until Matt told him it might take him a long time to get his doctorate because he was so valuable to the team. Even though we all assured him that Matt was only kidding, James was unusually quiet during the rest of the evening.

A week or so after the thaw, the trial of the school principal accused of child molesting was scheduled to begin. Beth had strong feelings about the case and had been confident she could get a conviction. She began to worry when, at the last minute, the defendant's wife, who came from a wealthy family and could afford expensive legal counsel, arranged to bring in a high powered defense attorney named Raymond Warren to represent her husband.

A day or two into the trial, Beth began coming home in a state of fury. Warren, who was notorious for his theatrical and successful defense of obviously guilty clients, launched an unmerciful attack on the prosecution's witnesses. The worst was when the young college woman who had volunteered to testify because of the earlier experience she'd had with the principal when she was in middle school took the stand. Raymond suggested she might have misinterpreted the situation because of her infatuation with the defendant. The implication that a thirteen-year-old honor student had been sexually attracted to a forty-year-old principal was almost too much for Beth to deal with. The two-week trial ended in a hung jury. After three full days of deliberation, two jurors refused to go along with a guilty verdict.

Knowing Beth as I do, it came as no surprise that she had difficulty dealing with the outcome of the case. On the other hand, I didn't expect such a strong reaction. She seemed to view the outcome as a personal defeat. She was as distraught as I'd ever seen her. When her mood failed to change in the days after the trial, I suggested we take a trip to Florida during the university spring break. She agreed it might be a good idea.

On Wednesday of the week before the spring break, students begin to leave. By Friday, the campus is virtually deserted. I refuse to cancel my Friday classes even though less than a third of the students can be expected to show up. As usual, I took attendance in my two morning classes. The students who were there seemed pleased that I recognized their presence. I worked in my office through the lunch hour to take care of some last minute details. Beth was packed and ready to head south when I got home a little after one o'clock.

Early Saturday afternoon, we crossed the Florida state line and took the shortest route to the Gulf of Mexico. Unfortunately, we ended up on a beach filled with spring breakers. Most of them were carrying beer cans as they crossed the highway, often causing motorists to slow down or stop. In the twenty minutes or so we spent driving through this enormous open air party, we observed a remarkable display of bizarre behavior, including a group of young women waving from a motel balcony clad only in the bottoms of their bikini bathing suits and two males standing in the back of a moving jeep drinking out of pitchers of beer.

When we finally left the festivities behind, I said to Beth, "From the reports of students, I've become aware that spring break can be pretty wild, but I guess you have to see it first hand to fully appreciate what actually goes on. The interesting

155

part of it is that the majority of the spring breakers become normal, well-behaved students when they return to their campuses."

"Do you suppose their parents have any idea of what it's like?" Beth asked.

"I doubt it."

After we finally left the festivities behind us, we drove along a stretch of beach that was completely deserted. We had driven an hour or so when we came to a shabby mill town on the edge of a large, quiet bay. Two blocks past the town's only traffic light, Beth noticed a real estate agent's sign on a small wooden building with the paint peeling from the siding and a rusting metal roof. She suggested we stop and ask if there were any houses on the beach available to rent for a week.

We had some trouble opening the door, which was sagging on its hinges. Once inside, we were greeted by a white-haired, neatly dressed gentleman with a heavy local accent. We inquired about a rental. He told us there was a pleasant, one-room beach house available three miles from the office that might be satisfactory. He offered to take us there, so we could see it before we made a decision. There was something about the agent's manner that led us to believe that wouldn't be necessary. We paid a week's rent and got a key and directions to the house.

It turned out that the agent's description of the house as pleasant was, at the very least, an understatement. It was built on a high dune two hundred feet from the Gulf of Mexico. The furnishings were more than adequate, and it was immaculately clean.

Every morning, Beth and I ran together on the beach. The rest of the day we acted like south sea island beachcombers. On our second day, we discovered a superb restaurant a few miles from where we were staying. We ate there three times, stuffing ourselves with fish from the local waters. After six days, we reluctantly headed north. By the time we left, Beth was in a much better mood.

- 35 -

We arrived home on Sunday to a cold rain, which made us appreciate our trip even more. For the first few days after returning, I was as lethargic as the students. By the end of the week, the weather had improved. The sight of students sunbathing on the porch roof of the fraternity and sorority houses on Friday afternoon was a welcome sight. It was a sure sign that spring had finally arrived.

On Saturday, when Beth and I were enjoying our morning coffee out on the deck, I commented that I thought the campus community was on the way to full recovery from the trauma experienced earlier in the year. It seemed the terrible memories had faded into the background, and the fear that had permeated the atmosphere throughout the fall and winter was subsiding.

I woke early on Sunday morning to a clear sky. It was such a beautiful day that I decided to run a couple of extra miles. Beth was still asleep when I left the house.

The edges of the road I run on are filled with litter of all kinds. In addition to the usual aluminum cans and discarded fast food containers, I see a variety of other types of trash. I find it so offensive that several times a year, I walk the route with a plastic bag and clean up as best I can. Occasionally, more sizeable objects are left beside the road—such things as large piles of disposable diapers, worn out mattresses, and old plumbing fixtures.

A few hundred feet beyond the old highway bridge, I could see that, since my run the previous morning, something had been thrown into the drainage ditch on the right-hand side of the road. From a distance, it appeared to be a bundle of old clothing. I was just a few feet away before I realized that it was a partially clothed, contorted human body. The exposed flesh on the legs and torso of the lifeless form were covered with dark stains.

As a reader of mystery novels, I'd come to believe that when viewing a mutilated body, the natural response was to throw up. In my case, there was no

157

gastrointestinal reaction. Instead, I immediately went into a state of panic—pounding heart, difficulty in breathing, and the feeling I was going to faint.

I ran back to the house at top speed. Beth was pouring a cup of coffee when I charged through the door into the kitchen. She looked puzzled at my dramatic entry. I was so out of breath that it took a few seconds before I could explain. "There's a body of a woman on the side of the road just across the concrete bridge." She listened as I gave the information to the 911 operator.

"I can't believe this," Beth said.

"I'm not sure I can either. I've got to get dressed and drive back."

I went into the bedroom and put on a pair of jeans and a flannel shirt over my running clothes.

"Is there anything I should do?" Beth asked, as I passed through the kitchen.

"You better call Russ. Since we're outside the city limits, the 911 operator's first call will have been to the County Sheriff's Department. It might be some time before he's notified.

I know he'll want to get to the scene quickly."

I parked the pickup at the side of the road fifty yards from the body. I had no desire to get any closer. In a few minutes, I heard sirens. I was out of the truck leaning against the front fender when the first Sheriff's Department car crossed the bridge. I waved the driver on to where the body was located. One of the deputies stayed by the body, while the other came back toward me. By the time I'd explained to him what had happened, an ambulance had arrived. A paramedic knelt by the body briefly, spoke to a deputy, and went back to the ambulance.

I was sitting in the pickup, not sure what to do, when the sheriff drove past me in his Lincoln Town Car. I recognized him from the pictures printed in the paper at election time. I had no idea about his expertise as a law enforcement officer, but I was impressed with his skill as a politician. In our part of the state, where there are always three or four individuals running for sheriff, he typically received more votes than all of the other candidates combined.

After a long conversation with the deputies, he headed my way just as Russ pulled up behind the pickup. He intercepted the sheriff, and they talked for several minutes before they walked over to me.

Russ introduced us and suggested to the sheriff that, since he was needed at the crime scene, he could wait until later to get my official statement. The sheriff nodded and went over to the deputies who were waiting for further instructions.

"Number three," Russ said.

"Number three," I repeated.

"You might as well go on home. I'll stop by later."

Beth must have been watching through the living room window because when I pulled into the driveway, she was waiting for me outside the back door.

"Number three," I said, as we walked into the kitchen.

Beth poured two cups of coffee. "You'll need to eat breakfast. How about some scrambled eggs?"

"I don't have much of an appetite. Just put a couple of slices of bread in the toaster."

I started to describe my experience of the morning but before I was able to complete a sentence, Beth interrupted me. "How many people know where you jog?"

"I have no idea. It's not something that comes up in conversation very often. Why is that important?"

"You know darn well why it's important," Beth said, looking very serious. "I've been sitting here going over this in my mind ever since you left. I don't want to sound melodramatic, but I'm scared. There are a lot of places to dump a body. I keep asking myself why this one was left on your jogging route."

"There's no reason to be concerned. It just happened to be an isolated spot that was handy. It doesn't have anything to do with my investigation."

After I said that, it occurred to me that in the years we'd been married, I'd never been anything but entirely honest with Beth. "Still, it's a remarkable coincidence the body showed up so close to our place. Russ will be stopping by. We can ask him what he thinks."

Russ pulled in the driveway an hour later. We filled coffee cups and went into the living room.

"There's no question. It's the same guy. The victim is a young woman, probably in her late teens or early twenties. The body was left where it could be easily found and, from what I could tell, the injuries were similar to the ones in the other two killings."

"Any clues at the scene that might be important?" I asked.

"Nothing that was obvious, but it's possible that something might turn up in the autopsy or the lab analysis. We've got to hope he made a mistake this time."

"Do you think my part in the investigation might have something to do with where the killer left the body?"

Russ didn't hesitate. "It's a possibility."

Russ caught Beth's look. "That doesn't necessarily mean that you two are in any danger. You have to keep in mind, this guy is killing for sexual kicks. It's reasonable to assume he's not into revenge. On the other hand, if he thought you were getting too close, that's a different story. For a while, it would be best for you to be cautious."

"How do we do that?" Beth asked.

"Beth, you shouldn't be in the house alone. Probably it would be a good idea if Tom drove you back and forth to work. Tom, you should find another place to jog. And stay away from this case. Let the professionals handle it. I'll keep you informed."

Russ finished his coffee and got up to leave. "I have work to do."

As soon as he was out the door Beth said, "That wasn't very reassuring."

"I guess we should've anticipated that there might be some risk if I got involved."

After a late lunch, I fell asleep on the sofa. It was after three when I woke up. I went into Beth's study where she was reading a book.

"I think Curley should be at the bar by now. I have to see him." I expected Beth to try to talk me out of it, but she just nodded and warned me to be careful.

At four fifteen, there were five cars and half a dozen pickup trucks in Smokey's parking lot. It appeared that Sunday was a big day. I wondered if I'd have a problem talking to Curley.

I pulled into the spot where I'd parked before and went in the side door. Only a few of the bar stools were occupied. Most of the customers were at the other end of the room watching a game of pool. Curley looked over in my direction and asked what I'd have. He showed no sign of recognizing me. I decided to stick with light beer.

I wanted to be sure I got out of the bar before Billy showed up, so I drank the beer quickly and signaled for another. When Curley returned with the change, I made my move. "Billy Wade is an old friend of mine. I live in Chicago now. I missed him last fall when I passed through town. You think he'll stop in tonight?"

Curley stared at me for a bit. "Oh yeah, I remember you. On Sunday night, you can count on Billy being here by seven."

"That late? I've got to make some phone calls. I'll do my best to get back, but I may not make it. Could be I'll miss him again. I got into town late last night. Maybe I should've come in then. Was he here after ten?"

"He sure was. He had a hot streak at the pool table. Must've won fifty dollars. He hung around until closing."

I felt a wave of relief. If Billy had no alibi for the evening, it might've meant I was responsible for another murder because I'd failed to tell Russ what I'd learned. And if he was the killer, it was hard to tell what he might have done when he learned someone was asking about him.

Beth didn't say anything when I gave her my report.

- 36 -

Identification of the victim proved to be a problem. There was no report of a missing young woman on the campus or anywhere in the city. It was a quarter past six on Monday when the police received a call from a female student who had learned of the murder on the evening TV news. An hour later, she identified the body. It was her roommate, a sophomore at the university. Her name was Jill Lawton.

The third murder had surprisingly little impact on the students. It appeared they had become resigned to the fact that violent deaths on campus were something to be expected. I found this attitude in my ivory tower to be very disturbing.

Russ called on Tuesday evening to bring me up to date on the investigation. Jill's official residence was a coed dormitory. Most of the semester, she'd been staying in her boyfriend's apartment. During that period, her roommate, Karen Ellsworth, who had taken a course with me the previous semester, saw her only occasionally.

Late Saturday afternoon, Jill showed up at the dorm and told Karen she was dropping out of school. She said she was going to call her parents the next morning and arrange to have them pick her up. She spent the rest of the afternoon and early evening packing. When Karen left at seven to go to a party, Jill told her she was going back to see her boyfriend. They'd a serious argument earlier in the day. She said she wanted to see him again before she went home.

The boyfriend said Jill called him around seven thirty to tell him she was coming over. At nine, he got tired of waiting and went to a bar to meet some friends. He didn't bother calling Jill to find out what had happened. He said they hadn't been getting along well recently, and he assumed she'd decided not to come to see him and would be spending the night in the dorm.

Karen wondered why Jill failed to show up with her parents on Sunday to pick up her things, but Jill had always been unpredictable, so she thought nothing of it.

Upon hearing the description of the unidentified victim on the Monday night news, the roommate realized it might be Jill.

For a few days after the murder, Beth and I followed Russ's advice the best we could. I drove Beth to her office each morning and picked her up in the afternoon. There seemed to be little else we could do. I considered buying a handgun but thought it would be carrying things a little too far. The precautions we took quickly became tiresome so, by the end of the week, we decided to go back to our old routines. However, this didn't mean we were no longer apprehensive.

In spite of Russ's recommendation not to get involved, on Wednesday night, I reached the point where I felt I must do something. I figured I could get some information about the victim in ways that wouldn't interfere with the police investigation.

Before my first class on Thursday morning, I called Alice Murray at the Registrar's Office and asked her to get me the name of Jill's academic advisor. This was a perfectly legitimate request. Occasionally, instructors might need to talk with the advisor of a student enrolled in one of their classes.

I was so eager to get started that I went back to my office between classes to check for phone messages. Alice had called. Jill was a history major. Her adviser was Charles Miller. I knew Chuck pretty well. He was an easy going, laid back guy who enjoyed working with students and spent a lot of time with his advisees. I was sure he'd be able to tell me quite a bit about Jill. I called Chuck's office and left a message. He got back to me during the lunch hour. We arranged to meet in the faculty lounge at four.

I explained my interest in Jill to Chuck without going into detail. I was relieved when he didn't ask any questions and seemed to see nothing unusual about my involvement in a murder investigation.

"Jill took my course in twentieth century U.S. history last fall," he explained. "Her class attendance was poor and her exams and papers were in the C to C minus range. I was surprised when she came to my office halfway through the semester and told me she wanted to major in history. She asked if I would be her advisor. I wasn't convinced it was a good choice, so I spent some time talking about other options. She insisted that history was the only subject that really interested her."

"Great teachers inspire students," I said.

"I think Jill needed more inspiration than I could've offered. When I got her folder from her freshman advisor, I saw problems. She barely made her grades the first semester of last year; she failed one course and got a D in another, which put her on academic probation. Registration week, she showed up at the last minute to work out a schedule. That was the last time I saw her outside of class. I felt charitable at grade time and gave her a C, which she really didn't deserve. She got a B and three Cs in her other courses. That was good enough for the registrar to give her one more trial semester. Ironically, on Monday, I received her mid-term grade report. She was failing in all of her classes."

"It sounds as though you didn't get to know her well."

"I just met with her a couple of times, and she wasn't the kind to talk about herself, at least with her advisor."

"The other two victims were very good looking women. Would you say Jill was attractive?"

"She was average height and maybe a little overweight. I remember she always wore quite a bit of makeup. I suspect it may have been to hide a bad complexion. I guess I'd describe her as being rather plain looking."

Before I went back to my office, Chuck and I spent some time sharing campus gossip.

Chuck hadn't been able to tell me much about Jill. However, from his report, one thing was clear. The murderer hadn't limited his choice of victims to attractive young women who were outstanding students.

On Saturday morning, Russ called and asked if he could come out to the house. He came in the door without knocking, poured himself a cup of coffee, and sat down with us at the kitchen table. "We've done about everything we can. Now we're waiting for a few more laboratory reports. We have nothing yet that provides any significant clues, and I doubt that the lab results will be of any use.

"We couldn't find anyone who saw Jill after her roommate left the dorm. The killer may have set up a meeting by a phone call or picked her up when she was on her way over to see her boyfriend. His apartment is on East Seamer Street, so she would've had to walk quite a distance after leaving the lighted campus.

"One of the first things I did was to check on Rutledge. The woman he was living with told me he'd moved to California. She'd just received a letter from him asking for money that was postmarked San Diego, so he's no longer a suspect."

Russ went on to describe Jill. According to her boyfriend, she'd been depressed for some time and had been drinking heavily. Russ suspected there might have been some drugs involved. He said he got the impression that the boyfriend wasn't too stable and was probably having a problem with alcohol and drugs himself.

I knew more about Jill's history of academic problems than Russ but saw no point in telling him about my conversation with Chuck. It was doubtful the information I had would contribute anything to the investigation.

"Jill was certainly different from the other victims," I commented, when Russ had finished with his report.

"Yes, she was, but you have to think the three had something in common."

"I know her roommate. She was in one of my classes last semester."

"You're thinking about getting in touch with her?"

"It did enter my mind."

Russ got up to pour himself another cup of coffee. "I see no reason why you shouldn't talk to her. Be sure and let me know if you come up with something."

"I will," I said.

Beth invited Russ to have lunch with us. He refused, saying he had to stop by the department and take care of some paperwork.

After he'd gone, Beth said, "I get the impression Russ is experiencing some stress."

"I think we are, too," I said.

We spent the rest of the weekend working in the garden. Because of our trip south during spring break, we were getting a late start. On Saturday afternoon, I spread fertilizer and worked the soil with the roto-tiller while Beth went to the greenhouse for plants. By dinner time on Sunday we had planted potatoes, cabbage, broccoli, cauliflower, spinach, and lettuce. The rest of the things we put in our garden could be damaged by a late frost, so it would be a couple of weeks before we would plant them.

- 37 -

At nine o'clock on Monday morning I began calling Karen Ellsworth's number. I finally reached her at four that afternoon and explained briefly why I wanted to meet with her. She appeared at my office door ten minutes later. She seemed so eager to talk that I saw no reason to go into more detail about my involvement in the case.

"What would you like me to tell you?" she asked.

"You probably got to know Jill as well as anyone. I'd like to learn as much as I can about her. What kind of person she was and the things that were going on in her life before she was killed."

"We were assigned as roommates when we were freshman. By the end of the year, I decided I wanted to room with someone else. When I mentioned this to Jill, she became so upset, I agreed to try it for another semester."

"That tells me she wasn't the easiest person to live with."

"She wasn't. All she wanted to do was party. You know how it is here. The weekend starts on Thursday night. She would start drinking then and keep it up all weekend. She'd come in drunk late at night and would be sick most of the next day. I didn't want to stay in the room when she was like that, so I usually went to the library to study.

"At first, she always came back to the room. Later, she might not show up for two or three days. She hardly ever studied. She was smart enough that she could do a little bit the night before an exam and manage to pass.

"Sometimes she'd get really depressed and stay in bed all day and not talk at all. I'd have to bring her food from the dining hall. At first, when I saw her like that, I tried to convince her to stop drinking so much and get some counseling."

"Sounds like good advice."

"Jill never listened. She said she didn't want to waste her time talking to some stupid shrink. Finally I gave up trying to help. There was nothing I could do.

165

"On that Saturday, she came back to the room and told me she was leaving school. She said she was going to call her parents in the morning to ask them to come and take her home. I said I thought it was a good idea."

I purposely hadn't mentioned to Karen that I was aware of what she had reported to the police. If she knew, I was afraid she might be less likely to confide in me. "Did you have a chance to talk to Jill after she told you this?" I asked.

"I stayed to help her pack. I was with her until about seven, when my date came to pick me up. She talked about looking forward to getting away from campus. She was failing in all her courses and knew she would be dropped from school. And I'm sure she and her boyfriend were having problems. I suspected they must have had a bad fight before she came back to the room. I wondered if they weren't on the verge of breaking up. She said she was planning to work for a year and then transfer to another school."

"Did she tell you what she intended to do that night?"

"She said when she finished packing, she was going back to her boyfriend's apartment. I had a feeling she was hoping they might be able to work things out."

"Do you think she might've changed her mind and gone someplace else?"

"I doubt it. I don't know where she would've gone. Jill didn't have any close friends."

"Had the murders on campus made her cautious about being out at night alone?"

Karen shook her head. "I don't think so. She was too wrapped up in her problems to worry about something like that. She told me sometimes at night when she couldn't sleep she left the apartment and took long walks."

"Do you know if Jill got any phone calls on that Saturday?"

"She didn't get any after she came back to our room."

"Were you with her the whole time?"

"Yes, except when I went to the dining hall to eat dinner. Jill said she wasn't hungry and stayed in the room. I was gone about a half-hour."

"Jill had adjustment problems from the time she arrived on campus. It seems that recently, these problems became more serious. Do you have any idea what might've been going on in her life to cause this?"

"It's true that the last few times I saw Jill, she was in bad shape. I really felt sorry for her. She was basically a nice person. I'm sure part of Jill's problem was her boyfriend. She'd only known him a few weeks when she began spending most of the time in his apartment. That was right after the beginning of the semester. He turned out to be a real jerk. He treated Jill very badly. When he got drunk, which was quite often, he was physically abusive. I saw the bruises. Jill had been with him a month or so when she showed signs that she was in trouble."

Karen paused for a moment. "There was something else. I guess it's okay to talk about it because I think I can trust you not to tell anyone."

"Of course, you can."

"I'm almost positive that I'm the only one who knows about this except for Jill's boyfriend. A couple of weeks ago, she came back to the room and stayed overnight. She'd just found out she was pregnant. She didn't get along well with her parents. She was afraid if she told them, they wouldn't let her come home. She was pretty desperate. She asked me if I knew where she could get an abortion. I didn't know of any place and even though I wanted to help, I was afraid to get involved.

"She left the next morning. I didn't talk with her again until she came back to pack. She never mentioned anything about the abortion. I wondered if part of the reason she was leaving school at that time was because of the pregnancy. Since her parents were coming to pick her up, I thought maybe she'd told them, and they were going to help."

"You didn't tell the police about this?"

"No. When Jill told me, she made me promise I wouldn't tell anyone. After she was gone, it probably wouldn't have made much difference, but I thought if I told someone, other people could learn about it. Her parents might not have known, and I didn't want to be responsible for them finding out. Later, I began to worry. Maybe it would help the police find the killer if they knew about the pregnancy. I guess that's why I'm telling you. At least someone involved will know."

"Karen, there was no need for you to tell anyone because the medical examiner would find out about the pregnancy. I appreciate your coming in to talk. Based on what you've told me, I have a much better understanding of Jill and what was happening in her life before she was killed."

Even though I promised Karen not to reveal the secret of Jill's pregnancy, I wasn't hesitant in telling Beth about it when I got home. She reacted immediately. "I think the pregnancy might be an important factor in this case."

"In what way?" I asked.

"I don't know exactly. I just have a hunch it's something worth following up on."

That evening, I sat down at the computer and opened the investigation file. I wondered why I hadn't deleted it earlier. I typed in a summary of the interview with Karen and then read through all of the previous notes looking for parallels in the lives of the victims. All three had experienced difficulties with their boyfriends. It was hard to make much of this because the types of problems seemed to be so different. In Whitney's case, the relationship apparently ended because of personality conflicts. Cheryl and John were able to resolve their differences and, at the end, they were very close. Jill and her boyfriend were obviously two troubled young people who might be expected to have a stormy relationship. I was feeling quite frustrated when I closed the file.

Earlier, Beth had called in to say she was going to bed. She was sound asleep when I joined her. I wasn't ready for sleep. I lay there going over what Beth had said about Jill's pregnancy—that it could be an important factor in the case. I knew I had to give her comment serious consideration. Beth has a remarkable talent for analyzing complex situations. It enables her to come up with insights that most would overlook.

I imagined that the pregnancy introduced stress in Jill's life that added significantly to the turmoil she was already experiencing. Coping with it must have been extremely difficult, and her boyfriend didn't seem to be the kind of guy who could offer her much support. In fact, the pregnancy may have contributed to the crisis in their relationship.

I thought about how I'd reassured Karen that her failure to tell the police wouldn't impede the investigation because they'd learn about it through the autopsy. If the interview served no other purpose than to relieve her worry, I considered it worthwhile.

Then something occurred to me. I felt a little foolish for not thinking of it sooner. If my explanation to Karen about the autopsy was accurate, why hadn't Russ told me Jill was pregnant? As far as I knew, he'd never withheld information before. It wasn't his style. I could see no reason why this issue would be so sensitive he couldn't reveal it. He knew I'd never repeat anything he told me to anyone else, nor would Beth.

Suppose Jill wasn't pregnant at the time of death. She might've lied to Karen about being pregnant, but that seemed highly unlikely. The only other possibility— she'd had an abortion. I began asking myself what significance this might have in the investigation.

By this point, I was too agitated to think about sleep, so I got out of bed and went into my study. There was no point in going back to the computer. I had the entire investigation file stored in my personal memory bank. I picked up a pad of paper and went into the kitchen to brew a pot of coffee. By the time I'd finished the third cup, I'd scribbled five pages of notes. I caught myself moving my lips as I read them.

Assume that Jill had an abortion. Could it be the thing the three victims shared was that they'd terminated a pregnancy close to the time they were killed? Support for the abortion hypothesis: Whitney and Cheryl had given indication that they were experiencing emotional turmoil in the weeks before they were murdered, which would be understandable if they were struggling with pregnancy. And it appeared that both began to show signs of distress at about the time they would've discovered they were pregnant. Also, I remembered Whitney had some physical symptoms that are common in the first weeks of pregnancy.

After giving this some consideration, I decided it was probably unlikely that Whitney and Cheryl had had abortions because they would've taken the necessary precautions to avoid getting pregnant. Besides that, their boyfriends seemed like responsible individuals who would also be careful when involved in sexual activity.

I was about ready to scrap the abortion idea when, for some reason, I began to think back to my interview with John, and the words he'd mumbled as he was leaving my office came to mind. He seemed to be saying that he'd lost more than Cheryl. Could he have been referring to the loss of his child? John might've been opposed to an abortion. Cheryl, on the other hand, could've been inclined to view a child as jeopardizing any plans she had for the future. I was always a little puzzled as to why John and Cheryl, who were so close and seemingly so well suited to each other, apparently went through a troubled period. A pregnancy would explain it. Even in a relationship as strong as theirs, an issue that serious could result in serious conflict and the distress Cheryl seemed to be experiencing.

I needed to know if Jill had been pregnant at the time she was killed. Finding that out could be a problem. The medical examiner's report would be in the case file, but I didn't want to risk asking Russ if I could examine it. He might become suspicious because I hadn't followed up on his offer to let me go through Cheryl's file. I could imagine him asking questions I wouldn't be able to answer.

I decided I'd have to get help from Beth. She worked closely with Walter James, the medical examiner. I knew they got along well, and she could probably get the information from him. However, I knew that she was always very professional in her dealings with her colleagues. If she thought it would be inappropriate to ask Walter for information about the autopsy report, she'd refuse. I'd have to wait until morning to find out.

- 38 -

I was tired enough by the time I went back to bed that sleep came quickly, even with the high level of caffeine in my system. I slept so soundly I didn't hear the alarm. When I finally opened my eyes, Beth was already out of the shower and in the bedroom getting dressed.

"Must have been a late night. I didn't hear you come to bed," she said.

"It was. I'll go make the coffee."

"It's ready. I put it on before I showered. By the looks of the coffee maker, you did some drinking last night."

"I did. Meet you in the kitchen. We need to have a conference."

When Beth joined me a few minutes later, I was still in my pajamas sitting at the kitchen table with a cup of coffee in front of me. "I take it you're not running today. This must be important."

"It may be." I told her about my thoughts of the night before. She listened intently while working on a bowl of shredded wheat.

"Your analysis intrigues me," Beth said.

"It was what you said about Jill's pregnancy that put me onto this. Now I need you to find out from Walter James if Jill was pregnant when she died."

Beth was slow to respond. Finally, she said, "Even though I'm a little uncomfortable about the idea, it doesn't appear that I'd be doing anything unethical. Walter would trust me with the information and probably wouldn't ask why I needed it. I'll give it a try."

"That's a relief. I was afraid you wouldn't do it."

"I really shouldn't."

"Why don't you go to work before you change your mind?"

"I'll get in touch with Walter as soon as I get to the office and call you when I have anything to report."

During the drive to campus, I began to feel uneasy about not running. It had become such a ritual—one I ordinarily missed only when there was bad weather. This was an absolutely beautiful morning, so I had no excuse. I decided I could make up for the lost day by running a few extra miles on Saturday.

Several students had appointments with me to discuss their term papers. The last one left my office a few minutes before I had to go to my ten o'clock lecture, so I didn't have time to think about abortions.

There was a phone message for me when I got back to the department after class. Beth had worked fast. "The test was negative. I'll be in court this afternoon and may have to work late. I'm looking forward to talking about this when I get home."

I hadn't thought about what I would do if it turned out Jill wasn't pregnant. I opened the lunch I'd brought from home and began to plan my next move.

It seemed reasonable to assume that Jill had had an abortion. I needed to find out if Whitney and Cheryl had also terminated pregnancies. I anticipated having difficulty getting this information, because the few people the two might've confided in would very likely be hesitant in sharing their knowledge with me.

First, I thought of Whitney. Scott would undoubtedly know. If Whitney were pregnant, he would've been the father. I remembered the problem I'd had earlier in contacting him. There was no reason to think it would be different now. This wasn't the kind of question to ask in a phone call, so I'd probably have to wait until the weekend, as I had before, to catch him at his apartment.

I wasn't patient at this point, so I decided to talk to the Richardsons. It could be they wouldn't have known if Whitney had been pregnant in the period before she was killed, and even if they did, they might not reveal it to me. Still, I had to try. If they were serious about finding the murderer, they should be willing to help. I dug into my desk and managed to come up with the Richardsons' phone number. Mrs. Richardson answered. She seemed surprised when I identified myself.

I explained that it was important for me to talk with her and her husband and asked if it would be convenient for me to come by later in the day. After some hesitation, she told me her husband was usually home by five thirty. She said I could come any time after that and not to worry about interfering with their dinner because they usually ate quite late. She gave me directions to their house.

I called Beth at her office and told her I'd arranged a meeting with the Richardsons and would be late getting home.

I'd been to the city where the Richardsons lived several times. Most of the way, I'd be driving on an interstate highway. I figured the trip would take two hours. At three thirty, I told Jean I was leaving for the day and headed for the pickup.

I made good time until I reached the city limits where the after work traffic slowed me down. The Richardsons lived on the far side of the city, so it was a few minutes before six when I finally reached the exclusive subdivision where their home was located. All of the houses in the area were large and beautifully landscaped.

The Richardsons' was one of the most impressive, if you happen to like nineteen eighties vintage architecture. It was on a cul-de-sac. The lawn sloped toward the street. Behind the house, there was a wooded area, which gave a feeling of rural tranquility.

I parked in front. The silver-gray BMW in the driveway made my pickup seem out of place.

Mr. Richardson opened the door before I had a chance to ring the bell. He was dressed in what I assumed were his work clothes, a dark blue suit, white shirt, and conservative tie. He greeted me cordially and led me into the living room, where his wife was waiting. She wore a long sleeve white blouse and black slacks.

Either Mrs. Richardson had a special talent, or she had hired an excellent interior decorator. The room was furnished with a large, comfortable, attractive sofa and matching chairs. The lamps on either side of the sofa had ceramic bases. I imagined they could've been custom made by a talented potter. On the walls, there were what appeared to be original watercolor paintings. I felt out of place, just like my pickup.

Mrs. Richardson welcomed me, shook my hand, and invited me to sit down. I chose the only upright chair in the room. It seemed more suitable to my mission than the others.

"Did you come to bring us news that there's been progress in the case?" Mrs. Richardson asked. There was an eagerness in her voice.

I avoided dealing with her question directly. "We've not talked in some time, so let me bring you up to date. I've been involved to a degree in the investigation of the other two murders, and the police have kept me informed about what they have found. To this point, there haven't been any clues that proved to be of value.

"Recently, I've come across something that could be significant. I called today and asked for this meeting because you may be able to help evaluate this new information. The question I have is a highly personal one. I assure you I'm asking it only because your answer could be extremely valuable in establishing the identity of the killer."

I paused, realizing that I hadn't decided ahead of time how I would phrase my question. I saw no way to soften its impact, so I decided to get directly to the point. During the brief delay, I got the impression Mrs. Richardson was becoming slightly uncomfortable.

"In the period prior to her death, do you know if Whitney had an abortion?"

I watched Mrs. Richardson. There was no obvious display of emotion. Her only reaction was to look away from me and focus her gaze on another part of the room. I turned to Mr. Richardson. He was clearly disturbed and seemed to be having difficulty in regaining his composure.

"Dr. Evers, I'm shocked that you would ask such a thing. It is insulting to me, and my wife, and our whole family. It shows a callous lack of respect for the memory of our daughter."

I interrupted before he could continue. "I'm extremely sorry you and your wife feel that way. In no way did I intend to imply anything disparaging about Whitney. You know I held her in the highest regard. She was a remarkable young woman. As I told you, I asked the question because the answer might be very important in the solution of the crime."

When I got up to leave, I started to apologize for upsetting them by raising the abortion issue but changed my mind. "I must go. Thank you for seeing me. I hope I haven't interfered with your dinner hour."

David Richardson got up from his chair. "Dr. Evers, you understand this type of investigation could seriously damage the reputation of our daughter and the rest of the family. I assume you will not pursue it any further."

"I cannot promise you that. If you recall, you and your wife are responsible for me becoming involved in an investigation of Whitney's murder. I intend to continue my inquiry. But let me assure you, I'll do my best not to tarnish the memory of Whitney. As a matter of fact, she had such a high degree of respect among those who knew her, I think it would be impossible to do so." I went out the door before there was an opportunity for further conversation.

During the drive home, I tried to sort out what had happened. If the Richardsons knew Whitney had had an abortion, their response could be interpreted as an attempt at a cover up. It was equally possible that my question simply came as a shock because it brought up an issue they knew nothing about. Whitney may not have terminated a pregnancy. Or, if she had, she hadn't told her parents. Knowing the kind of reaction she might expect from them, that would seem to be a reasonable decision on her part. If they didn't know, their indignation would be understandable. The curious thing about the way they'd reacted was that neither of them made any attempt to assure me that Whitney *hadn't* had an abortion. If they had, I might've left with the idea that the abortion issue was a false lead not worth pursuing.

I decided I'd have to talk to John Baxter.

- 39 -

I pulled the pickup into the garage a few minutes after eight. Beth brought a plate of sandwiches and a bowl of homemade potato salad out of the refrigerator. While we ate at the kitchen table, I told her about my talk with the Richardsons.

When I finished, Beth said, "It's possible Whitney had an abortion."

"That's the way I see it. I've already decided I need to talk with John Baxter. I'm a little uneasy about asking him to see me. He was really struggling at the time of Cheryl's murder. I wouldn't want to stir up any unpleasant memories, but I don't see how I have much choice."

Beth responded without hesitation. "You have to follow through on this."

I glanced at the clock on the oven. "It's still relatively early. I'm going to try to call John. I'd like to meet with him tomorrow. Even if he lives on the other side of the state, I can take part of the day off to make the trip."

I went to the drawer where we keep the phone books and got the University Directory from the year before. I found John's home address. He lived in a city that was an hour and a half drive away.

I'd been able to get Julie Woods's phone number with only her last name and home address, but she was from a small town. John lived in a much larger community. I called long distance information. A polite operator found a Baxter listed at the address I gave her. I dialed the number. A pleasant sounding woman who answered told me John worked in an electronics store and had to stay late because one of the other clerks had called in sick. She expected him in a few minutes.

I called back in a half-hour. John picked up the phone. When I identified myself, he remembered me. Because the recent murder had received so much publicity, I assumed there was no need to acquaint John with any of the details. I began by explaining that the investigation had turned up something that could eventually lead to the identification of the killer. I told him he might be able to provide some additional information that could be important. I asked him if it would be convenient for him to meet with me the next day. He said he would be home from work at five thirty and gave me directions to his house.

The next day, I locked the door to my office at three thirty. Jean was away from her desk. I left a note saying I was leaving for the day. I was familiar with the city where John lived. On several occasions I'd attended meetings at Western State University, which was located there. The campus was attractive. Its buildings were nicely designed and the grounds well maintained. Unfortunately, it was near the center of the city in an area that had fallen into a state of urban decay. The streets were lined with boarded up store fronts and homes that had once been owned by prosperous members of the community but were now either abandoned or occupied by people who lacked the desire or the resources to maintain them. Students were warned of the potential dangers that awaited them if they were to venture outside the boundaries of the campus. As I drove down the main street, it seemed that the area had deteriorated even more since my last visit.

John lived in an older residential area about a mile south of the university. The Baxters' house was typical of the type built in the Midwest in the period after WWI. It was a story and half with a dormer extending across the front of the upper floor. Facing the street was a large porch with heavy pillars supporting the roof. The condition of the house and the small yard suggested considerable effort had gone into maintaining the property.

I arrived a half-hour before my appointment, so I drove on by. A few blocks down the street there was a park with a baseball diamond and basketball courts. I pulled into a parking area and watched some teenage boys in a half court game. A couple of the players showed the kind of talent that might pay their way through college some day.

By the time I returned to the house, there was an older model, Japanese-made sedan in the driveway. I parked the pickup at the curb thinking that it fit into this neighborhood better than it had the day before at the Richardsons. As I climbed the steps of the front porch, it occurred to me that I was feeling more comfortable than I had when I'd approached the Richardsons' front door.

The tall, distinguished looking woman who answered the door was dressed in a uniform that hospital workers wear. Her quiet, gentle manner reminded me of John.

"Dr. Evers, I'm John's mother. Please come in." She led me into a small, spotlessly clean living room filled with comfortable furniture and motioned for me to sit down. I chose a large recliner. "John isn't home yet. He should be here any minute. I just got in from work myself. I was about to make a pot of tea. Would you like a cup?"

"Yes, I would," I said. When she left to get the tea, I looked around. There was a TV set in the center of one wall with shelves on either side. The lower shelves were filled with books. On the top shelf, there were photographs of three children, two boys and a girl, at various ages. Two obviously recent pictures showed a young man in a military uniform and a young woman in a graduation gown. Both were smiling.

Mrs. Baxter came back with a tray. On it were two mugs of tea, cream, sugar, and some interesting looking, light-colored fudge. "You have to try that fudge. It's a secret family recipe. I'll have to put it away before John's father gets home. He can't resist it. Our doctor told him he has to lose some weight." She smiled. "I have to keep an eye on him all the time. He has no will power when it comes to food."

I took a bite of fudge. While I'm not a big fan of candy, it was so delicious I quickly finished the first piece and picked up another. "I can understand how your husband might have a problem with this."

Mrs. Baxter nodded knowingly and set the tray down on the coffee table. "I noticed you were looking at our family pictures." She motioned toward the one I had noticed of a young man in a military uniform. "That's our oldest son. He's in the air force. He likes it very much and plans to make it a career." She pointed to the one of the young woman. "That's our daughter when she graduated from Western last spring. She teaches first grade in one of the elementary schools here in town. In June she's getting married and will be moving to Chicago where her fiancée works. Of course, you know John. That's his senior yearbook picture."

Just as I was about to ask a question, I heard a door close in the back of the house. "John, Dr. Evers is here," Mrs. Baxter called out.

When John came into the living room a minute or two later, she got up. "I have to start dinner. I'll leave you two alone to talk. It's been nice meeting you, Dr. Evers."

John looked a little uneasy as he sat on the couch across from me.

"How have you been getting along since we last talked?" I asked.

"I'm doing all right. I have a good job, and my boss is going to make me assistant manager at the store where I work and arrange my hours so I'll be able to begin taking some courses at Western in the fall."

I was concerned that John would have difficulty in getting his life together after Cheryl's death. Obviously he was making progress. "It sounds as though things are going well for you. I'm especially pleased to hear that you'll be going back to school. It's very important for you to continue your education."

I decided to get to the point. "As I mentioned in our phone conversation, you may have some information that could be of considerable importance in the investigation. The question I have for you is a very personal one. I can understand completely why you might not want to answer it."

John nodded.

"There's reason to believe that at least one of the victims had terminated a pregnancy a short time before she was killed."

John spoke before I could continue. "Cheryl had an abortion." His quick response caught me by surprise.

"John, I appreciate your telling me this. I want to assure you that I'll keep this confidential. No one else will need to know. However, if the killer is found, there's a possibility it could become public information."

"I understand. I've thought about this quite a bit. I decided Cheryl would want me to tell someone if it would help in finding the murderer."

"I can imagine that based on what I've learned about her," I said, nodding my head. "I have one other very important question. Do you know what doctor she went to?"

"Once Cheryl had made the decision, it was hard for her to talk about it. She never mentioned the doctor's name. I wanted to be with her that day, but she insisted on going alone."

"She must have gone to a place fairly close to the campus."

"Yes, she took a cab. I think it might've been some sort of clinic across the river on the other side of town."

"John, thank you for giving me this information. I realize it was a difficult thing to do. I have to be going, but before I leave, I want to ask one more question. Do you think you'll ever be coming back to the university?"

John shook his head slowly, as though he was having trouble answering the question. "I doubt it because it would remind me of the time Cheryl and I were there together. I know Western doesn't have the same prestige, but I can get a good education here, and I'll be able to keep my job."

"You probably had a financial aid package that included a scholarship."

John nodded.

"If you ever decide to come back, contact me. I'm certain I can help you get the scholarship reinstated."

"I appreciate that. I'll keep it in mind."

John offered me his hand when I got up to leave.

The meeting with John convinced me that the thing the three victims had in common was that they'd all had abortions in the period before they were murdered.

Aside from confirming the abortion theory, John had revealed something else that was significant. Cheryl's abortion had been performed at a facility in the city. Based on what Karen Ellsworth had reported, Jill also must've had her abortion close to the time she was murdered. Since there was no reason to believe she'd left campus during that period, it was likely she'd had it performed locally.

It appeared the killer was somehow able to find out that his victims were scheduled for an abortion—or that they'd recently had one. I wondered how that could happen. Personal medical information is considered to be confidential. In the case of abortions, this policy certainly would be honored, since there is so much stigma associated with the termination of a pregnancy.

I was fairly confident I knew where Cheryl had gone for her abortion. There was a clinic in the part of town John described that had come about through the efforts of Anne Watkins, a local physician specializing in obstetrics and pediatrics.

Anne became concerned about the lack of services available for women in the area who were unable to pay for medical care. With financial support from several community organizations and a few wealthy citizens, she was able to start a free clinic. It was located in a remodeled storefront in a run-down area of the city. An anonymous donor paid for the rent and the utilities. Everyone assumed that donor was Anne. All the nurses who worked in the clinic donated their time. On a number of occasions, I'd done psychological evaluations in cases where a child of one of the patients was showing signs of emotional disturbance.

When the clinic opened, Anne made it known that she would be performing abortions. It wasn't long before a relatively large number of women were taking advantage of the service. As time passed, women who could afford to pay for an abortion began asking for appointments. Anne couldn't bring herself to turn them away, so she asked them to give a donation. I'd known for some time that, occasionally, university students received abortions at the clinic.

Beth had consulted with Anne when the fertility problem developed. During that time, they'd become close friends. They met for lunch regularly, and Anne would have us to her house for dinner several times a year.

Had the other victims gone to Anne's clinic for their abortions? I wondered. If they had, it might be easier to trace the killer. But I felt very uneasy about asking Anne to violate a professional obligation by revealing privileged patient information. I needed Beth's advice.

I drove through a driving spring rain on the last half of my trip, so I got home even later than the night before. Beth met me at the door. "I hope you appreciate that you have a doting wife. This is the second evening in a row she's had dinner waiting when you arrived home late. There's a pasta and sausage casserole in the oven. All I have to do is heat it for fifteen minutes. Grab a Molson and tell me what you found out."

I finished the report of my conversation with John with a question. "Can I talk with Anne about this?"

"I think you should. If any of the victims were her patients, I'm sure she must be terribly upset. Don't worry about putting her on the spot. I think she'll feel free to talk to you because you've worked with children who were being seen at the clinic, so you could be considered a staff member and have legitimate access to patient information."

Beth was unusually quiet during the meal and ate very little. After the kitchen was cleared, she said she was tired and went to bed. It took me a while to realize what was going on. Abortion is a difficult issue for Beth. On the one hand, she feels that a woman should have the right to choose. At the same time, she has trouble dealing with the fact that we were denied the opportunity to have children while others get into a situation where they feel it's best to terminate a pregnancy.

- 40 -

The next day, as soon as I finished my run, I dialed Anne's office number, hoping to catch her before she left for morning rounds at the hospital. I was in luck. She answered the phone.

"Why the early call? Is Beth all right?"

"She's fine. Her only problem is that she works so hard she's tired most of the time."

"That sounds familiar."

"I need to talk with you. It's not a crisis, but I'd prefer we meet as soon as possible. It's something I can't discuss over the phone."

"You've aroused my curiosity. How about late today? I ordinarily finish with my last patient about half past five. We could meet at the clinic. Would that be convenient for you?"

"Yes. I'll be there at five thirty."

Beth had come into the room and overheard my side of the conversation. "I'll make dinner," she said.

"Make something that you can keep on the back of the stove. I may be late for the third day in a row."

I arrived at Anne's office just as a mother was leaving with her young child. The waiting room was empty, so I assumed it was Anne's last patient of the day. The receptionist, who was gathering her things together to leave, said Anne would see me as soon as she was off the phone. Five minutes later, Anne emerged from the examination area. "Let's talk in my office."

Anne is in her early 50s but looks much younger. She is tall and slim, and there isn't a trace of gray in her reddish blond hair. She moves with the grace of an athlete. She's such a fine tennis player, few men risk facing her on the court.

The office was small. Shelves, which covered one wall, were filled with medical texts. On another wall, there was a file cabinet and a computer. Anne's gray, metal desk was completely clear. We sat on inexpensive, vinyl-covered chairs.

"I'll get right to the point. At the beginning of the fall semester, Whitney Richardson's parents came to see me. Whitney had told them she'd taken courses with me and had worked as my undergraduate teaching assistant. They were disturbed at the lack of progress in finding Whitney's killer. Because they were convinced that the person who'd committed the crime was a disturbed individual, they came to the conclusion that someone trained in psychology might be able to accomplish more than the police. They asked if I'd be willing to do some investigating. My initial reaction was to refuse, but the more I thought about the idea, the more tempting it became. I talked it over with Beth. I'm not sure she was entirely happy with me getting involved, but she didn't discourage me. I interviewed a number of students who might've had some information that would provide clues. I had no success at all."

I hesitated before continuing because I was uneasy about raising the abortion issue. "I did some more investigating following the other two murders and wasn't able to come up with anything of significance. Then a couple of days ago, I stumbled on something that might be important. I have reason to believe that the victims had abortions a short time before they were killed."

"Tom, you needn't go any further. The women were my patients."

I nodded. "I didn't mean to pressure you into violating confidences."

"Don't worry. I welcome the chance to talk about this with someone I trust. I've kept the matter to myself for too long. There was no reason to discuss it with the staff. We have volunteers who work a limited amount of time. Most of them have no contact with the women who come for abortions. One of the nurses who happened to know Cheryl Martin had been to the clinic, commented on how tragic her death was. That was the only time the issue came up. Rita Carey, our receptionist, made the appointments for all three women. She never mentioned anything about it, so I never brought it up with her. Rita is a good worker, but she's not terribly bright. I'm not sure she realized the possible connection.

"Of course, it never occurred to me that Whitney Richardson's murder was in any way related to her abortion. Cheryl Martin's murder raised some questions, so I decided to go through the files on the abortions we had performed.

"We don't have many college women taking advantage of our services because most of them can afford to pay. Some probably go to one of the physicians in this area who perform abortions while others choose to return to their hometown. Since the first of last year, four other university women had been to the clinic. Three came during the winter or early spring before Whitney's appointment. I saw the fourth in July. She was a local woman who attends another university. She was living at home for the summer. I was reassured by what I found, and I was able to convince myself the killings weren't related to the abortions."

Richard Kelly

"I understand how you'd see it as coincidence," I said.

"There was something else that kept me from becoming more suspicious. I couldn't imagine how anyone would be able to identify patients who came to the clinic. We have very strict rules about confidentiality. I've known each of the staff members for a long time, and I'm absolutely certain there isn't a person in the group who would give out patient information."

"Is there anyone else who had access to the clinic files?" I asked.

"Only Rita. She was one of our first patients who came for an abortion. At that point, she was in her early twenties. The man she'd been living with had recently left her with two young children and no means of support. She needed a job badly. I felt sorry for her. We had money to pay someone on a part-time basis, so I offered her the position. She was overjoyed and has performed very well. After a year, we were able to put her on full-time and provide medical benefits. She understands completely the need for guarding the privacy of patients. I think she's particularly sensitive when it involves abortions because she's been through it herself. I trust her as much as I do our professional staff."

"This year, did you perform abortions on other students besides the victims?"

Anne frowned slightly and nodded. "Yes. Even though I assumed it was mere chance that both Whitney and Cheryl were our patients, when a university student came to the clinic in early December and requested an abortion, I was slightly apprehensive. With some hesitation, I went ahead and terminated the pregnancy. Of course, nothing happened to her. In mid-January, I performed another abortion on a university student. Once again, there were no dire consequences. After that, I put the whole issue out of my mind."

"I suppose it's possible that the woman who had the abortion during the summer escaped because she wasn't living in campus housing," I said. "It could be the killer relies on the University Directory to identify his victims. Or maybe he didn't bother looking because most students leave campus for the summer. Do you have any explanation for the woman in December?"

"Yes. She was very depressed at the time. It's likely that she went home right after the abortion and didn't return. She never came in for the usual follow up visits."

"It might be worthwhile to know what happened to her. If you'd be willing to give me her name, I could check with the Registrar's Office to see if she withdrew before the end of the semester."

"Before you leave, I'll get it for you from the files."

"Do you think the woman in January might also have left campus?"

"She failed to come in for a follow up appointment, but I doubt that she dropped out of school. She seemed to handle the situation well. As I recall, she was from somewhere in the east. If she'd gone home so soon after the semester started, she might have had to face questions from her parents that would be difficult to answer. I'm sure she hadn't told them about the abortion."

"During much of January, it was bitterly cold. The murders apparently all took place outside. Do you suppose the terrible weather protected this woman from attack?"

Anne seemed to ponder the question for a moment, then nodded. "That could be the reason. I remember the abortion was at the beginning of a particularly cold spell. The weather was so bad that day I had Rita drive the woman back to campus."

"So you have no idea how the victims were identified?"

Anne shook her head slowly. "I do not. For a while I wondered if the killer might've watched the clinic while sitting in a parked car, but that doesn't make any sense. How could he be on the street for so long without being noticed? Or, for that matter, it would seem unlikely he'd be able to spend that much time locating his victims."

"You're right. He must have found some other way."

"Tom, as you can imagine, this has been a devastating experience for me. I'm going to do everything in my power to prevent it from happening again. You're the first person I've mentioned this to. I intend to close the clinic. I'm going to wait until our fiscal year ends in July. If I acted before that, some might wonder about the reasons. Now I'll have a couple of months to prepare people. We have strong support from a number of individuals in the community who I know will be surprised and disappointed. I plan to say that the workload has become more than I can handle. I'm also going to refuse our services to college women. That may not be much of a problem. The semester will be ending in a few weeks—after that, it's doubtful we'd be getting requests from students."

"It must have been a tough decision," I said.

Anne sighed. "It was terribly difficult. I wish I could come up with another solution. Unfortunately, I can see no alternative. I feel that we've been offering important services to women in need. I've gotten a great deal of personal satisfaction out of my work here. I'll miss it."

"How about keeping the clinic open but refusing to perform abortions?"

"I've thought about it, but I couldn't face the possibility that people would think I'd changed my philosophy about a woman's right to choose, or that I'd been intimidated by the anti-abortion activists. They've certainly become more aggressive over the past year, and it is generally known that I've been receiving personal threats on my life."

"Have you considered the possibility that the killer might try to find another source for his victims?"

"Yes, and it's a dreadful idea. I can only hope he won't be successful. Unfortunately, there are facilities in other communities that only perform abortions.

Patients leaving one of those clinics would certainly be vulnerable. However, it would be very difficult, if not impossible, to determine if a woman was a college student."

"Anne, you must keep in mind that you've done all you can. Whatever happens in the future cannot be on your conscience." I stood up. "I'd better be getting on home. Beth said to tell you to expect a dinner invitation in the near future."

Anne nodded. "I'll be looking forward to it."

During dinner, I told Beth what I'd learned in my meeting.

"When I found out about the abortions, I thought it might eventually lead us to the killer. Now I don't see how it could be of any help. It doesn't tell us anything about his identity, nor does it suggest any way of tracking him down."

"It does seem like another dead end," Beth said. "I don't know what more you can do. The situation is frightening. The closing of the clinic doesn't necessarily mean the killing is over. As you suggested, the killer can easily find other women who have had an abortion. I guess one thing we can hope for is that in order to satisfy his bizarre impulses, his victims must be university students. With the clinic closed, they may be very hard to find."

"I don't want to sound too pessimistic, but we shouldn't underestimate this guy," I said. "He was clever enough to identify students who were receiving abortions at Anne's clinic, so he may be able to find a way to locate college women who've had abortions at other facilities."

"I don't want to talk about this anymore," Beth said, frowning. "Let's go to bed."

- 41 -

Looking back, I'm surprised how quickly Beth and I were able to put the events of the past months out of our life. I think it was because we realized there was nothing more to be done, and we were tired of spending so much of our time thinking about killings and murder victims.

The following Sunday evening, Beth and I reflected on how much we'd enjoyed the weekend. Friday evening, we had grilled steaks and ate out on the deck. On Saturday, we went to dinner at Dominic's. We were in bed early each night, slept late, and relaxed during the day. We were living a normal life again.

Wednesday afternoon at four o'clock, Anne called me at my office. "Tom, something has come up. We need to talk. I'm at the clinic. Can you come over?"

I knew if Anne needed to see me on such short notice, it had to be about something important. I locked the door to my office and moved quickly through the reception room. Jean was on the phone, so I waved as I passed by her desk.

I pulled the pickup into a parking place in front of the clinic at four twenty. The waiting room was empty, which was unusual at that time in the afternoon. I found Anne back in her office.

"Tom, I didn't hear you come in," Anne said, looking up from some papers on her desk. "I wasn't expecting you to get here so soon. Sit down. I'll be with you in a minute. I want to lock the door so we won't be interrupted."

Someone had come into the waiting room. It sounded like a mother with a small child. Anne explained that the clinic was closed for the day and told the woman to come back the next morning.

"I canceled my late afternoon appointments and sent Rita home early," Anne said when she returned.

"What's happened?" I asked.

"I think one of my patients may be in danger. Last Thursday, I had an appointment with a young woman who asked for an abortion. She was nice looking and well dressed. When I saw that she had given an address near the campus, of course, I asked her if she was enrolled at the university. She told me she'd dropped out two years ago and was working full-time in the chemistry department. She's twenty-two years old and seemed mature. After the usual interview, which involves quite a bit of counseling, I saw no reason to refuse her request. I performed the abortion this morning.

"I always spend some time with a patient after completing the procedure. She was a little groggy. While we chatted, she let slip something that made me suspicious. When I pushed her a little, she admitted that she's a full-time student. She made up her story because she'd gotten the impression the clinic didn't perform abortions on university students. She does work in the chemistry department but as a part-time lab assistant."

Anne sighed. "I checked the student directory. She's listed. We don't have her identified as a student in our files, so she may be in no danger, but if the killer learns her name, he can do what I did."

"It looks like she's a potential victim," I said.

Anne nodded. "I called you because I'm at a loss as to what to do. I considered notifying the police and asking them to put her under surveillance. It's not something I'd feel comfortable in doing because it would violate a basic rule of medical practice, but unless you have any other suggestions, I'll have to do it to protect her."

"You'd have to tell the police everything that's happened in order to convince them the woman was in danger. If you were able to do that, an officer would probably be assigned to keep an eye on her with instructions to follow her wherever she goes to make sure she reaches her destination safely. This would have to begin by Friday. She probably wouldn't be in danger until then. The killer has shown he has a preference for weekends."

As I thought about how hard it would be for Anne to ask the police to become involved, another possibility occurred to me. "I have a suggestion. Let me do the surveillance. I could keep watch on her just as well as the police. If something suspicious happened, I could use a cell phone to call 911 or notify the police directly. If this turned out to be a false alarm, no one would have to know."

Anne shook her head. "I'm not sure I could let you do that. You might be in danger. We're talking about a vicious killer. Don't take this in the wrong way, Tom, but you're an amateur in this business."

"I don't think we need to be concerned about me being exposed to any danger. There's no way I'd become directly involved. As soon as anything developed, I'd call in the reinforcements. I have to agree with you that I'm lacking in experience with this type of thing, but I don't see it as a difficult task."

"You make it sound simple. I don't know what to say."

"Maybe we need more time to think. Why don't you come to our house for dinner?"

"That's a good idea. We could get Beth involved in this. She might be able to help us decide what to do."

"As a health conscious physician, how would you feel about a meal loaded with cholesterol, fat, and sodium—like pizza?"

"I love pizza."

"Good. Why don't you plan to come about seven o'clock. Beth's working late, but she should be home by then."

"That would be good for me. I have to go by the hospital to see several patients."

I used Anne's phone to call Beth to let her know we were having company for dinner. She wasn't in her office, so I left a message. On the way home, I picked up two large pizzas.

Anne arrived before Beth. She was wearing jeans and a T-shirt that had "Tenth Annual Run for Children" written on it. "Still competing?" I asked.

"I wouldn't call it competing. I run for the exercise now. I limit myself to five Ks. The knees aren't what they used to be."

I poured Anne a glass of wine and a Molson for me, and we sat down at the kitchen table. Beth came in a few minutes later.

"Something serious must have come up. I want to hear about it as soon as I get into some more comfortable clothes."

Beth was back in the kitchen quickly and joined us at the table with a glass of wine.

I looked at Anne. "You go first. Beth knows everything except what's happened today."

Anne went over what she'd told me earlier. When she finished, Beth said, "I understand your concern. This woman *is* a potential victim. She needs protection."

"Beth, Tom has suggested a way of dealing with this. I'm anxious to hear what you have to say about his plan."

"I think I'll get another Molson before I start."

"You'd better fill my glass while you're up," Beth said. "Any more for you, Anne?"

Anne covered her nearly full glass and shook her head.

I explained what I'd proposed to Anne.

Beth took a moment before responding. "I'm not sure I like the sound of this."

"There is one other option. The police could be contacted. Russ would be willing to take over, but he'd need to know why the woman was in danger. Also,

187

he might feel it necessary to inform her that she was a potential victim. That would be a problem for Anne."

"I understand," Beth said. "Tom, I have to be convinced you'd be in no danger. This guy is an animal. You'd have to keep your distance from him, whatever happens."

"I don't see how there would be any risk in it for me," I said. "Anne and I want to hear your opinion."

"I'm too hungry to think clearly," Beth announced, as she stood up and opened the boxes of pizza.

While we sat at the kitchen table eating, Beth came up with possible scenarios and asked how I might deal with them. I kept repeating that my only involvement would be to notify the police if I felt that the woman was in danger.

Finally, Beth said, "Even though I don't like the idea, I'm beginning to think that maybe it would be best for Tom to watch the woman."

"I still have some serious reservations," Anne said.

"I agree with Beth. I want to do it."

Anne shrugged. "It seems I'm out voted."

Beth made the point that the operation had to be well organized. We spent the next hour working out a detailed plan. Anne told us the woman's name, Carol Rogers, and described her. She was tall, rather thin, and had long blond hair. It sounded as though she would be easy to recognize. Anne didn't know her address, so I checked the University Directory. She lived on Maple Street, just a few blocks from the edge of the campus.

The plan was for me to park the pickup on the street where I'd have a good view of the entrance to Carol's apartment. Because finding a parking place could be a problem, we decided it would be a good idea to locate a suitable spot as soon as possible and leave the truck there. Beth would transport me to and from campus in her car.

I'd follow Carol whenever she left the apartment. If she met up with anyone suspicious, I'd call 911 on a cell phone. We didn't have one, so Anne suggested I use hers, but in order to keep her completely out of the picture, we decided I should get a phone in my name before the weekend.

I planned to start my surveillance early Friday evening and continue the watch at least through late Sunday night for the next two or three weekends.

Anne left at a quarter past ten. By that time, all three of us were nearing exhaustion.

"I think Anne was a little uneasy when we were making the plans," Beth told me later, while we were getting ready for bed. "She's not accustomed to that type of thing."

I shrugged. "Neither are we."

- 42 -

I woke up the next morning before the sun was up and lay in bed for a while thinking about the next few days. There was no way I'd be able to go back to sleep, so I got out of bed quietly and went for a run.

I'd showered, dressed, and made the coffee by the time Beth came into the kitchen, still not fully awake. Her nightgown was one of my worn out Chicago Bulls T-shirts. It came down almost to her knees.

"Nice legs," I remarked, as she went by me on the way to the coffee pot.

She joined me at the table. "What did you mean when you said 'nice legs?'"

"Just that you have nice legs."

"You think I'm getting fat and my legs are too heavy?"

"You have beautiful legs."

"I'm going on a diet."

"Have you gotten on the scale recently?"

"Yesterday morning."

"How much did you weigh?"

"One hundred and fourteen."

"That sounds just about right for a woman who is five-four."

"I'm almost five-five."

The way the conversation was headed, I decided it was best not to respond.

Beth took a few more sips of coffee, and her eyes seemed to focus. "The plan we worked out last night made more sense to me then than it does now. It could be I wasn't thinking clearly because of the three glasses of wine I drank. By the way, don't let me do that again. I've got a headache."

"Things look a little different to me this morning, too. Do you remember a quote in that cookbook someone gave us for a wedding present? It was something to the effect that alcohol doesn't give you courage, it merely allows you to see things as they really are."

189

"I remember. What does it have to do with last night?"

"I've no idea. It just popped into my mind." I got up and put my coffee cup and plate in the dishwasher. "I'm going to leave as soon as I make a sandwich for lunch. I want to check out the place where Carol lives on my way to campus."

As Beth headed for the shower, I mentioned I might need to call her later. She said she'd be in her office all day.

University Avenue runs east-west. It passes through the campus, dividing it in half. On the east side of the campus, there are four or five blocks lined with two-story buildings, which date back to the early 1900s. Most of them are occupied by merchants who sell books, computer supplies, athletic equipment, and a variety of other products essential in the lives of students. Also there are two restaurants, a bar, and a coin operated laundry.

Carol's address on Maple Street was in an area north of this stretch of University Avenue that I think of as the student ghetto. Large, stately, older homes have been divided up into as many as five apartments. The majority of these are awkwardly arranged, the furnishings tend to be shabby, and the plumbing is often inadequate to serve the number of occupants. In most cases, they aren't very nice places to live. However, students who want to be free from the rules and regulations that are imposed in the university housing units seem to find them highly attractive. Even though the rents are exorbitantly high, the occupancy rate in the area is usually near one hundred percent.

Carol's apartment was in a large, two-story house. From the outside, it appeared to be in good condition. This, along with the fact that there were only three mailboxes by the front door, suggested that her apartment was superior to most in the area. It occurred to me that her landlord might've been shrewd enough to rent only to women who would treat an apartment more gently and cause fewer problems than their male counterparts.

After my eleven o'clock class, I went to an electronics store in a mall on the other side of town and bought a cell phone. On my way back to campus, I turned on Maple Street to get a second look at the place where Carol lived. I pulled into an empty parking space across the street from her apartment. From that location, the view of the house was unobstructed, and it was just far enough away that it seemed unlikely I'd be noticed by anyone entering or leaving. I decided to leave the pickup there and walk back to my office, which was five blocks away. Beth picked me up on her way home from work that afternoon and dropped me off on Friday morning.

I ate an early dinner that evening in the campus cafeteria. It was a few minutes after six when I settled into the pickup and called Beth on the cell phone. She wished me luck.

Fifteen minutes after I'd arrived, two college age women approached from the direction of University Avenue carrying grocery bags and went into the house. Neither matched Carol's description. I wondered if they were her roommates.

At seven, a car pulled into the driveway and a couple got out. The young woman was tall and slim with shoulder length blond hair. It had to be Carol and her boyfriend.

The car was so loaded with beer cases and grocery bags that they each had to make two trips to get everything into the house. Carol seemed to be moving slowly. I wondered if she was still feeling the effects of the abortion. They used the side door, so Carol's apartment had to be on the first floor. After about ten minutes, the boyfriend came out a third time and moved the car down the driveway toward the back of the house, I assumed to allow for more parking. It looked as though there was going to be a Friday night party on Maple Street.

In the next two hours, a steady stream of guests arrived by car and on foot. Some of them brought their own beer. Because of space limitations, those arriving after eight thirty had to stay outside on the front porch, which didn't seem to prevent them from entering into the party spirit. A little after nine, I decided Carol wasn't in immediate danger and called Beth. I met her at the corner of University and Maple, though I can't imagine anyone at the party would've noticed if she'd picked me up at the truck.

Beth left for her office early on Saturday to prepare for a trial that was coming up. I ran an extra two miles, ate breakfast, and went into my study. I needed to work on a draft of an article I was writing with a colleague at another university. When the words wouldn't come, I decided to get a head start on preparation of the final exams for my classes. That didn't go well either. Finally, at lunch time, I gave up trying to get any work done. I spent the afternoon reading a biography of Abraham Lincoln I'd begun when we were in Florida. Beth came home at five. We ate an unexciting meal of leftovers, and I was back in the pickup at six thirty. I brought Abe along for company.

When there was no sign of activity in the apartment for almost an hour, I began to wonder if Carol had left before I'd arrived. At seven thirty, I saw her come out the side door carrying a black trash bag, which she put in a small dumpster beside the garage.

I found I could read and keep my eye on the house at the same time, because Abe's law practice and political activities in Illinois weren't interesting enough to hold my attention for very long. I was looking forward to the Civil War.

About the time there wasn't enough light for me to continue reading, the car Carol had arrived in the night before pulled into the driveway. She came out the front door and got in. I followed, staying a block or so behind. Three minutes later, the car turned into a fraternity house parking lot. Several couples were standing on the porch. The women wore dresses and the men, jackets and ties. I thought the dress up type party had gone out of style on campus. Obviously, I hadn't kept up with the current fashion trends.

I assumed Carol would be safe in the company of her boyfriend for the rest of the night, so I headed back to Maple Street. My parking place was still empty. I pulled in and called Beth for a ride home.

Beth spent most of Sunday working in her study, leaving me alone with Abe. She refused my offer to prepare dinner. She announced it was ready just as Abe and I got to the Civil War. She'd made a gourmet casserole with ingredients from a specialty store near her office. Unfortunately, I couldn't enjoy it to the fullest. My mind was on other things besides food. I kept thinking about how the killer seemed to have a preference for Sunday night.

Because I was eager to get back to my surveillance job, I had Beth drop me off a half-hour earlier than the night before. I wanted to give my full attention to the Civil War so, instead of Abe, I brought a book of crossword puzzles to keep me company.

There wasn't any sign of activity in the house. I imagined that, after such a hard weekend, the occupants were getting caught up on their rest. I was trying to come up with a four-letter word for pitcher beginning with the letter *E* when one of the women I'd seen on Friday came out of the house with a book bag on her shoulder. I imagined that she was probably headed to the library or to study with a friend somewhere. I glanced at my watch. It was seven twenty.

A half-hour later, the lights began to come on inside the house. By that time, it was too dark to work on the puzzle, which was a relief because I had an excuse for not being able to finish it. I got stopped at the point where I needed a five-letter word for a rabbit's relative.

For the next forty-five minutes, I sat in the dark thinking about rabbits while I watched the house. It appeared as though the occupants were getting back to their studies. I kept looking at my watch. I was getting bored. At nine o'clock, I began to wonder how much longer I needed to stay. It seemed increasingly unlikely that anything was going to happen. I decided to wait another hour just in case.

A few minutes later, Carol came down the front porch steps. She wasn't carrying a book bag, and it was fairly late to leave for the library. She walked south toward University Avenue. I waited until she was almost to the corner of the block before starting the engine. I pulled away from the curb and drove slowly. For a moment, I lost sight of her. When I reached the intersection, I saw she'd turned right and was heading toward the campus. She didn't seem to be in any great hurry.

There weren't any cars behind me, so I was able to wait at the corner until she was further down the block. I was fortunate there was no parking on the side of the street she was on, so I could follow her driving slowly. If a car came up behind me, I'd be able to pull over and let it pass. Just as I was about to make the turn, a car coming from my left caused me to hold up. As it went by, I noticed that it was a white sedan with a campus security emblem on the door. Not far behind it were several other cars.

When I was finally able to turn, I saw that the security vehicle had stopped at the curb next to Carol. From a distance, she appeared to be talking to the driver through the passenger side window. I didn't want to pass for fear I'd lose sight of her, but before I had a chance to slow down, Carol opened the door of the car and got in. I was impressed. One of the security officers had seen a young woman alone on the street after dark and offered her a ride to campus. Carol was safe for the evening. I could go home.

- 43 -

I was behind the security car when it got to the next corner, so I decided to follow it through the intersection instead of turning and heading home. I was curious about where the officer would be taking her at that late hour on a Sunday night.

Two blocks further on, the car crossed the street that ran along the east edge of the campus. By the time the traffic cleared, allowing me to follow, it was several hundred feet ahead and moving slowly. I caught up to it when the driver stopped at a crosswalk. The campus is well lighted, so I could see inside the car. There was no one visible in the passenger seat.

I was sure the car hadn't stopped to drop Carol off. I glanced in the rearview mirror to double check. The area behind me was deserted. Had the officer forced Carol to the floor so it would appear he was alone? A ridiculous idea, but I couldn't help thinking there was something strange going on.

I stayed well back, not wanting to arouse suspicion, as the driver patrolled the campus. After fifteen minutes, the car headed north toward the football stadium. Beyond the stadium, there was a large, wooded area and the university golf course. All of the land was owned by the university. There were no private residences. I was beginning to become alarmed.

It was an ideal location for a murder.

As I drove past the stadium parking lot, I thought about a 911 call, but I knew I'd have to wait until the security car reached its destination in order to be able to give the police directions. Then it occurred to me that the operator would probably put me through to the dispatcher at the city police station or the county sheriff's office. If whoever was driving the car had the police radio on, he might intercept the dispatcher's message and be alerted to what was happening.

I considered calling campus security. With luck, Rod Dudley would be on duty. He'd be the ideal person to handle this type of situation. I quickly discarded

194

the idea. It was unlikely Rod would be working on a Sunday night, and it might be difficult to convince the person who took the call that a woman was being abducted by someone driving one of their cars. I couldn't afford to waste time with a long explanation.

The only other thing I could think of was to call Russ. I dialed his number. After four rings the answering machine came on, and I remembered that Rose and Russ played bridge on Sunday night.

The security car had turned onto a road that ran through woods on the south side of the golf course. There was little traffic in the area, even during the daylight hours. At this time of night, it was completely deserted and very dark. My headlights would be clearly visible from the car in front, but there was no reason the driver would suspect he was being followed.

Panic had begun to set in. I seriously doubted I'd be able to deal with what might be ahead of me by myself. Then I remembered the earlier conversation with Matt, when he'd volunteered to help if I ever needed any. Just as I picked up the cell phone to dial his number, the tail lights ahead disappeared. The road was straight with no hills. The driver must have turned off. I couldn't imagine where. It was at least a mile to the next crossroad.

I drove on slowly. At the point where I lost sight of the lights, there was a narrow gravel road that went off to the right through the woods. Fifty yards beyond the road, I pulled onto the berm and dialed the cell phone.

Matt answered.

"This is Tom. Don't ask any questions. You got a cell phone for Rachel to use when she's out alone at night?" Matt said he did. "Get in your car as fast as you can and drive toward the golf course. Call me when you're on the way." I gave him my number. Two or three minutes later, he called back. I explained as best I could what had happened and told him where I was.

Matt's house is on the south edge of the campus. I figured it was about three miles to the spot where I was parked. Even in light traffic on a Sunday night, it could be ten minutes before he could get to me.

I sat in the pickup imagining what might be happening back in the woods. After fifteen minutes, and no sign of Matt, I decided I couldn't wait any longer. If the killer moved rapidly, Carol might already be seriously injured—or even dead. I picked up the cell phone. I wanted to let Matt know what I was going to do. Then I realized I'd neglected to get his cell phone number.

I moved the pickup to a spot a few yards from the entrance to the gravel road. I told myself Matt would figure out where I'd gone. In the meantime, I needed a weapon.

There was a jack under the seat. I got it out and worked the mechanism until the shaft was fully extended. The base was heavy with sharp corners. I held it at the end of the shaft and tried a practice swing. There was a layer of grease on the shaft that made it hard to grip. I managed to get most of it off by rubbing it on the leg of my jeans.

A full moon showing through the partly overcast sky provided enough light for me to make my way along the drive without difficulty. I'd walked only a short distance when I saw light through the trees. A little further on, I came to a clearing where there was a Quonset shaped building several hundred feet from the edge of the woods. There was a light mounted over the door that illuminated a parking area. I'd reached the edge of the golf course. The building was probably used to store maintenance equipment.

The security car was in the grass beyond the corner of the building. I couldn't see anyone, but I thought I heard voices coming from somewhere nearby. I worked my way slowly around the edge of the clearing, staying in the darkness close to the trees hoping to get a better view without being seen. When I reached a point about a hundred and fifty feet from the car, the voices were more distinct, and I recognized the sound of sobbing.

To get closer, I had to leave the protection of the trees and cross an open area. I'd gone about a third of the way when I saw someone kneeling beside the car on the passenger side. I moved to my left so I'd be hidden by the corner of the building as I approached.

By the time I reached a spot a short distance from the rear of the car, my clothes were wet with perspiration, and I felt like I had run ten miles. I went down on one knee to catch my breath and tried to decide what my next move should be. A scream made the decision for me.

I jumped up, grabbed the jack by the shaft, and went around the car. There was enough light for me to see clearly. Carol was on her back fifteen feet away. Her long, blond hair was spread on the ground. The figure kneeling beside her with his back to me also had long, blond hair; it came down below the collar of his security officer's uniform. Rod Dudley.

I was so startled, I hesitated. It was only for an instant, but it proved to be costly. I moved forward, holding the jack over my head with both hands. As I started to bring it down on the back of Rod's head, he turned toward me and leaned to his left to avoid the blow. Instead of hitting my primary target, the base of the jack caught Rod on his right shoulder. At the point of contact, I heard a crunching sound. This time, Rod was the one who screamed.

I put so much effort into the blow that I lost my balance and fell. I scrambled to my feet quickly and turned toward Rod. He was sitting upright, holding his shoulder with his left hand. I picked up the jack that I had dropped and moved toward him with the intention of getting in another blow before he could recover, but by the time I stepped around Carol, who hadn't moved, Rod was on his feet and backing away.

The blow to the shoulder must have done some serious damage. Blood was beginning to show on his uniform shirt, and his right arm dangled limply at his side. With his good arm, he reached down and pulled at his right pants leg, just above the boot he was wearing.

When Rod bent over, I stepped closer and aimed a swing of the jack at his head. I missed. The jack, still coated with a film of grease, slipped from my hands and landed in some weeds twenty feet away. I stood motionless, waiting to see what Rod would do. He began to circle around me. His facial features were contorted. He was grinding his teeth and making a growling sound. I had the distinct feeling I was face to face with a madman.

A wild thought came to mind. I had not been in a fight since the fourth grade, and I had taken a pretty fair beating from a kid who was smaller than I was. Even though Rod had the use of only one arm, I knew I was no match for him. I began to retreat.

I focused my eyes on his one good arm, hoping I'd be able fend off a blow. That was a mistake, because I didn't see his right leg come up until just before a boot hit me in the ribs. It felt like the whole side of my body had caved in. The force of the kick knocked me to the ground. I was on my knees struggling to get up when Rod's boot make contact again, this time on the side of my head. The next thing I knew, Rod was sitting on my chest, his hand pressing down on my throat. I did my best to pry it loose, but his grip was too strong.

I was close to losing consciousness when I saw his limp arm hanging down. I grabbed it with my left hand and pulled as hard as I could. Rod grunted in pain. When he reached for my hand, his weight shifted enough for me to push him off my chest.

Before I could get to my feet, Rod was on top of me again. He rolled me over on my stomach and got on my back. He reached around and used his forearm to cut off my supply of oxygen. I was about to lose consciousness for a second time when Rod's arm pulled away from my throat. A moment later, the weight was off my back. Moving very slowly, I managed to lift myself into a sitting position. A few feet away, I saw Matt and Rod facing each other.

Rod began circling as he had done with me. He was making that growling sound again. Matt leaned forward, his hands at his sides, his elbows bent slightly. Rod faked a swing with his good arm and then kicked with his right foot. He must've thought it was his best move. It didn't work this time. Matt was so tall that Rod's boot only made contact with his hip. Matt stood with his feet planted as though nothing had happened.

Rod backed off and began feinting blows with his left arm. Suddenly, he lunged forward and aimed a chop at Matt's neck. Matt blocked it with a forearm and countered with a left fist to Rod's ribs. Rod staggered. Before he could regain his balance, Matt hit him with a solid right to the jaw, followed by another left to the body.

Rod spit out a tooth and began to retreat. There was no more growling. His expression was one of desperation. He may have realized he was no match for Matt, even with two arms. He glanced over his shoulder, as though considering a retreat, feinted a few more times, and then charged Matt with his head down. Matt grabbed his shoulders and threw him aside like he might've handled an opposing lineman who was trying to keep him from sacking the quarterback.

Rod ended up sprawled on the ground. When he finally managed to get back on his feet, Matt rammed a fist into his stomach. While Rod doubled over in pain, Matt grabbed his long, blond hair with both hands and brought a knee up into his face. Rod collapsed on the ground and lay motionless. Blood poured from his mouth and nose. Matt stepped back and kicked Rod in the rib cage with such force, it rolled him over on his back. He unleashed a second kick. This time, his size fourteen Nike caught Rod on the side of the head.

Matt stared down at Rod for a few seconds. It looked as though he might be considering another kick when a moan from Carol distracted him. He went over and knelt beside her. He spoke to her softly and touched her on the cheek. When she didn't respond, he got to his feet and came over to where I was struggling to get up. "Tom, we have to get her to a doctor. Do you feel up to walking?"

"I think I can manage, but what about Rod?"

"He won't be going anywhere for a while. The cops can come back and take care of him. Let's get moving." Matt picked Carol up gently and headed toward the road. Every part of my body seemed to hurt when I tried to stand. I leaned against the car for a moment to steady myself and then followed.

Matt laid Carol down in the grass beside his car, which was parked behind the pickup. I used my cell phone to call 911. Then I dialed Russ's number. He must have been asleep because it took a while for him to answer. There was no point in trying to explain what had happened over the phone, so I told him there was an emergency and gave him directions to where I was. He hung up without asking any questions.

I eased myself out of the pickup and went over to where Matt was sitting beside Carol, who was still unconscious. She was covered with a blanket he'd gotten out of the trunk of his car.

I've never known Matt to use profanity. He told me once that even the insults and taunts he hurled at his opponents on the football field would've qualified for a "G" rating. He said the English language was so rich he didn't need to use obscenities to express his feelings, but when he looked up at me, he said, "That bastard. I should've killed the sonovabitch back there."

"It looked to me like you came close."

"I guess I might've gone a little too far. Some unnecessary roughness?"

"Not the way I see it," I said, rubbing a painful spot on my throat.

Just then, we heard sirens in the distance. "Matt, would you do the talking when the police get here? Right now, I don't feel up to explaining what happened."

Matt nodded. "I'll do my best to keep them away from you."

- 44 -

A Sheriff's Department car was the first to arrive, followed closely by an ambulance. Matt walked over and intercepted a young deputy who was headed toward us. Matt talked, and the deputy kept nodding.

The paramedics did a quick examination of Carol while she was on the ground before lifting her onto a stretcher. Matt was still talking to the deputy when the ambulance pulled away.

Another sheriff's car pulled up, which was fortunate since the first deputy couldn't seem to decide what he should do. The second deputy went directly over to Matt. He listened for a minute or two and then got back in his car and drove up the gravel road.

Russ and the sheriff arrived at the same time. They went over to talk with the deputy who had stayed behind. Matt joined the group. The deputy gave a report on the situation. Matt didn't say anything. After a brief conference on strategy, the deputy got in his patrol car and headed toward the golf course.

Russ left the sheriff and started walking toward me. Matt tried unsuccessfully to cut him off. "I want to know what in the hell has been going on," he said.

"It's a little complicated," I said. I began by telling him that I had been on the way to my office about nine o'clock to pick up some folders I'd forgotten to take home on Friday when I got behind a university security vehicle that stopped to pick up a female student. I said I was still following the car when we reached the campus. I decided to stay with it because I was curious about where the student was going.

After this slightly deceptive start, I detailed the rest of the facts as they had happened. I'd just gotten to the part where Matt came to my rescue when the sheriff called over to Russ. "I just talked to the boys on the radio. They checked the security vehicle and the area around the building and couldn't find anything. I'm going to call for reinforcements."

Russ looked back at me. "Does Beth know where you are?" I must have answered with the look on my face because he said, "Go call her and tell her to meet you at the hospital emergency room."

"I'm all right. I don't need to go to the hospital."

"You don't look all that good to me, and I want you out of here. Your story stinks, and the sheriff is pretty sharp. If you tried it out on him, in about thirty seconds he'd be asking questions you'd have trouble answering. I'll get Donovan to drive you to the hospital. Someone will drop the pickup off at your house."

Beth picked up the phone immediately. I could tell she was frightened. I gave her a quick summary of what had happened. I assured her I was fine except for a few cuts and bruises. I think she believed me until I asked her to meet me at the hospital. That's when she really got upset.

Beth was waiting in the emergency room when Matt and I arrived. We had a chance to talk briefly. I did my best to convince her I wasn't seriously injured, but I don't think I was successful.

The doctor who examined me looked like he'd been on duty for thirty hours without a break. He wasn't the least bit sympathetic when I explained I'd been in a fight. He poked the sore spots and put some stuff on the cuts. It burned. He said I probably had some cracked ribs and should have X-rays taken. I said I'd drop around tomorrow. When I was getting dressed, the doctor commented that either the guy was a lot bigger than I was, or I must be a lousy fighter. He warned me that I was showing signs of having an alcohol problem and recommended I go for counseling. I didn't see any point in telling him that I hadn't been drinking or that the guy I had fought had been about my size and had the use of only one arm.

When the doctor finished his lecture, he wrote out a prescription and handed it to me. "This is for something that will help with the pain." I gave it back and told him I was perfectly capable of handling pain without resorting to medication.

Beth got up from her chair when I walked into the waiting room. She looked worried.

"It's just like I told you, a few cuts and bruises, and maybe some cracked ribs."

"Are you sure you're telling me the whole story?"

"If I had any serious problems, wouldn't they be keeping me here at the hospital?"

"Okay, I guess I believe you."

On the way to the car, I asked Beth if she would mind driving. I could tell by her look she thought it was a dumb question.

We arrived back at the house at two thirty. By that time, I wasn't feeling at all well. Every part of my body hurt. I began to question the wisdom of refusing the doctor's prescription. Beth must've thought I didn't look too good because she left the living room and came back with an aspirin bottle and a glass of water. "You'd better get to bed. I want a full report on what went on tonight, but it can wait until morning."

"I'm a little too wound up to be able to sleep. I'd like to talk about it now."

By the time I'd finished telling Beth what had happened, there were tears in her eyes. "I can't believe how stupid I was to let you do this."

"I was the stupid one. I should've considered more seriously the possibility that there might be danger involved. I don't even want to think about what would've happened if Matt hadn't shown up when he did."

"Neither do I. But thankfully, it turned out all right. I assume the sheriff's crew has caught up with Rod by now. Finally, there'll be an end to the killings. Do you think you're ready for some sleep?"

"I believe I can manage."

It took some time for me to get into the bedroom and out of my clothes. The aspirin hadn't had much effect.

- 45 -

I woke up to bright sunshine coming through the bedroom window. I found Beth in the kitchen drinking coffee. "What time is it?" I asked.

"Almost nine o'clock."

"I have a class at ten. I'd better move fast."

"Don't bother. I've already talked to Jean and explained what happened last night. She's going to cancel your classes. She asked how you were. I told her you were all right, but you didn't look too good. I called my office and said I wouldn't be in today."

Beth brought me a cup of coffee as I sat down at the kitchen table. "The phone has been ringing all morning. A reporter from the newspaper wanted an interview. I said you weren't able to come to the phone. He was very insistent. He finally gave up when I resorted to some strong language. I think I may have shocked him."

"I wouldn't be at all surprised."

"Then a guy from the TV station called. He wanted to send a mobile unit out here and talk to you on camera. When I told him to stay away, he got nasty. He informed me that there was no way I could stop him."

"Is he coming?"

"I don't think so. I said I was your attorney and that if any of his people came near the house, I'd have charges brought against them, and I threatened the TV station with a lawsuit."

"Could you do that?"

Beth laughed. "Of course not. Rachel called a few minutes ago to find out how you were doing. I told her you were all right, but you didn't look too good. She had a funny story. Apparently, while they were eating breakfast, a TV crew arrived. I guess they'd decided it was a bad idea to call ahead when they wanted

203

Richard Kelly

an interview. They had their camera set up and were waiting for Matt when he went out the door.

"Matt must've had a heated conversation with the person in charge. Rachel said he kept talking, and the guy kept shaking his head. Finally, Matt grabbed him by the shirt and walked him back to the truck. Then Matt went over to the cameraman, who ended up handing him the film cartridge. Matt threw it down on the sidewalk and stomped on it."

"I would've liked to have seen that," I said, grinning.

"Russ called just a few minutes ago. He's dropping by later this morning to bring us up to date on what's happened."

After eating a couple of pieces of toast, I eased into the shower and washed very gently. I found some mud still caked in my hair. I got out my razor with the intention of shaving but one look in the mirror and I decided against it. There was a long cut on my upper lip, and the left side of my face was swollen and deep purple in color.

I was dozing on the sofa when I heard Russ come in the back door. As usual, he didn't bother to knock. In a minute or two, he came into the living room carrying a cup of coffee he'd picked up when on his way through the kitchen. He settled into a chair while Beth joined us.

"Donovan filled me in on what happened after he arrived. It was quite a night. Even though there were half a dozen deputies, four of our guys, and three state troopers involved in the search, Dudley managed to elude us until a little after sunrise.

"Steve Albright, one of the deputies, finally spotted him on the golf course hiding in some trees on a hill overlooking the clubhouse parking lot. Steve circled around so he could approach without being seen. He was only a few yards away when he stepped into Dudley's view.

"It turned out that Dudley had a gun. It was a small caliber automatic he carried in a special holster that fitted in the top of his boot. Steve had his weapon drawn. He saw the gun in Dudley's hand and was about to fire when Dudley put the muzzle of the automatic in his mouth and pulled the trigger. The shot blew off the back of his head and spread his brains all over the tree behind him."

Beth groaned. "Russ, it wasn't necessary to give us all the details."

"Sorry, Beth. Dudley probably figured he could talk a golfer who arrived early at the clubhouse into driving him out of the area. Since he was wearing a uniform, he might have been able to pull it off. If that didn't work, he could've hijacked a vehicle. We were lucky Steve found him when he did."

"Russ, which leg was the holster on?" I asked.

"You thought of the same thing I did. It must've been on the side where you hit him with the jack. That would explain why he didn't use it on you and Donovan. It would've been difficult for him to get the automatic out of its holster

204

reaching across his body. He obviously didn't need it to handle you. Don't take that personally, Tom. But Donovan was a different story. Fortunately, he caught Dudley by surprise. In the fight that followed, there would've been no opportunity for Dudley to get to the weapon. If you'd caught Dudley on the other shoulder, you wouldn't be sitting here talking to me. I hope you realize how lucky you were."

Russ took a sip of coffee. "Tom, since the case is closed, I was able to convince the sheriff that there was no need to get an official statement from you. I guess you're off the hook."

"Thanks, I appreciate that."

"You're welcome. I'd like to ask why you were driving around near the campus at that hour on a Sunday night, and how you just happened to see a woman being picked up by a campus security vehicle, and what made you decide to follow it. I'm pretty sure you wouldn't give me a straight answer, so I won't bother."

Russ paused for a moment. I think he was hoping I'd tell him what he wanted to know. When I didn't say anything, he got up and left.

After he was gone, I said to Beth, "I don't think Russ is happy with me, and I can't blame him. I kept things from him he feels he had a right to know about."

"Russ is upset right now, but I'm sure he'll get over it in time," Beth said.

"I hope so."

"Now that Rod is gone, I guess we'll never know how he was able to identify his victims," Beth said.

"I'm sure it'll remain a mystery."

"Aren't you curious?"

"Of course, but I don't see any possible way we could find out. And with Rod out of circulation, it doesn't seem to matter all that much."

I must have looked a little dilapidated because Beth suggested I stay on the sofa and rest for a while. I took her advice, and within thirty seconds, I was in a deep sleep. When I woke up, I looked at the clock on the VCR. It was a little after two.

I was in the process of easing myself into a sitting position when Beth came into the room. "You were really out. How are you feeling?"

"I'll let you know in a minute."

"Anne called while you were asleep. She'd just heard the news. She asked how you were doing."

"Let me guess. You told her I was all right, but I didn't look too good."

Beth smiled. "That's exactly what I said. She wants to get together as soon as you feel up to it so she can hear about what happened."

We were sitting at the kitchen table eating a late lunch when Matt called.

"You took some pretty fair shots last night. How're you doing?"

"Not too bad."

"It seems like everybody wants to hear the inside story. I made it through my morning classes without having to deal with questions from students probably because they hadn't heard the news yet. By twelve o'clock, a crowd was gathering at my office door. I got out of there quickly.

"I expect we're going to receive a lot of attention in the next couple of days. I'm not looking forward to it. I thought we might go over some strategies. I refuse to spend a lot of time answering questions about what happened. The editor of the student newspaper called a few minutes ago, and I agreed to an interview tomorrow. That's about all I'm willing to do. You'll be getting a call from the editor soon. I was wondering if we could talk with him at the same time."

"That sounds fine to me. It would be good to get it over with in the morning. My first class is at ten. I'm free until then."

"How about meeting him at nine?"

"I'll see if I can set it up with the editor. We can meet in my office."

"I'd like to get together with you before we see him so you can fill me in on what happened before I got involved."

"I'll be in my office by eight, so anytime after that would be okay. By the way, I hear you've already had some contact with the media."

"I did, and it wasn't an entirely friendly interchange. Some TV reporter said he was going to file charges against me. Something about assault and battery. When I told Rachel, she just smiled and said I deserved some jail time for acting like such an idiot." Matt laughed. "Let me ask you, what kind of a wife is that?"

"A remarkable one. How many women would be able smile when their husband acted like an idiot?"

"I just remembered why I don't like psychologists." The line went dead.

206

- 46 -

I woke up feeling better. Jean was the only one in the department when I got there at a quarter past eight. She looked up from her desk. "Beth was right. You don't look too good."

I tried to look serious. "It seems a guy deserves a little more sympathy from a friend after he's had a traumatic experience."

Jean's face broke out in a smile. "You know me, Tom. I'm a very understanding, empathetic person. It's just hard for me to express my true feelings. It's good to have you back safe and sound. Starting after lunch yesterday, people of all ages, sizes, and shapes came through here looking for you. Most of them wanted to know how you were doing. I said you were all right, but you didn't look too good. I told them you'd be in today. You can expect some visitors."

"Matt Donovan will be here in a few minutes. We're meeting with the editor of the student newspaper in my office at nine. Don't let anyone else get by you. Make up some excuse for me."

"I can handle that. I've been doing it for years."

"Jean, I don't know how I'd get along without you."

"Seriously, Tom, I want to say that a lot of people, me included, are grateful for what you and Matt did."

I surprised myself when I said, "No problem." It's an over used phrase I find objectionable. I don't remember ever saying it before.

When Matt arrived at eight thirty, I told him basically the same thing I'd reported to Russ.

He was silent for a moment and then said, "There's more to this than you've told me. I know there must be some important reasons why you can't talk about it, so I won't ask any questions."

I nodded. "I knew I could count on you to understand."

I'd intended to spend some time planning what I'd say in my classes. I expected the students would be curious about what happened. I couldn't face the prospect of a question and answer session. I didn't have a chance to work out my approach because the interview with the editor lasted so long I had to rush to get to class on time. The students were sitting in quiet anticipation when I arrived. There had to have been one hundred percent attendance—something that occurs only on the first class meeting of the semester.

There was no way I could begin lecturing as usual, so I started by saying, "I understand how disappointed you must have been yesterday when you came to class and found it had been canceled. You know it's my policy never to cancel without giving notice. However, something unexpected came up over the weekend that made it necessary. I'm certain much of what you've heard about what happened is untrue, or at least grossly exaggerated."

The smiles on the faces of a number of students indicated they were beginning to realize I wasn't being entirely serious. "I don't think it's appropriate to spend valuable time boring you with the details, particularly since we missed a class yesterday. I suggest that if you would like more information, you talk to my friend and colleague Matt Donovan. As a teacher of literature, he is far more articulate than I am and could give you a much clearer picture of the recent events."

The response I got told me most of the class knew of Matt's reputation. There were smiles, some laughter, and a significant amount of head nodding. The group seemed satisfied, so I went on with the lecture. A few students that I knew well came up at the end of class and politely asked how I was feeling. I answered by saying that I felt better than I looked. I used the same approach in my eleven o'clock class. It worked fairly well there, too.

The next edition of the campus newspaper carried the story. Though I thought the writer did a respectable job, I would've preferred that he not make Matt and me out as such heroes. There were articles published in our local newspaper and others throughout the state. I had no desire to read them. For the rest of the week, Jean did a remarkable job in keeping people away from my office door. Unfortunately, whenever I left the department, I wasn't able to avoid being confronted and questioned. I answered the best I could and found myself frequently saying, "No problem."

Matt got progressively more irritated as the week went on. I heard he was sometimes less than polite with those who insisted on questioning him.

A note from Joan Richardson arrived late in the week. She said that she and David experienced a deep feeling of relief upon hearing that Whitney's murderer would never again harm anyone, and they both wanted to express their appreciation for what I had done. She said that she hoped I had not been offended by anything David had said, as he had been going through a very stressful time. I wrote a reply on the word processor, which simply said, "No problem." I never mailed it.

On Friday morning, I was sitting alone at the kitchen table drinking a third cup of coffee and wondering if I might be able to start running again in a day or two when the phone rang. Beth had been taking all the calls. She was in the shower, so I answered. It was Russ. He wanted to know if I had time to have lunch with him at the Downtown Deli. I said I did. "Meet you there at noon," he said and hung up before I could ask why he wanted to get together.

Russ was sitting at a table by the front door when I arrived at the deli. He didn't say anything until we'd gone through the line and taken our trays to a table in a far corner of the room. "You're looking better than when I last saw you."

"I'm doing fine," I said. There was another silence while Russ took a drink of iced tea. Since he had called the meeting, I waited for him to start talking. Anyway, I didn't have anything to say.

"I talked with the Rogers girl at the hospital on Tuesday. She was able to clear up a few things. Dudley called her on Sunday afternoon. He identified himself and said that because of the recent killing, he was getting a group of women students together to discuss what kind of additional safety measures might be instituted on the campus. He told her she'd been recommended to him as a mature person who could make a significant contribution to the discussion. He asked if she'd be willing to attend the first meeting of the group, which was scheduled for that night. She felt highly complimented by the invitation and accepted immediately."

"Knowing Dudley's reputation, I can understand why it never occurred to her that she might be in any danger," I said.

"Dudley explained to Carol that if word got around about the meeting, it might raise the level of fear on campus. He asked her not to mention it to anyone, even her closest friends. He offered to pick her up in a campus security vehicle. Because the meeting was secret, he said it would be best if they met at a place away from her apartment. He must've used some variation on that approach with the first two victims. The third victim was a different type, and she was murdered on a Saturday. Somehow, he found another way to get to her."

"That must've been difficult. I can't imagine how he pulled it off," I said.

"There's no question about it; Dudley was clever. On Wednesday, I went through his apartment. It was one big room in a basement over on Wilmont. It was clean and neat. The furnishings were limited to a table and chairs in the kitchen area, a futon, and some bookshelves. There was a big screen TV, a video recorder, and an expensive stereo system. One end of the room was filled with high-tech exercise equipment.

"He had a large collection of porn video tapes. The two or three I checked out were really rough. The bookshelves were filled with magazines, mostly porn, and some body building stuff."

I took a bite of my sandwich and said, "I guess it was the kind of thing you'd expect a sex murderer might have around."

Russ nodded. "There was a file cabinet back in a corner with neatly labeled folders. In one section, there were articles on the campus murders that had been cut out of newspapers. Another big section, and this is where it gets interesting, was filled with anti-abortion publications. There were a couple of folders containing reports of attacks on the staff of abortion clinics. Dudley must've gone through the stuff carefully. Parts were highlighted with a felt marker, and there were notes in the margins. The stuff on abortion doesn't surprise you, does it?"

I was relieved when Russ continued without waiting for me to answer.

"There were things I hadn't been able to figure out. What were you doing driving around the campus on a Sunday night? You said you had to pick up some folders. I can't imagine what would be so important that you had to make a special trip to your office at nine o'clock. Besides that, the spot where Dudley picked up Carol wasn't on the shortest route between your house and Coomer Hall. Then there was the cell phone. I remember you telling me once you couldn't imagine a reason for ever needing one.

"Last night when I went to bed, I wasn't able to sleep. I kept going over in my mind what I'd found in Dudley's apartment. Then, all of a sudden, the whole thing began to make sense."

Russ hesitated, as if he were organizing his thoughts. "Let me tell you what I think happened. Somehow you found out what the victims had in common. All three had had abortions shortly before they were killed. Dudley believed that women who had abortions were murdering their unborn children and sadistic porn turns him on, so the murders accomplish two things. He punished the victims for what they'd done, and he got a sexual high at the same time."

"You're talking like a professional psychologist," I said.

Russ seemed to be so engrossed in what he was saying that he didn't hear my comment. "You couldn't tell me what you'd pieced together because it was confidential medical information. For the same reason, you weren't free to ask for help when you learned that Carol might be in danger after she had an abortion, so you decided to do something on your own. Beth and maybe one or two other people knew. You got a cell phone. You parked your pickup outside Carol's apartment and followed her wherever she went. If you saw something suspicious, you could call for help.

"Carol told me Rod picked her up a couple of blocks from her apartment. You were following and saw her get into a security vehicle. It would seem like she was getting a ride to campus by a conscientious officer and was safe. I can't understand why you followed the car, but fortunately for Carol, you did."

As I listened to Russ, I was amazed at what he had been able to deduce.

"At some point, you realized the officer wasn't going to drop Carol off on campus and that she might be in danger. You tried calling me, but I wasn't home. Then you probably thought about calling the department, but you couldn't risk it because the driver of the vehicle might have his radio on and pick up the message from the dispatcher. As a last resort, you called Donovan and got lucky.

"Maybe I didn't get all the details right, but I'm pretty sure that was about the way it happened. The one thing I haven't been able to figure out is how you were able to identify Carol as a potential victim. The only way I can see to explain it is that all of the girls went to the same place for their abortions. After Carol had hers, some insider got concerned about her safety and asked for your help. I suspect that somehow you uncovered the abortion tie in before Carol had one. By the way, I'm fairly sure I know where the abortions were performed."

While Russ was talking, he hadn't touched his lunch. When he paused and started eating, I thought about what a shame it was I couldn't tell him how impressed I was with the accuracy of his analysis. After finishing part of his sandwich and downing a few mouthfuls of potato salad, he said, "There was another folder in Dudley's file cabinet you ought to know about. In it were clippings from the local paper, which reported court cases Beth had been involved in—and her name was always underlined. There were also several articles from the campus newspaper where your name appeared, also underlined. The spot where the last victim was left wasn't chosen randomly."

Russ began to work on his lunch again. I could tell by his manner that he knew I wouldn't be free to confirm or deny his reconstruction of the events or to tell him how I'd learned that Carol was a potential victim. When he finished everything on his tray, he looked at his watch. "Tom, I gotta tell you. That was one fine piece of work."

"I know what you're thinking. I didn't handle the situation well. Things seemed to get out of control. I made some dumb decisions. I'm sorry."

Russ just nodded. "I have to get back to work."

"Me too."

As we were walking toward the parking lot, Russ said, "Rose was just saying that we hadn't gotten together with you and Beth for a while. She was thinking about calling Beth to invite you over to dinner. That sound okay?"

"That would be nice. We'd really enjoy an evening with you and Rose."

- 47 -

Due to the many distractions in the past few days, I'd gotten behind in my work. It was after six when my desk was finally cleared, and I was able to get away from the office. Beth was in the kitchen preparing dinner when I got home.

"I'm working on a special occasion meal. Pull up a chair and tell me what Russ had to say." She opened a Molson, poured herself a glass of white wine, and joined me at the table.

After hearing my report, Beth shook her head slowly. "I work so closely with Russ I tend to take for granted how remarkably good he is at his work."

I nodded in agreement. "I think maybe he's not so upset with me after he figured out what happened. He said Rose will be calling to invite us for dinner."

"That's good to hear, and it reminds me that Anne called a little while ago. She wants us to come to dinner tomorrow night."

Dinner at Anne's was always a special occasion. After her parents died, she moved into their beautifully maintained Victorian home where the family had been raised. It was furnished with valuable antiques, and the walls were lined with bookshelves. Anne greeted us in an outfit suitable for a celebration. She wore an elegant, full-length gown, and a necklace that must have been a family heirloom. It was in stark contrast to the casual outfits she wore on most occasions.

I settled into a rocking chair, and Beth sat on the sofa. There was a tray of appetizers on the coffee table. Without asking our preferences, Anne brought out two glasses of wine and a chilled mug of Molson. "I want to hear about Sunday night. Then I have something I need to discuss with you."

Since Anne had been an accomplice, I felt it was appropriate to describe the events in detail. I noticed that Beth stared at her wine glass the entire time I was talking, and Anne looked very serious.

"Tom, there was nothing on TV or in the newspaper accounts to suggest how dangerous a situation it was for you. If I had any idea that this might happen, I certainly wouldn't have gone along with the plan."

"I guess all three of us were unrealistic not to consider that there might be some risk involved," Beth said.

Anne looked me over with a clinical eye. "Fortunately, it appears you escaped without serious injury. I must say, I'm grateful to you on two counts. You ended the career of a monster, and I won't have to close the clinic."

Anne took a breath and let it out slowly. "Now, I'll get to my news. Rita Carey has disappeared. I know you are aware of how the clinic operates. It's staffed by part-time volunteers with the exception of Rita, who was on duty full-time to take phone calls and schedule appointments. Two days a week, I come in after my morning hospital rounds and spend the rest of the day. Monday evening, I got a call from Jenny Rust, one of the nurses who works on Monday afternoon. She said that when she got to the clinic a few minutes after one, the door was locked, and there was a patient waiting outside. Rita should have been on duty at twelve thirty. She never showed up. Jenny wondered if I knew that Rita wasn't at work. Of course, I didn't, but I wasn't terribly surprised because, in the past, Rita had taken days off without letting anyone know.

"When I arrived at the clinic on Tuesday at nine o'clock, there was no sign of Rita. I tried calling her at home and got no answer. Whenever I had a free moment during the day, I called again. I was never able to reach her. By late afternoon, I became concerned that she might be having some sort of trouble."

Beth spread some pate on a cracker. "Were you beginning to wonder if this was in some way related to what happened on Sunday?"

"It did enter my mind," Anne said. "On my way home, I drove out to the trailer park where she lives. Her trailer was closed up, and the blinds were down. I got no response when I knocked. While I stood on the steps wondering what was going on, a woman came out of the trailer next door and started to get into her car. I asked her if she knew where Rita was. She told me that during the afternoon the day before, she'd seen Rita loading her van with clothing and toys. When Rita's children came home from school, she put them in the van and drove off. The woman said that was the last she had seen anyone at the trailer. She assumed that Rita had moved out. I know Rita originally came here from a southern state where she grew up. She mentioned that she still had relatives in the area. That must be where she went.

"Because of the timing, the Dudley situation had to have been the cause of Rita's quick departure. There seems to be no question as to how he identified his victims. Rita gave him their names. We can only speculate about what kind of relationship Rita had with Dudley, and how aware she was of what was going on.

213

It's possible she didn't connect the information she gave Dudley with the murders. I'd prefer to believe that was the case, but somehow I can't."

Anne set her wine glass down on the table and frowned. "I have a question for the two of you. Do I have an ethical or legal obligation to report what I've told you to the authorities? Of course, you understand why I'm hesitant in doing that. It could have a negative impact on the clinic."

Beth spoke first. "You don't."

"Is that Beth the attorney speaking?" Anne asked.

"No, it's a friend who respects your judgment and integrity. As an attorney, I don't see any problem."

"Tom, what about you?"

"I agree totally with Beth."

"I'm still a little uneasy about the situation, but you've helped relieve a burden on my conscience. Let's go into the dining room. It's time we had some food."

After reflecting a moment, I said, "Not just yet. I think we should talk some more. The female students seemed to feel that Rod Dudley was extremely attractive." I turned to Beth. "I remember you saw him when we were eating at that Italian restaurant near the campus, and you expressed a similar opinion."

Beth nodded. "I did. Anne, I assure you he was a very good looking man."

"Also, Rod could be very charming. He got along well with the students and the people he worked with. Let's suppose Rod discovered Rita could be valuable to him because of her position. It wouldn't have been difficult for him to meet her, and there's no doubt she'd be taken by his good looks and charm. As a single parent who was responsible for raising young children, attention from a man like Rod could be especially gratifying."

I picked up my mug of ale and took a drink, carefully piecing the events together. "The two begin spending time together. Most likely they have an affair. He makes an effort to be attentive and affectionate. Rita begins to rely on him, and she trusts him. So when he questions her about patients who come to the clinic, she gives out information freely without ever considering she may be doing something wrong. Then a student is murdered. Rita doesn't think it's related to the fact that the victim had recently been a patient at the clinic. The second murder may have raised a question in her mind.

"At some point, she might've mentioned this to Rod. He suggests to Rita that she give him the names of all the students who come to the clinic so he could keep an eye on them and maybe prevent any more murders. This makes sense to Rita. After all, Rod is a campus security officer. On Monday, when Rita hears the news about Rod, she suddenly realizes what's been going on. She's frightened and sees no alternative but to pack up her children and leave town."

"So, you think it's possible Rita may have been used by Rod and was entirely innocent?" Anne asked.

"Yes, I do."

"What Tom has suggested makes sense to me," Beth said.

"Tom, I trust you didn't conjure up this explanation of Rita's role just to make me feel better."

"I guarantee you I did not. And let me point out one other thing. Rita worked at the clinic for a number years. I'm sure you got to know her well. Can you imagine she'd provide the names of patients to Rod if she had any idea how he was going to use them?"

With a hint of a smile on her face, Anne said, "All right, I'm convinced. Let's eat."

Anne is an excellent cook, and she loves good food. Because she's busy with her work, she can't afford the time to prepare elaborate meals for herself. When she has guests for dinner, she goes all out. During the next hour and a half, we ate our way through four superb courses.

Anne's day begins at a very early hour, so Beth and I make it a point not to stay late when we visit her. We left right after helping her clear the table. When we got to the door, she hugged us both.

"How about your ribs? Are they still sore?" Beth asked, as we pulled in our driveway.

"Hardly at all. In fact, I'm planning to run in the morning. Why do you ask?"

"No particular reason. I was just wondering."

Later in bed, I was thinking how relaxed and content I was feeling, though my ribs did hurt a little, when Beth said, "You already know this, but I'm going to say it anyway. I'm really proud of you for what you did."

I smiled into the darkness and said, "No problem."

Epilogue

Graduation Day One Year Later

At our university, faculty members are required to participate in the graduation ceremony decked out in their academic robes. Due to the limited seating space, not everyone is obligated to attend every year. There's never been a complaint about this because sitting through the ceremony is the equivalent of spending two hours in a sauna while watching the grass grow.

Matt and I show up every year. We have the absurd idea that our presence adds dignity to the occasion. Aside from that, we have the opportunity to see some of our favorite students one more time and to meet their parents. This might seem to be a little strange, but it's important to us.

The university invites a dignitary to give the graduation address—a high profile politician, renowned literary figure, nationally recognized humanitarian, or occasionally an individual from the entertainment world. He is rewarded for the effort with an honorary degree and some attention from the media. I use the male pronoun because females are seldom, if ever, asked. I've learned through years of experience that the addresses are incredibly boring, with the possible exception of those given by entertainers.

This year, I was guardedly optimistic. The speaker was one of our state representatives in Congress. He was an intelligent, articulate young man, and I agreed with his political philosophy. When he was only a few paragraphs into his speech, I began hearing the same self-serving rhetoric and familiar platitudes. My attention wandered. I reflected on the past year after Rod Dudley's homicidal career had come to an end.

Matt gave me a scare. At the beginning of the spring semester, he received an unsolicited offer for a professorship at a prestigious university on the west coast. He asked my advice. I told him he'd be an absolute fool not to accept it, and if he did, I wouldn't have to put up with his childish obsession with intramural basketball. I was sure he'd be leaving. A few days later, he called to tell me he'd turned down the offer. He and Rachel decided that the Midwest provided a healthier environment for their children, and they'd miss Beth and their other good friends among the faculty. He didn't mention me. Redheaded gorilla.

We won the intramural championship again, but it was close this time. I'm definitely retiring, and Matt should, too. A man his age just can't compete with the younger guys.

Beth and I get together regularly with Russ and Rose for a home cooked meal. As usual, Russ is working overtime to keep the city safe from the criminal element.

217

A couple of weeks ago, Don Reynolds announced his resignation as head of Campus Security. The Dudley episode had a serious impact on the security staff. Rod always conducted himself in a professional manner, and the other officers viewed him as a leader and role model. When he turned out to be a vicious killer, they responded with shock and disbelief. Several key men and women resigned. Don became frustrated when he was unable to hire qualified replacements, so he decided to retire.

Anne is very pleased with the progress that's been made at the clinic during the year. She's recruited several more professional volunteers and obtained additional financial support from the community. As a result, the services are available to more women. There have been several violent demonstrations at the clinic by anti-abortionist groups, and Anne has received threats on her life. This hasn't diminished her determination. She recognizes that these are the realities physicians in her position must face.

Patti made the dean's list both semesters. She decided to major in psychology and asked me to be her advisor. I said I would on the condition that she treat me with the respect a college professor deserved. She told me that was asking too much. In spite of what she said, I agreed.

Julie Wood, Whitney's research partner, is getting her master's degree in social work. She called to tell me she'd accepted a position as director of a program that offers services for women who have been abused by their spouses. She also announced her engagement to a medical student. She assured me that when he finished his degree, he wasn't going to be like other doctors. I didn't bother asking what she meant by that.

Diane Jason, a.k.a. Archie, is enrolled as a graduate student in physics here at the university. She taught an introductory course this past semester. She said she was not at all pleased with her performance but might consider an academic career. I'm fairly sure her first effort in the classroom was highly successful.

I've picked up a new advisee. Mark Breland decided to major in psychology. He's working as a volunteer in the local EMS unit and is looking forward to a career as a paramedic.

I run into Amy Price on campus from time to time. We always exchange a few words. Cheryl's name never is mentioned. I guess we both prefer not to be reminded of the conditions under which we first met.

John Baxter stopped in to see me when he came to the campus during spring break. He was considering coming back to the university, but as a result of the visit, he decided it would be best if he continued his education at State. Sadly, I doubt if he'll ever be entirely free from the memories of Cheryl and the relationship they had.

A week after the thing with Rod was over, I asked Karen Ellsworth to come and see me. I assured her I hadn't told anyone about Jill's pregnancy—Beth didn't count—but my knowing about it provided some important clues in the case. When I told her she had made a major contribution to the identification of the killer, something only the two of us would ever know, there were some tears in her eyes.

After the graduation ceremony ended, Matt and I spent a half-hour congratulating students and being introduced to parents. On our way to the lot where the pickup was parked, Carol Rogers came running toward us, still wearing her graduation robe. When she got close, I saw that there were scars on her face, but they weren't obvious enough to detract from her good looks. I'm sure there were deeper psychological scars that would never disappear.

She hugged Matt, which wasn't an easy thing to do because of his size, and then me. She stepped back and in a whisper said, "I guess I really don't know how to thank you." At that, she turned and walked slowly toward a middle-aged couple who must have been her parents.

Matt pulled one of those red bandana handkerchiefs out of his rear pocket and wiped his eyes. "This time of year my hay fever always kicks up."

"I know what you mean," I said.

In the drive back to Matt's house, he said, "We'll be leaving for Michigan at the end of the week. Rachel wanted me to be sure and tell you to call as soon as the baby arrives."

"You and Rachel will be the first to hear," I said.

"Have you picked out a name yet?"

"We chose one when we found out it's a girl. We're naming her Whitney Cheryl. I know the names don't go particularly well together, but it's what we wanted to do."

"That combination sounds just fine to me," Matt said emphatically.

I guess I hadn't mentioned that Beth and I are adopting an Asian orphan.

About The Author

Richard Kelly has a Ph.D in clinical psychology. He taught at a university for twenty-five years and has worked in psychiatric facilities in the U.S., Canada, New Zealand and Australia. He and his wife divide their time between a beach house on the Gulf of Mexico in Florida and a home on a hundred acres in rural Indiana.